TRANSMISSION

ATIMA SRIVASTAVA

Library of Congress Catalog Card Number: 91–61204

British Library Cataloguing-in-Publication Data
Srivastava, Atima
Transmission.
I. Title
823(F)

ISBN 1–85242–228–9

First published 1992 by
Serpent's Tail, 4 Blackstock Mews, London N4
and 401 West Broadway 2, New York, NY 10012

Set in 10/12 Walbaum by Selectmove Ltd., London
Printed in Great Britain by
Cox & Wyman Limited of Reading, Berkshire

This volume was published with assistance from
the Ralph Lewis Award at the University of Sussex

CHAPTER ONE

'I don't know how you do it, Angie.' Chloe unfurled the cellophane from her packet of Bensons and held out a cigarette for my attention with a 'you're incorrigible' look on her face. As though she was my grandmother or something.

'Which *one*!' urged Hugh casting his eyes blindly around the smoke-filled pub.

I drew long and mysteriously on my cigarette and blew out the smoke slowly for maximum effect. Chloe tapped the ashtray with her cigarette. 'I mean you were only *in* here for half an hour last night!' she grumbled.

'Skill, pure skill,' I smirked, turning to look at my fingers, exhaling, then polishing my nails on my lapel in a flurry. It was one of those stupid things we always did at school. Well, other kids did it anyway. I usually observed. Listening and learning the ways of cool. How funny that almost ten years later it would be amusing a bunch of ex-university students.

Chloe rolled her eyes.

'She's not gonna tell you who chatted her up last night, Chloe, so just give up.' Hugh grinned and stretched his legs out from the red vinyl seat. The pub was already sticky with heat, smoke and attitude. There was a sudden rush of cold air. We all turned automatically to see who had come in. I shouted over, 'All right, Maggie,' and Chloe moved up to make room. At the bar I was smiling as the barmaid refilled the same-again orders plus a brandy and babycham. Hugh and Chloe were quizzing Maggie. She kissed her teeth so loudly that I could hear it above the band tuning up. I had to laugh. I had a lot of time for Maggie.

'A skinhead, Angie, are you out of your mind?' said Chloe when I came back.

I took another of her cigarettes and waved her attitude off with it. 'It was a laugh, Chloe . . . chill out man!' I said.

Maggie snorted into laughter. The band started up and true to the tradition of the Dog and Trumpet, they made up for lack of talent with the maximum of volume. It was so loud that you couldn't even shout at your neighbour how bad they were. Maggie kissed her teeth. I looked around and smiled again. It was good to see her, we never seemed to catch up with each other these days. When we were at school we used to chat non stop to the bus stop and then ring each other up when we got home. In class we'd always sit in the back row and be told off for talking all the time. God knows what we found to talk about! She was my best friend for a couple of years, especially after she stuck up for me when the bovver girls decided it was my turn for in-the-bin.

There were a number of qualifications for in-the-bin, and you never quite knew what they were. The bovver girls wore make-up, jewellery (hoops) and skirts more than one inch above the knee, all of which were totally illegal. Boyfriends picked them up after school in Ford Escorts and you had to get out of their way at three twenty-five in the loos, where they changed into clingy cheesecloth tops with little buttons, and five-inch high platform shoes.

Maggie's mum couldn't afford such luxuries, so even though they never met, both our mums had a tacit solidarity. I used to plead with ma to let me have a Saturday job but she always said homework was more important. That's how I got into talking on the phone to Maggie — as soon as the family had left for shopping at Tesco's on Saturday, my finger was in the dial.

On my thirteenth birthday, a Saturday, Maggie and I were allowed to visit Brent Cross, the new shopping centre just opened in Hendon. It had been billed on the tv and local newspapers as the Oxford Street of North London, and for days the kids at school had been shouting, 'I'm going to *Brent Cross!*' On the word Brent, you thrust one fist up in the air, and on the word Cross you stuck the other one up in the opposite direction so that your face was framed in a triangle.

It was packed out. No one had ever seen anything like it. We swaggered up and down the shiny floors gawping at the glittering shops that dominoed ahead of us: Miss Selfridge, Top Shop, Marks and Spencer, Saxone. Once we'd finished riding the escalators and running up them the wrong way, we sat exhausted opposite the huge fountain on yellow plastic seats and unwrapped our pineapple turnovers. Fifty pence each from the American bakery but money was no object that day.

It was round about lunchtime the trouble started. Half the school was in there of course and one of the blokes in the fifth form was standing around smoking in a crowd — some of whom we noted weren't even from our school! We were suitably impressed. All the fifth formers had friends outside school. Maggie warned me not to do it but when Trevor Fairweather sauntered over our way and offered me a cigarette I wasn't going to refuse. He stayed for a while talking to me and then said he'd see me at the school disco the following Saturday. I lay awake that night planning what I was going to wear the following week and for once Dad's incessant radio blaring out the World Service in the next room didn't bother me.

On Monday the word was out. We had just set foot in the playground for morning break when a six girl delegation stomped down from the fifth formers' hut. A lot of the girls (segregated playgrounds) stopped what they were doing to have a good look. They couldn't have been more attentive if they'd been at a bloody public hanging.

'Oi!' said one of the girls and I knew the order had my name written on it.

'You been talking to my boyfriend, you paki?'

'No,' I said.

The playground teacher was way over the other side and scared of her own voice anyway.

'Yes you were, you lying git.'

I'd seen her before in the corridor, jewellery jangling, and in the summer I'd noticed a tattoo on her arm saying 'Pauline loves Trev 4 ever'. That's why she always wore a black scarf wrapped around her wrist because if the teachers had seen it they would have had a heart attack.

I used to wonder what it must be like to be her. I used to wish I had the guts to slouch and laugh in the back row of the special girls-only assembly where Mrs Powell the assistant headmistress would tell us how the loos were getting jammed because 'some girls weren't disposing of their STs in the bins provided'. And Pauline said brazenly, 'What's STs, Miss?' Everyone burst out laughing and Mrs Powell had been really annoyed.

'Fuckin' paki, you're going in the bin,' shouted Pauline's friend with the blonde hair.

They grabbed my legs and arms and started hauling me toward the corner of the playground where there was a large metal rubbish bin, five feet high. Although Maggie ran across to the teacher for help, I still got dumped in the bin, shaking as I tried to scramble out, my skirt scrunched up around my middle.

'Miss,' said Maggie, 'it was Pauline Metcalf, I saw her.'

She was brave, Maggie. My attackers had scattered by then but Pauline looked over disdainfully.

'Don't know what she's talking about, miss,' she said. There was no point anyway. It couldn't be undone.

'Angie! Did you give him your number?' said Chloe with big eyes.

'Please!' I said

'He'll have to crawl. You know how she is. Likes her men under manners,' said Maggie deadpan.

Everyone laughed and we were all back on familiar ground, talking of how we'd met Chloe at university and she was all into feminism and guilty about fancying this bloke. I'd gone straight up to Hugh and said, 'My mate fancies you.' Just like that, why not? They'd been together ever since.

'There he is,' pointed Maggie and we all looked over to the door. Blond hair, leather jacket, Mr I'm-so-cool. We burst out laughing like schoolgirls, even Hugh, the 'New Man' as Maggie called him because he'd read more feminist books than any of us and didn't mind boring things like cooking and washing up.

'He's not really a skinhead,' said Hugh.

Oh yeah, I thought, you know all about it don't you? I'd hardly seen this lot since leaving university a year ago but in the past week I'd seen them twice and suddenly all their predictable attitudes began to wind me up: working class people were like this; middle class people were like that; black people were oppressed; meat is murder etc. etc. Because that guy didn't look like a member of the National Front then it was all right for me to talk to him. Maggie was just as bad. By the time we'd got to university she was already behind the Black Student

Alliance stand at Freshers week. She'd started hanging around with big rastamen and calling white people pasty. It was all politics with Maggie. She said that Brent Cross thing was like the stance of prisoners handcuffed at the wrist. Everything was to do with being black and coming from Africa.

I remembered once when Maggie had come back from a trip to Morocco in our first year and we'd travelled down to London together for the rest of the summer holidays. Her mum had met us at Wood Green bus depot and taken one look at her daughter and screamed, 'Waalaa . . . you look like a damn African Maggie.' Maggie's mum and I had doubled up laughing but Maggie had remained poker faced. Her mum was a right laugh and she had always given me extra large helpings at school where she was one of the dinner ladies. Never mind Africa, Maggie's mum would have a jumping fit if anyone tried to suggest she came from Jamaica. 'Us Baijans have a better culture than those feisty Jamaicans,' she'd say.

Maggie and I had too much in common to fall out over politics. We'd sit in the union bar at university talking North Londonese — about the Music Machine and 'All right, John' and never about in-the-bin. Chloe and Hugh who'd never been to London thought we were 'dead streetwise'.

Everything was so different now and sometimes I wished it wasn't. Everyone was talking so I sneaked a look across to the bar. Lol was in the middle of a conversation with a tall Jamaican guy wearing a wide brimmed hat and a camel coloured coat. Stoke Newington was full of hoods.

'So anyway, how come big media woman visitin' the masses two nights running?' said Maggie with a smile. Chloe and Hugh chuckled. I wagged my finger at her — one of her own mannerisms — as if to say 'you're Bad!' At university we had an unspoken pact not to talk about politics because we liked each other. She had given me lots of books and pamphlets to read but I was always too busy having a good time.

'She has to come up here to get her weed,' said Hugh, 'and a piece of rough!'

Everyone laughed while I narrowed my eyes at him. It was just like the old days with kindly insults being thrown around.

'Guess who works behind the bar at the Hackney Arms,' said Chloe. 'Ruth Walters.'

Maggie and I gave little murmurs of recognition. The problem with reunions was that everything revolved around the shared experience of having spent three years together. Some boring person on campus now had significance because she was working in a pub in Stoke Newington.

'Yeah,' said Hugh, 'she signs on at my office.'

He thought he was really in touch with the real world because he worked behind a glass screen to protect him from desperate people with UB40s.

'Stupid bitch,' I said. 'Fancy signing on two streets away from where you work!' I could just hear my mum: 'Ungelliee, you are too much hard on people — you'll never get through life being smart alec.' She had picked up English expressions over the years but only by chance used them appropriately.

There was a tap on my shoulder. I jumped. I started to smile. It was Lol. I knew he was bound to find an excuse to leave his conversation at the bar and talk to me at some point in the evening. But this was not the case.

'Listen darlin', why don't you say it a bit louder, tell the Social about it,' he said, threw me a scornful look and walked back to the bar.

In the short silence that followed my ears began to burn and my face felt hot. The band was thrashing away regardless. My mum seemed to have taken up residence inside my head. Now she was doing a mannerism that irritated the hell out of me. She was patting the air in front of her in the middle of something I was saying, indicating I should turn the volume down. 'I am not sitting in New Delhi, Ungelliee.'

'Bloody nosey parker,' I said

'He's right, you know, especially round here. You don't know who's in the pub, and I do work there,' said Hugh looking at the cigarette he was rolling. He had a little tin full of tobacco and a lettuce leaf to keep it moist.

'Huh, all you're worried about is your job,' I spat at him.

'Well, it's a bit different round here you know'. He licked one side of the roll up and looked at his feet. 'You're lucky to *have* a job . . . not like in North London.'

That was it. I went mad. 'You think you're so great, don't you, squatting in council flats. You've always had something to say about me living in Finchley. You make me sick, as though you're not just looking after yourself, just like everyone else . . .' I got up noisily and stormed off to the loo.

As I brushed past Lol towards the Ladies, his friend at the bar was shouting, 'Gimmie two saaarf drink.' He saw me and blocked my way putting his foot out. I glared at him. His lazy smile showed a gold tooth, his skin was matt, like black smooth clay.

'Hey, darlin'. Yuh wah jukk?' he said.

'Fuck off.' I said even though I didn't have a clue what he was talking about.

In the toilet there was graffiti and no toilet paper. Standing sitting to avoid touching the wet toilet seat I thought about Lol. Bloody cheek.

I looked at myself in the mirror and zipped up my trousers. The music was pounding at the door. So I'd made a silly mistake about a faceless number in a little pub in Stoke Newington. So what? I was a successful television researcher on the way up and I was earning more money than all of them . . . and damn goodlooking to boot. On the way back, Lol stopped talking and looked straight at me. I stared right back, flicked my hair, and was about to walk past him when he caught my arm. Who did this guy think he was anyway? He was standing there in red label Levis, looking cocky.

'Wanna shoot some pool?' he smiled.

'No thanks,' I said, although I would have loved to thrash him on the pool table.

Hugh winked at me as I sat down. Chloe and Maggie were gossiping. 'Hey, Hugh, you know I've been a bit under pressure lately . . .' I started to lie but he shrugged it off. 'So what new film you working on?' he asked. This was just politeness. Chloe and Hugh thought I lived in a world full of superficial manners and trendy people. They were in the Socialist Workers Party.

'Not sure yet, I'm going for an interview tomorrow.' I obliged. It was so difficult to explain to them, and my folks and anybody else, about being freelance. The idea of working ten week contracts at a time was something they couldn't understand. Maggie had a well paid job with Hackney Council but it was structured and there was a ladder to climb, grades to move up. Chloe and Hugh just worked to live. Lol was tapping me on the shoulder again. I looked up and nearly drowned in his grin. 'You're on next,' he said. All right, I thought, I'll show *you*! I wagged my finger at Maggie who was laughing into her hand and followed him into the back room.

The air was so thick with weed smoke you had to hack your way to the pool table. Nearly all the men in there were black, standing talking or taking aim, resplendent in majestic dreadlocks and long coats. There was a soft buzzing of conversations in the air and the band in the main room was reduced to a distant baseline. Lol was the only white man there but he seemed to know most of them.

'This is Lundy,' he said and winked at me. His friend from the bar was now seated at a table rolling a joint. He looked up and extended a large lined hand. 'All right?' I said sheepishly, glad that he seemed to have forgotten my earlier retort. Lol was setting up the balls inside the triangle at the other end of the table. A few faces turned to look at me but my confidence stayed put as I went to select a cue.

'She gon' trash ya, bye,' said Lundy.

I watched astonished as Lol wagged his finger at him. Lundy smiled at me. It made me laugh the way black people said 'boy' all the time and the way Chloe and Hugh couldn't ever bring themselves to say it because it smacked too much of 'a colonial past'.

Lol motioned that I should break, which was his first mistake. I used to play pool every day at university and I was good. I'd done so many things at university which would have been impossible at school: slept with people's boyfriends, been 'streetwise', learnt arrogance . . .

I was about to clear up on the black and Lol still had two balls left.

'You've played this game before,' Lol said standing so close I could smell his aftershave. I knew his game. Trying to distract me. But I was all concentration and as the black rolled easily into the pocket I looked straight into his eyes and smiled triumphantly.

He looked at me for a moment his face completely dead-pan as if we were playing poker.

'You like to win, don't you?' he said.

I shifted my weight from one foot to another.

'So?' I said defiantly.

'Sooo . . .' he said and shifted his position, looked at the floor, then looked at me again. 'So, winner stays on.'

'You were going to say something else.' I was well and truly flirting with this man now but I wanted to see how far he was going to take it.

'Well,' Lol smiled, 'I was gonna say yuh wah jukk but it probably isn't a good idea, right?' His face seemed to become so serious that it warranted an honest answer. I knew what it meant now anyway. It was the kind of request men made to women on the offchance.

'Well, I don't really sleep with people soon as they ask me.' I didn't care who was listening. People were too busy doing deals and minding their own business anyway.

'Yeah, I've got a problem with that too,' he said. We must have spent five minutes looking at each other without blinking. At last embarrassment began to nudge me.

'Uh-huh,' I said. 'Don't tell me you're married, misunderstood, lonely. . . .' I reeled off the list like I was some kind of woman of the world and not a 25-year-old smart ass trying to cover up.

'Nah, I've been all of those. Now I'm just HIV positive.'

'*Time*, gentleman and ladies, please!' Ray the landlord was shouting as if he was going to pick a fight with anyone who wanted to give him an argument about it.

No one was paying any attention and people were still crowding at the bar. Probably because there weren't any ladies *or* gentlemen in there as far as I could see. If the kind of people I worked with ever came to a place like this they would probably have a heart attack. It was full of old black men swaying at the bar, young dudes in knitted tams wrapped around their thick dreadlocks, dirty looking white punks wearing torn leather jackets . . . If not a heart attack then they would have said dreamily that the place had such 'atmosphere'. I began to chuckle to myself but that was because I was drunk.

'Come *on*, darlin',' Ray was poking me in the shoulder. His pink face was mottled up with purple rage. Every time

I had seen this man he was either miserable or in a rage over something. There was too much dealing going on — which of course he allowed, because while the punters were waiting for their gear they had to drink. Or else there was a fight, or Spurs had lost and then there was universal misery. If they had won then there was serious drinking but then the filth, as he called them behind their backs, would pay a visit. Or else his beautiful but exceptionally dim daughter Tracey was allowing herself to be chatted up by some unsavoury character instead of attending to her job of pulling pints. I could see her now through the haze, laughing at some joke Lol was telling her at the bar. I found my lip curling up disdainfully betting it wasn't the one he had just told me.

Maggie was standing next to me. 'Come on we're going up the Four Aces, Ange.' She was shaking me and I brushed her aside because I was concentrating on the bar and now a number of people had started to get up and make for the door, all of them blocking my line of vision.

She kissed her teeth loudly and said, 'I don't know what you see in them pasty men, Ange.' Now Chloe and Hugh were threading their way toward us carrying my coat and bag. I slumped against the pool table and gave up looking.

'Hey, Angie, let's go to the reggae club.' Chloe was pulling her cardigan on. Hugh was standing next to me playing around with the two balls left on the table knocking them against each other until finally one of them careered into a pocket. 'I've got some blow,' he said to me. They were all waiting on me and Lol was chatting away to Tracey and I couldn't think of a way around it.

The cold air rushed into my brain as soon as we stepped onto the pavement. I felt a little unsteady on my feet but the others were rattling away in front of me so I held on to Maggie's sleeve for support.

'. . . and I said to him, you look well out of your box, man, and you know what he's like.' Chloe said to Maggie while Hugh walked along beside her, his arm casually around her shoulder.

'. . . and I said, well, it's not on the gear you sold me the other week man coz that was shit, you know.'

Maggie nodded her head. It was just like being at university. Conversation about the quality of grass, how out of it you were, who you fancied. Police cars ee-awed past us and the wind blew us closer together. Maggie was so good at this kind of thing, at diplomacy.

She hadn't always been that way. After being friends for most of the first year Maggie had started a big argument with Hugh in the bar one day. The night before, some skinheads had come onto campus and slashed up an African student at a reggae gig. All hell had broken loose. The Black Student Alliance wanted to set up vigilante groups to patrol the grounds. Hugh said that was a dangerous thing to do and Maggie had said it was dangerous already being black and who was he, a public schoolboy, to be telling them what to do. Maggie went her own way for a few years until we all left university. Chloe felt her loyalties had been split. It didn't take much to upset Chloe, she was like a little girl.

Hugh had been upset too, but Maggie was hard as nails and none of that 'New man shit' cut any ice with her. I thought she was crazy because apart from anything else, Maggie was brighter than Hugh. She had always been conscientious and worked much harder than I did. On graduation day when she stepped up to get her degree — a first in Sociology — I'd felt almost as proud as her mum who was sitting on the other side of the huge, hushed hall of parents. I'd craned my head past ma, dad and maama ji to catch that woman sitting black and proud beaming in her new hat with white people all around her. What a story she would tell back in Wood Green.

Hugh had got a 2:2, same as Chloe, and I'd said to Maggie in the bar later, she could tell them to stuff it now. For me it had been a long day of getting stoned and trying not to laugh at the whole charade. I had always been expected to do well at university and like everything else in life, the Literature degree had been another thing that had come my way.

The Four Aces was packed out. Clumps of people were waiting around outside, black girls with straightened hair in high heels and lurex skirts, stylish black men in suits and spats, and about ten rastas standing at the door.

'This place is full of pimps!' I hissed at Maggie. She giggled, nodded and pushed me past a bouncer, telling him Chloe and Hugh were ok. We all shuffled downstairs to the basement. It was an illegal, after-hours bar like a number of others along the street. The air was smoky with the smell of saltfish and rice that they were serving at the bar, along with cans of Coke and Red Stripe. Dead cans were being used as ashtrays. People just didn't think they were having a good time unless they were in a place that was a fire risk, about to get busted any minute, and full of people you wouldn't want to look in the eye in case they got the wrong message. Bodies were moving to the heavy reggae baseline from the big speakers. Black prostitutes rubbed shoulders with nice middle class white girls; political activists and drug dealers danced next to squatters and rastamen. 'Stokie people,' Chloe called them. Hugh was skinning up in a corner. Maggie had met someone she knew and was laughing about something. They were all on their own patch, even Chloe and Hugh who had become bona fide residents of 'Stoke Trenchtown'. I decided suddenly it was time to go home. The evening felt stale and humourless.

'Maggie, I've got to get up tomorrow, I'll call you,' I shouted over the noise. She stopped talking long enough

to make a face that said we just *got* here. I pressed her arm
and said I would call. Walking back to Chloe and Hugh
I kissed them goodbye. 'See ya, Huge,' I said, using the
nickname from college to show he was still my friend.
'Don't pick up any strange men, Ange,' he winked back.

It was a relief to get out of that place. The car was
parked outside the pub. Kissing was something else I'd
learnt at college. English people grew up knowing about
kissing people hello and goodbye, like they knew which
knife to use in posh restaurants.

Thank God I was nearly at the car. I wanted North
London and home and bed. Just as I was rooting around
in my bag for the keys a familiar voice called over. I looked
up and saw Lol coming out of the Dog and Trumpet. For
a split second I felt sick, shy and nervous but it must have
been the dope making me feel paranoid. He crossed the
street and stood smiling at me under the street lamp. His
eyes seemed so blue I thought it must be a trick of the
light.

'You didn't say goodbye,' he said, grinning.

'You looked like you were too busy,' I said curling my
lip.

'Yeah, I was . . . I had some unfinished business.' He
had the cheek to continue to smile.

If he thought I was going to ask what he meant by that
he was very much mistaken. As if I didn't know.

'That's not much of a motor for a Yuppie, is it?' he said
nodding at the orange Datsun, his face deadpan.

'Pardon?'

He started to laugh. I tried to put the key in the door
but it wouldn't fit, because I was too angry. Lol was still
laughing.

'Something amusing you?' I said viciously.

Lol stepped back, folded his arms, smiling as though it
was joke of the century.

'Yeah,' he said innocently, his eyes fixed on mine.

That was it. I was in a rage.

'Can't you think of anything nice to say to me?' I blurted angrily.

He had that grin on his face again. 'Of all the bars in all the world ya hadda walk into mine.'

I laughed. For one stupid drunken moment I wanted it to stay just like this. The key turned.

'Listen right,' he said and his face was deadpan. 'The Trumpet's my old man's pub, I'm always in there. Maybe I'll see you, yeah?' Then he was gone.

Drinking and driving is not a good idea. I know it. I also know all the speed traps, the slowest traffic lights, the shortest routes from Stoke Newington to Finchley. I've always made it my business to know what I need to know so no one could get the better of me.

It started to rain. I knew he must be running down the street somewhere getting soaked. I spent the whole journey concentrating on the road and going over and over in my mind everything he had said. I kept seeing his face. He was exactly the kind of man whose name would have been scratched on a girl's arm at school. There had been no such thing at university, and certainly not at Direct Vision, where talking to me was the nearest any of them ever got to meeting 'working class people'. What a laugh. I had always played on it though, I thought ruefully. In a strange way they seemed to be impressed that this girl in a hurry who never stopped dropping aitches and tee's was actually a graduate of literature. Lol would have known better. I could tell by the way he looked at the car, at my friends, at my retorts, that he thought I was well off. Things seemed to be topsy turvey. Hugh at ease in Stoke Trenchtown, a skinhead chatting up a 'paki', Maggie hanging out with 'new men'; me in a world of 'darlings' talking bullshit. Talking about the Dog and Trumpet as if I knew the place inside out. I had only been there half a dozen times and already I had it down in my pool of knowledge. Like reading a book review, then talking about the book as though you'd read it. I mentioned it to Phil, once in the restaurant, and Phil had laughed and said everyone did it. Talked bullshit.

Maggie and I had grown so far apart over the past year that Phil had become my confidante. On my second day at Amigo's restaurant I'd bumped into her as we were all practising carrying four plates on one arm.

'Sorry, Annabelle,' I'd said.

'It's Phillipa, actually,' she'd said.

'Sorry,' I'd said, thinking how could I have forgotten what a face like that was called. Phillipa looked and walked like a model. Silky wavy brown hair tumbling around her shoulders and perfect make-up.

'That's ok,' she'd said, 'all prissy Jewish names sound the same.'

We'd both laughed.

Phillipa could never have been called Tracey like the girl behind the bar at the Trumpet. Then I felt guilty, but thinking of Lol made me smile.

CHAPTER TWO

I turned the wheel into the drive and noticed the light was on in the front room. Ma had given up waiting up for me months after I had returned from university. The 10 was hanging off the door. No one had bothered to fix it. It was the subject of another one of dad and maama ji's jokes. Finchley was the constituency of Mrs Thatcher and this was the 'other' No. 10 they'd say and slap each other's backs.

I put my key in the door. Rax was standing in the hallway looking in the mirror.

'You're going to wear it out,' I said. He carried on combing his hair and smiling at himself.

'Give us the keys, Jelly.' He was wearing a black polo neck and a pair of denim dungarees five sizes too big. Only one button on the bib was fastened, holding the whole thing together — but this was style according to Rax. After combing his hair for the fifth time he put on his baseball hat and started folding up a small white towel into a long rectangle which he then placed carefully around his neck. He would have spent hours ironing every single item including the towel and the red printed scarf that hung out of his bib pocket like a tongue. Only to get it all soaked up with dance sweat within a few hours.

'Where're you off to?' I asked, disinterested. It was always the same thing but different venues.

'Vauxhall Art Centre tonight,' he said bouncing up and down as if he could already hear the music.

South London, I thought. Abroad.

'Keys, whistle, and hard tunes,' he was muttering as he picked up the plastic box full of records and started dragging it into the driveway.

The tv was on and I poked my head round the door. maama ji was sitting in the middle of the settee, his feet on the coffee table.

'Yaar, that brother of yours. Used to be he did not come in till midnight. Now he does not go out till midnight,' he said and tilted his head to one side. 'Hi, Maama ji,' I said laughing. For years I had tried to train the family in simple behavioural habits: hello, goodbye, thank you, please, knocking on doors, not opening my letters. . . all to no avail. They continued to have conversations without breaks, to make judgements as if we were not living in a different country, in a different world.

'Can I turn the heating down?' I asked. As usual it was up full blast. As if the *desi* vegetables, Indian videos of trashy films, Indian friends were not enough of a re-creation of the life in Delhi.

After turning the thermostat down regardless, I sat down next to him. 'Rax's gone to a warehouse party, Maama ji, they don't start till gone midnight,' I explained. 'He's DJing up there.'

'Warehouse, yes,' he said and ran his hand through the white hair that hung past his collar — as if that explained everything. Next to his feet was the chessboard with a game midway. He and dad would continue it tomorrow night.

I strolled into the kitchen to make some tea. A mild shiver went through my stomach as I remembered the interview, although I had worked out what to wear.

Maama ji and ma weren't alike at all. He was her younger brother. Like all good Indian girls she had looked after him as if she were his mother, especially when my gran left the family for long periods of time to go on marches and meetings against the British. Maama ji had been more or less brought up by ma and she indulged him in ways she never did us.

I have a hazy memory of maama ji meeting us at the airport, his woollen scarf tightly wound, his hair in need of a cut. He had been living in London for a year in a bedsit in Dulwich where the meter never worked.

Making tea (bought from The India Tea Centre in Oxford Street) in the little room overlooking brick walls and washing, he told ma and dad about the weather and about jumble sales. He told them how there were people in this country who gave away clothes and furniture that wasn't even soiled or broken, good solid things from Aquascutum, Liberty's and Harris Tweed. Names and shops they had read about in their English classes.

We had arrived in London, armed with advice about how we would never see the sun again. I was five and Rax was only a baby but that white Christmas is fixed in my mind like the plastic snowstorm that maama ji bought from a jumble sale.

I don't remember hardship, or the cold, just being spellbound by the air being alive with huge flakes of dandruff that turned the horrible patch of grass outside our flat into a soft fluffy white carpet. Snow and jumble sales.

We had found a flat just minutes from his bedsit in a big Victorian house. Upstairs lived an old Sri Lankan couple. The wife showed ma how to gut a chicken and where to buy Basmati rice. Every Saturday maama ji, dad and ma would queue outside church halls feeling vaguely ashamed that anyone back in Delhi should know they were buying secondhand clothes. Rax and I were dumped upstairs and had to sit silently while bedridden Mr D'Souza watched the sport on the black and white tv from morning till the football results at five. Rax snored through most of it and Mrs D'Souza fussed about in the kitchen cooking the evening meal. When dad had the money to buy a house it was unthinkable that maama ji should carry on living in his room so we all moved together to the leafy suburb of Finchley.

Over the years ma and dad gave up the Saturday rituals. Once ma was working and they had been able to afford a house in North London, middle class sensibility moved in. What would people think? But maama ji continued to seek out the never ending bargains; he didn't give a damn what people thought.

After jumble sales he graduated to Oxfam shops and Help the Aged. But for the past few years he had concentrated solely on car boot sales. Instead of becoming more selective, his net had widened to anything that was solid and useful. Now he did not bother with clothes or trinkets. He'd moved on to household items which he explained were plentiful at the car boot sales. Consequently the house had turned into a bit of a car boot sale itself.

'Bargain!' Maama ji would smile slyly as he dragged a telephone seat through the door. Although the telephone had been quite happy on a little shelf by the front door, it was decided that it would be so much more convenient to sit and use the phone, instead of having to stand by the door. And so it went on like that. Every new object found its own rationale and gatecrashed its way into the house. Hatstands and coathooks; nests of tables and paintings; ice buckets, typewriters, encyclopedias, vases, lamps, and a vast paraphernalia of wedgewood, crystal and glass figurines. Every available surface was cluttered up with the junk. The rest of the dining room was full of the piles of magazines that dad collected. *Time* magazine, *India*

Today and oddly, *The Independent* colour supplement.
And what with Rax's overflow boxes of records, No. 10
was teeming.

Another coffee percolator had appeared in the kitchen.
Tomorrow ma would find a space to store it. I made the
tea properly, with tea leaves and in the pot, because
no one apart from me and Rax used tea bags.

Maama ji smiled and shifted over on the settee as I put
the tray carefully down on the table so as not to disturb
the chess game. The tv room was littered with newspapers
and magazines. No one bothered to clean up seriously,
not even ma. She wasn't interested in housework.

'Want some food?' Maama ji asked. 'I can make some
chapattis.' He was sitting with that far away look in his
eyes that I saw sometimes. I never knew how to ask
him what he was thinking. He had come to England in
1969 for further study, his head full of Wordsworth and
Shakespeare. He had taken various menial jobs in order
to live but somehow this land of opportunity had evaded
him. He never gained entrance into an English university,
and like so many other disillusioned men he had drifted
into an aimless bachelor existence. The family in India
despaired at his dwindling letters until dad was suddenly
accepted for a job in the English civil service which he
had applied for as a matter of routine. Now Nirmal and
Tara were going to London with their Ungelliee. Shankar
would be looked after, at least there would be family with
him.

'The television is rubbish *yaar*,' said maama ji. We both
laughed. 'It is only good when I see your name on it,' he
said grinning at me.

I rolled my eyes. 'Cooking with Guinness in the
Yorkshire Dales. Great,' I said. 'Hardly prime time tv
is it?' Direct Vision had the monopoly on *Cooking around
the British Isles* — mainly because no one else could think
of anything else to say about it.

'Listen, *arrey*.' He nudged me, 'it's a start, *yaar*.' I loved it when he said that, because men only said yaar to other men.

I woke before the alarm. Lying in bed for those last few minutes caught up in dreams I listened to the soft sounds downstairs. Ma cooking for tonight; dad flushing the loo after being in there for half an hour with the paper, smoking. Two years ago ma had insisted on having another loo built downstairs. Now it was full of books like *Symptoms — a self diagnosis encyclopedia*, Bertrand Russell's *A History of Western Civilisation*, and various Indian novels. Dad's heavy reading was combined with hypochondria. He and I were the only smokers in the house and the only ones who ever used the downstairs loo. Often I'd leave my eyeliner or mascara brush by the toothglass on the sink, after a quick repair job. The alarm bleeped and I shouted at it. It was a voice activated alarm clock that maama ji had found at some jumble sale. '*Arrey*, now you are in television business, you must be having these modern conveniences,' he'd said gleefully. Needless to say, it hardly ever worked. It continued to nag on just as ma used to do when I was at school and could never get my back off the warm sheets. 'Shut *up*,' I screamed and leaped up.

The sunshine was leaking in through the curtains. Today no one needed to coax me out of bed. All unnecessary thoughts left my head as I put myself into that single minded interview frame of mind, and stepped into the shower thinking only of how I was going to present myself to these people. Direct Vision was history, I was going to meet Davis Films and impress them with my star quality.

Pulling on my Katherine Hamnett jacket over my silky trousers I squinted in the mirror. Last night's sweaty Levis lay on the floor. I dumped them into the cupboard. Earrings! The look should be sophisticated, fashionable, with a touch of individuality. Silver gypsy earrings, £7.99 from a stall in Camden market. Everyone assumed they had been handed down by my grandmother. As if once they'd lain in a gaping jewellery box next to heavy dowry gold and rubies and silver filagree necklaces that some bored Maharani had fingered languidly on a sun spangled marble step. Very Jewel in the Crown! An upwardly mobile young woman of confidence peered back at me from the mirror.

'What lovely earrings,' Lindsay Paris had smiled at me that night I was doing a late shift at Amigo's. She was sitting at table twelve and was about to change my life.

'Ungelliee,' ma screeched from downstairs and I tore myself away from the mirror and ran downstairs. Dad was turning the pages of the newspaper; the little black and white set in the dining room was on breakfast tv; maama ji was leafing through the E to H book of the encyclopedia; sitar music was coming from the cassette recorder; pots crashed into the sink in the kitchen, samosas sizzling in hot ghee. In the kitchen ma, partially obscured by smoke, was putting two slices of bread in the toaster while keeping an eye on the hob.

'What's all the cooking for, Ma?'

'The peanut butter is on the table, now hurry up or you will be late.' I walked through to the dining table and sat down carefully, so my jacket wouldn't crease. When I told dad how much it cost he'd taken a sharp intake of breath, even though I'd halved the price. 'But it's a *designer* jacket, Dad,' I'd explained. He'd looked at me as though I were some kind of imbecile and said that everything was designed by somebody. There was never any point trying to argue a point with my dad. When I had asked for a filofax for my twenty-fifth — a '*real* one not one of those market efforts' — he stood next to me in the shop trying to beat the price down, finally accepting a free address insert, still insisting it cost as much as a three piece suite. 'Yeah, Dad,' I'd said, 'but we're not talking rupees here,' and rolled my eyes at the shop assistant, a greasy haired Indian man who was siding with my father. 'Well, my daughter she is a television researcher now — she has learned to waste money like an English girl,' said dad.

Ma came in with my toast, lifted her cup of tea from the tray in front of dad's newspaper, stared at the tv for a minute and wandered back into the kitchen again.

'Shankar, have you read what has happened last night?' dad asked maama ji in Hindi. 'Killings yaar, both Sikhs and Hindus killed. Yesterday around Model Town.'

Maama ji looked up and called out to ma. '*Arrey*, Tara di did you telephone?' Ma couldn't hear because the extractor fan was on.

'Yes, yes I tried earlier, but as usual the line is down,' said dad answering for ma. I realised they were talking about riots in Delhi, in Model Town where my other Anand maama ji lived, ma's elder brother. Ma came back in and said had anyone tried to telephone.

It was incredible the way they carried on sometimes: saying each other's thoughts, anticipating each other's anxieties, talking across continents over the breakfast tv. 'And today of all days,' she said and sighed. She was worried but dad didn't hold her hand or say don't worry sweetheart as my English friends' parents would have done. He put the paper down and dialled the number again.

'. . . And as Britain's Asian community prepares to celebrate its new year police warn that recent unrest in India may escalate violence . . .' The tv was blaring and dad put down the receiver and said 'shh' and then ma came in wiping her hands on a towel to listen.

Shit! It was Diwali tonight. That was why ma was cooking as much food as she could before going to work because people would be visiting tonight. Shit, that meant I had to stay in. I wavered for a minute by the tv and listened to the short broadcast. My uncle's face flickered across my mind for a second and with it a wave of anxiety from somewhere. But then I bit into my toast happy in the knowledge that others were doing the worrying, knowing what to do, making sure things would be ok. Dad was dialling the number again. I waited but no answer. He said I should go to my interview or else I would be late and that if I rang home or his office or ma's office someone would let me know how it was in Delhi.

Even though it was called the Misery Line I didn't mind the tube that morning. I was relieved that ma and dad were obviously going in late, so we didn't have to travel together. I needed to sit quietly on the train and concentrate on the interview. *The Independent* had devoted part of its front page to the fighting in Delhi and Kashmir. Inside there was an article warning of the dangers of communalism which I tried to read but somehow the information would not sit in my mind.

Lindsay had smiled at my 'I'm . . .' badge. At Amigo's we had to wear badges with our names and greet the customers with: 'Hi, I'm so and so and I'm going to be your waitress tonight.' Many of us wrote silly things on the badges like I'm available or I'm knackered. I'd written 'I'm overworked and underpaid'. It was just a way of making those long hours go faster but some of the staff really took it seriously. Alex, who had just left school like the majority of the waitresses, ran into the changing rooms one day, crying. 'I'll never be a good waitress.' Phillipa and I had become the 'grandes dames' of Amigo's in only three short months, mainly because we were older than anybody else there. We consoled her and asked why. 'Because I just can't do an American accent and no one likes me,' Alex said between howls. I tried to stop laughing while Phillipa explained patiently that just because the Americans who had trained us in waitressing—Hank and Sheryl—sounded as though they had stepped out of *Dallas*, *that* didn't mean ... But Alex wouldn't have it. Hank and Sheryl had been flown over to teach us all about waitressing because Amigo's was the first of a string of American Mexican Restaurant Bars about to be launched all over London. For four weeks we practised carrying four plates; were tested on the contents of fifty cocktails; memorised what a tortilla, a chimichanga and an enchilada were, how they were cooked, which salads accompanied which dish. Hank and Sheryl had been at pains to explain to us that waitressing was a skill, an art, a whole approach to life in fact. Alex and her friends recently ejected out into the world had watched open mouthed as Hank demonstrated and role played; as Sheryl lectured and wrote on the blackboard standing erect and sensational in her stilettoes.

Lindsay was deep in conversation with a woman in her early thirties. I was opening a bottle of wine at their table, about to reccommend our 'loaded potato skins.'

'We really need a researcher straight away, Lindsay,' the woman said tearing her garlic bread daintily so that the butter wouldn't ooze into the cups of her long scarlet nails.

'Christ, you're not telling me any of the ones interviewed were right, oh thank you very much,' said Lindsay looking up at me. She must have been forty-something and I liked her smile and manner. So it seemed easy enough, after all I was on my own territory and could always scurry about my business if it became embarrassing, or 'serious shame' as Rax would say.

'Why don't you give *me* the job,' I said and flashed the two women my most 'I deserve a good tip' smile. English people can never resist a smile.

I half expected them to ignore this loud mouthed waitress who was edging into informality instead of remembering her place, which was to serve. Only I never believed all that stuff they told us about how the skill of waitressing was an art and something to be proud of. You are a good waitress, ergo you are a popular/interesting person. However I certainly didn't expect Lindsay to stop talking, look at me thoughtfully and say, 'What makes you think you could be a television researcher?'

It was a serious question and I knew instinctively it was an ad hoc interview. Honesty and guts were the only way out.

'Well I can read, I know how to use the telephone . . . and I'm nosey.' This made them laugh and I felt relieved that they hadn't put me down as an idiot.

'Ok, let's see you prove yourself, young lady,' said Lindsay scribbling out the address of Direct Vision. 'We'll give you an interview and take it from there.'

I was so shocked that all I could think of saying was, 'Do you want some coffee?' I even forgot the rest of it. Normally when the punters said 'yes' you suggested they try a cappuccino [£1.00]. When that seemed like a good idea you reeled them in nice and easy: 'Well why not try our special liqueur cappuccino?' [£1.80], and if they even started thinking about that one then you were home and dry because all you had to do was toss in the idea of the special Amigo's cappuccino in which there were five liqueurs [£2.50] — each of which I could name of course . . . By this time they had forgotten all about the measly 80p filter coffee they had originally asked for, or were too embarrassed to backtrack. Result: extra pounds on the bill and therefore extra tip. That evening Amigo's lost out on two extra strong liqueur cappuccinos because Table 12 got them on the house.

'The rest as it were,' said Phillipa six months after I had left Amigo's and was working at Direct Vision, 'is history.' We had laughed and drank some more.

I kind of missed working alongside Phil in that tacky crowded restaurant but it was absurd — I was in a crazy exciting world, being paid more than ever, and people were impressed by what I did.

Tottenham Court Road station jolted my thoughts and I breathed in. Perfumes mingled with stale air; people wheezed as they climbed the moving escalators, scrabbling for travel passes, cigarettes, money. For once it felt good to be part of that mundane nine-to-five army. Direct Vision had employed me as a freelance researcher and for the past year I had worked for weeks at a time with gaps in between, during which I sat around the house smoking and ma fidgeted anxiously about my next assignment. She would scan the job pages of the newspapers daily and photocopy them for me; talk incessantly about her friends' children who had regular jobs with guaranteed sick pay and holidays. When all else failed she would turn the subject to marriage.

'Ungelliee, you are such a lazy bum and see if you got married then you could spend all your life doing nothing but then we wouldn't have to worry.'

I would giggle and leave the room to avoid yet another lecture on how at my age she and dad were married and dad spent all hours on his PhD, working the rest of the time to support them in that tiny flat in Delhi.

'You, you don't know what hardship is, what scarcity is,' she would say. Thank God, at least Rax had his full time job at British Telecom.

However it had been two months since I'd got my last pay check from Direct Vision, and even I'd started to wonder what I was going to do with the rest of my life.

I knew a job would come up sooner or later but it never felt urgent. Sometimes I thought I wasn't cut out for a career at all because I just didn't care badly enough about it. There were no bills to worry about and sometimes work felt like another fashion accessory. Yet when Lindsay had called me last week saying a job was coming up and that she had personally recommended me, I was filled with a sense of urgency and excitement. Another job, new people, another challenge . . .

Direct Vision had dwindled down to a small production office over the past year, with only the receptionist assured of her job. Most of the researchers and directors had scattered into the freelance market that sprawled across the various film and television companies in Soho.

'Things are getting thin on the ground, Angie,' said Lindsay. Two months ago, she'd called me into her office, lit up another Ultra Silk Cut. 'You've got a good record at Direct, you've done a number of films now — she'd paused, trying to soften the blow, then exhaled noisily — 'time to check out the big wide world.' We had just finished a series for Channel 4 but no more commissions had come through. So. No more work in the foreseeable future.

Suddenly Lindsay Paris with her family like atmosphere wasn't going to exist any more. My heart skipped a beat. I didn't tell my folks, who would have panicked. I was busy panicking by myself. The receptionist had told me in confidence that Lindsay seemed to have lost interest in the company because her mother was dying of cancer. I was shocked that such a tough businesswoman could have buckled under.

'You'll do fine, my girl,' said Lindsay, 'it's just a question of contacts.' I'd wanted to run out of her office, away from this elusive unreal world, far away from some dreaded quicksand that threatened to engulf me and belch me out stamped 'Not enough experience'.

I haven't *got* any contacts I wanted to scream at her. I don't know any film people. How can you leave me to fend for myself . . .? But she was already answering two phones at the same time and it would not have done to act like a child. That evening I smoked casual cigarettes and boasted to ma about how freelancing was a great way of working, because you could have time off, you weren't tied to a nine to five routine . . . Rax said that he was soon not going to be tied to *any* routine. 'Oh yes, big shot,' said ma and carried on making chapattis, 'cannot even make his bed, now he is ready to make his kismet . . .' 'Yeah!' I'd snorted in unison and escaped into the tv room to avoid the lecture starting 'And as for you . . .'

I was smiling as I picked my way through Soho past the big Cinema Distribution houses, their windows full of posters about forthcoming attractions. Walking down Wardour Street I looked at my reflection in the shop windows. There were shops selling director's chairs, light gauges, cameras, movie posters, books and postcards. Boys with walkmans trundled past me pushing trolleys piled high with film cans; men in dark glasses crossed the street, deep in conversation about budgets. And above me the sun was spilling into all the hubbub and activity. Even the few pornographic houses left in Soho had faded pictures of Marilyn Monroe in the window next to posters proclaiming 'Live Sex Show' as though bowing to the superior pulling power of the moving image. I sighed as taxis hooted and belched fumes into my lungs. I was part of it again. Meshed in with all those people about their business, heads buzzing with ideas, angles, stories, unaware of the mundane tourists and prostitutes. I smiled sneakily into a glass window proclaiming a new film. I knew what a best boy was. I was back in the fray. Waiting for the entryphone to buzz I breathed in a gulp of courage. Lindsay had recommended me for this job. I had to make a good impression.

CHAPTER THREE

'Hi, I'm Madeleine.' A woman with a broad New York accent and expensive diamante earrings extended her hand. She was wearing a suit with padded shoulders and too much Poison.

'This is Charles, the director.' Charles was tall with a mess of blond hair held back in a pony tail — one strand had already escaped and was trailing the side of his face. And what a face!

'Hey, let's go to Valerie's and do this interview there — I'm starved,' said Madeleine. Swishing skirts and people explaining ideas with their hands — Valerie's was full of conversations and newspapers. The aroma of freshly baked croissant filtered into the half darkness of the coolest patisserie in town. The French waitress weaved her way around the tables and perfumes setting down cappuccinos, shouting through to the kitchen.

'So, ok.' Madeleine tore a piece of croissant and deposited it into her mouth. 'We have six weeks to make this film. It's for Channel 4, part of their Contemporary Dilemmas series.' She paused and looked at me.

'Sounds really interesting,' I blurted out eagerly. Both of them looked bored. I realised I had betrayed my lack of experience in the media. I'd never heard anyone in the

industry, what little I had seen of it, praise tv programmes
effusively. They clearly thought it strange that I even
watched television. I'd noticed over the past year that
almost every one in this business only ever watched
television if it was a film they had worked on. If a
programme was discussed, it was usually to do with the
problems on location, or who had slept with whom or
who'd got what commission. Otherwise, television people
tended to drone on about how they couldn't wait to leave
television ('tape') and work in features ('35mm or 16mm')
. . . 'The *quality* was so much better, the *images* had more
depth . . .'

'You'll be shooting on video I suppose,' I said casually
as if, oh dear what we professionals have to put up with.

Madeleine immediately put on a glum look and
nodded. 'Yeah, 16mm is out, too expensive.'

'Yeah right,' I shrugged, easily slipping into her
Americanese. It had been the same at Amigo's. People
saying 'Yay' and 'Riiight' instead of yes.

'Oh well, I'm really into video, I mean it's the future,
right, I mean we're the new generation, right?' said
Charles mischievously glancing at me and laughing. I
liked the way he had included me. 'Ok, hot shot,' said
Madeleine digging him in the ribs, 'let's move on, huh?'
Charles smiled at her. She was the boss all right.

'The film is supposed to be about AIDS but we want to
make a different kind of thing, you know, not the usual
catalogue of open wounds and lesions.'

He looked at Madeleine who was looking at me and
nodding.

'Right, depression city,' she said and smiled.

I guessed that neither of them smoked so it wouldn't
have done to light up at that moment. But I had to do
something about my heart which had suddenly begun
to beat at an alarming rate. For some reason visions
of last night in the pub came swooping into my brain

and somehow Lol's face and the stench of the smoke wouldn't dislodge themselves. I sipped carefully as if to do anything more would have made me open my mouth and blurt out crazy mad things that would have sent these civilised people running screaming out of there.

'Yeah,' Charles put his elbows on the table. 'You see Madeleine doesn't want yet another film about gay love and friendship in the face of adversity.' They exchanged tired smiles and rolling of eyes as if it was all really too tedious for words.

'I mean, ok you know, but it's been done and we want something a bit sexier than that.' He lifted his eyes at me to see if I understood that sexy meant sensationalist.

'Something young people can relate to, not a big bad wolf kind of thing.'

I nodded into my coffee cup. Now I'm just HIV positive, he had said. Wanna shoot some pool, he had said. Darlin', he had said.

Charles's hands were moulding air. 'The way I see it is that no one wants to watch another film about AIDS ok, and so I want to do something different, something a little risky . . .' He put the strand of hair behind his ear and grinned at me. 'I mean it's like condoms with chips at the moment.'

Madeleine let out a short burst of laughter and nodded.

'And really,' continued Charles, 'it's like sex has become a . . . a hippy concept. Well you know, I want to put sex right back there where it always was anyway.'

He stopped mid flow to see if I was with him.

I was looking straight into his face.

'I mean sex has *always* been about danger and guilt and dirt and power. It's always been irrational and subliminal, sweat and blood and pain, deceit and manipulation. . .'

'Yeah, and *that's* only when it's *good*,' interjected Madeleine. She roared with laughter and looked at him sideways. They both laughed.

I was pretty sure they had slept together and somehow this tacit knowledge made an absurd impact on me. I felt as though they were not only interviewing me but as if they were dangling their private joke in front of me as a test. Suddenly I wanted to take that test. Jump onto their platform, be smart and blasé, not coy and unprofessional.

And an old memory of a cheat I had hidden in my sleeve in an exam came to mind. I'd guiltily flushed it down the toilet unread, because dad would have been not only furious but contemptuous — as if it wasn't worth winning then . . . I smiled at my own naïvety. This was the world, not a classroom and anything could be had if you were smart enough.

'You mean perhaps centering the film around a normal, er, straight person or something like that.' I had to hold my hands underneath the table to stop them shaking, excitement surging in the pit of my stomach.

Madeleine pushed her croissant aside, leaned over as though we were in the Dog and Trumpet, making a deal. 'Yeah, you got it . . . but.' She made a face as if the air had suddenly gone bad: 'We need an angle.'

Hugh would have said, 'Do people really *say* things like that?'

'The problem is that we really don't want to go through the usual agencies like the Terrence Higgins Trust etcetera because you know, that's not the story we want,' said Charles. 'We want to find an ordinary person who . . .'

'. . . is carrying on as normal, like they've got this disease but they're still chatting people up, hanging out, having fun . . . sort of dicing with death.' I was stunned at myself for coming out with a statement about something I knew nothing about.

Madeleine rapped the table with her palm and laughed. 'Hey, right,' she said. Charles smiled right into my face and I felt the old glow returning. I realised in a flash that they had seen an idea in my words, an idea that I was going to make happen.

'I think I know someone . . . a contact,' I said carefully and for the first time that morning I looked straight at Madeleine and took out my Bensons. 'Do you mind if I smoke?' I asked. In a funny way it wasn't a dissimilar feeling to turning tables at Amigo's when you had managed to subtly coax the customer into spending twice the money.

'Welcome aboard,' said Madeleine.

Amigo's was empty. The faint smell of oil lingered in the air and someone was hoovering round the back. It was cool in there and most of the waitresses were having their well deserved afternoon break. I remembered the delicious hours between eleven and twelve-thirty. Time to rub your feet, count your breakfast tips, make a phone call before the madness of the lunch hour started. Walking into the bar area I winced again at the décor. The walls were covered with stuffed animals and American car number plates, interspersed with potted plastic plants. 'Tacky was not the word,' Phillipa used to say, 'more like tacked on.'

'Hi!' I called to her.

She turned from the till and flashed me a smile, and pressed her palm in the air indicating five minutes. I nodded and lifted myself onto a stool by the bar. I was so excited and restless I thought I would burst. I wanted it all to come tumbling out in a rush so every time the story of the successful morning threatened to form itself into a coherent story in my head, I pushed it out. To distract myself I scanned the place to see if anything had changed. Only an American company could have thought that making a restaurant look like a swamp was a good idea. The dark green walls and dusky pink tablecloths seemed even murkier when illuminated by daylight fighting in through the windows. Stuffed birds in mid flight nestled among plastic aeroplanes; film posters for American classics like *Gone with the Wind* were taped next to baseball hats; various bits of old American cars — fenders, side doors, handles and steering wheels had been added onto any spare space on the walls. No constant theme or guideline. Just a series of whacky, unrelated items. Hypnotic muzak played through the speakers. Phillipa was serving at one of the two tables still occupied, so I proceeded to tear up three beer mats. She must have been cursing the straggling customers but I watched her smile sweetly as they sipped their coffee. Bored and restless I turned my attention to the door and gazed at the still street outside. Time seemed to be on hold. As if, while people beavered away in dark offices, the world had turned into a ghost town with litter whistling across empty pavements to piped muzak. The world was standing still, waiting for the workforce to kick, shove and cough it into reluctant life.

The door opened and Lol walked in.

I stared as he opened the second door and started to walk toward the bar. He was squinting in the sunlight so it took a second before he saw me. I couldn't believe it.

'Not you again,' he said grinning at me. I was grinning like an idiot.

'What are you doing here?' I asked.

'Working,' he said, easing himself onto a stool next to me. Why the hell couldn't I stop smiling? Instinctively I reached for a cigarette.

'You smoke too much,' he said, his face blocking out the table in the background. My mind had gone a complete blank. He was wearing old faded 501s ripped at the knee and a white t-shirt soiled with grass stains. The battered leather jacket hugged his shoulders as it had done last night.

'Working?' I asked, thankful to have thought of something to say. 'Yeah, I'm a gardener. God this place is really the pits, isn't it?' he said, looking around and coming right back to look into my eyes. I shifted around my stool and stared at the row of bottles behind the bar but not a single recipe for a cocktail came to mind. 'Please,' I thought, 'please don't let Phillipa finish her work, please don't let the world start. Not before I've had a chance to say something brilliant.'

'Have you seen the Gents?' I said suddenly, nodding in the direction of the toilets. 'Go on,' I urged when he frowned.

Without questioning me, Lol got up off his seat and followed my gaze, out of the double doors. I stuck my tongue out at the video camera above the bar.

The men's toilet was painted brilliant white with three television monitors mounted in the walls above the urinals covering the bar, restaurant, and lobby area. When I'd worked there we had amused ourselves by making faces in the restaurant whenever a goodlooking guy went to the loo.

Within minutes Lol was back chuckling. 'It's like the Starship Enterprise in there,' he said and we both laughed.

'Yeah right. Beam me up, Scotty,' I said rolling my eyes and Lol laughed out loud.

We talked for a while about how come it was the men's toilet that had monitors and not the women's, even through women spent more time in the toilet. I told him I used to work there, and that reminded me about being excited about my new job and how there were other things to talk about with him.

'Look, I've got a few things to do but um, can I have your phone number?' he said, and you could tell he was experienced in asking girls for their phone numbers. 'I haven't got a phone,' I said looking straight at him. I had a private rule about giving out No. 10's phone number to attractive men. There was also the double advantage of never having to wait by the phone. 'Well, I'll give you mine then,' he said scribbling down a number on a serviette.

'Maybe we can have a beer sometime?' he winked. 'See ya.'

'See ya,' I said and the noises of the restaurant started up again, like a car suddenly accelerating into action.

For moments I felt as though I had forgotten which piece of information was the most important, and I was putting my thoughts in order as Phillipa came up behind me, saying 'At last.'

I turned towards her and we smiled at each other.

'Did you get the job?'

'Of course,' I said. Job and telephone number. It was a good day.

'Great. Let's celebrate. I've got a half hour break, you want a red wine?' Phillipa didn't do conversations without alcohol, even if it was the middle of the day. I watched her pour out two large glasses of Côte du Rhône and marvelled at how she always managed to look as though she had just walked out of the hairdresser's. Whenever I had moaned to her about it she had always waved me off and said, 'A perm and years of practice in front of the mirror is all it is, Angie. And years of thinking I was the ugliest beast on earth.'

We both said 'Guess what . . .' at the same time. Then we both said 'You first' and laughed. It was like old times. 'Well,' she said, clasping her hands underneath her chin, 'the most amazing coincidence happened today. This guy I was at school with suddenly turns up to weed the garden outside . . .'

Before she'd even finished, I knew it was going to be a crazy day for coincidences. The world was tearing along at high speed dragging me by the scruff. All I had to do was stand still and things would happen.

'Was it Lol?' I asked and it was her turn to look surprised.

'Yeah, but?'

'I met him in Stoke Newington last night,' I said, unable to conceal my smile.

'Oh yes?' she said, arching her left eyebrow.

'So, you tell me,' I shrugged. For probably the first time with Phillipa, I was acting cool. 'He's nice, isn't he?' she said, and we both nodded. She wiped her lipstick away from the corner of her mouth. 'He's a bastard of course,' she added matter of factly. I couldn't bear the suspense. I reached out and grabbed her hand. 'Tell me *everything*!' I shouted and we burst into laughter. 'Phil, I'll kill you if you don't stop. Tell me!'

So she stopped laughing and composed herself, wrinkling up her brow.

'Well, you know we used to live in Hackney, well we were at the same school . . . He was a, well a skinhead, I suppose. Anyway he went around looking tough and you know all the girls were crazy about him. Then he started to go out with Kathi Smith and that was that really.'

'And?' I demanded. I had to know every detail.

Phil shrugged. 'Well they got married, you know. We moved to Hendon and I never saw him again.'

Married! Of course he was married. But there was something else to explain. How the hell could I have forgotten? People didn't make jokes about HIV, did they? Did they? Suddenly I felt sick. Had it been some sort of ghastly joke that I had half-believingly passed off as knowledge to Charles and Madeleine. I felt a panic rising in the pit of my stomach. There was no contact, no story. I would turn up on Monday with my tail between my legs and they would laugh at me.

What on earth was going on? One minute I was thinking he was a contact for a film about AIDS and next minute I was depressed because he was married. The two things did not make sense. If he had AIDS, or even if he was HIV positive there was no question of, well it was out of the question, so what on earth . . .

'Of course, I saw *her* a few times,' Phil continued.

'What?' I almost screamed. Phil looked up at me to see what all the fuss was about.

'Sorry,' I softened my voice. 'What do you mean you saw her?'

'Oh, she came in here a few times when it opened. Strange really, it's so far from her end of town. But it's like the nearest there is to Covent Garden I suppose. You know, zany-wise,' Phil said rolling her eyes.

'You mean, when I was here?' I stared at her.

'Yeah,' she shrugged.

Well, it would have been too ridiculous to ask Phillipa for a rundown of this woman's looks, style of dress, personality . . . and yet I wanted to know. I wanted to know everything.

But Hank had turned up. He was standing next to me doing his usual 'hi!', as if he didn't hate my guts for walking out of that place without giving any notice.

I'd chosen the busiest time on Saturday evening six months ago to march up to him. 'I wasn't sick yesterday, Hank, I went for an interview . . . with a film company,' I'd boasted.

'Uh- huh,' he'd said, counting money.

'So, I'm leaving, ok?' I really wanted him to be put out about it but he was irritatingly oblivious.

'Not for two weeks, honey,' he'd said to the cash register.

'No, in two minutes, Hank,' I'd said, thrown my apron on the floor and walked out.

'Now, just hang on little lady . . .' I could hear him shouting but I'd closed the door behind me.

Now he was talking boring stuff to Phillipa and I drummed the bar with my fingers and looked over my shoulder at the door.

'I don't believe it,' said Phil when he'd slithered away. 'He said I've been double booked on my shift, and Alex is doing it. I've got the afternoon off,' she said drinking some more.

'Brilliant,' I said, 'let's get out of here.'

I knew better than to talk to Phil when she was driving. The day she passed, her test, Mischa, her ex-husband, insisted that she drive him to work. Since Mischa worked in the West End, Phillipa had to negotiate the horror of the Marble Arch roundabout where there was pure traffic.

'Afterwards,' said Phil, 'I was shaking so much that I dropped him off, parked the car and caught the tube home. I put my licence in the kitchen cupboard. I said to him, ok I've got the licence already, I'll look at it now and again.'

The car had been towed away and Mischa was furious. He'd spent the whole night telling her what a selfish, neurotic woman she was.

'What a jerk,' I'd said.

I was biting my bottom lip off by the time we got to the driveway of her parents house. We walked in to the living room to the blaring tv. The house was immaculate as usual. There was lots of wood and Jewish stuff on the walls. Auntie Miri was glued to the tv in a cloud of smoke.

'Hello, darlin',' she croaked without looking up. Her voice sounded like she chain smoked, which she did.

'Hello, Miri, anything to report?' asked Phil.

'No darlin'.' Davey's gone for that job today but I dunno if he'll get it. Tilly's at the hairdresser's. Again.' Auntie Miri was a flesh mountain topped with jet black hair. Her lips which were decidedly pursed at the moment were always bright pink. Phillipa was the only one in her family who sounded like she'd actually grown up in suburban Hendon. All the others — auntie Miri, uncle Davey, Tilly and Morris, even cousin Geoffrey the accountant only confirmed that: 'You can take the family out of the East End but you can't take the East End out of the family.'

Phillipa was looking sympathetically at her aunt. 'What did Tilly say to you, Miri?'

'Nothing. Who am I to complain? All I want to do is help.' Auntie Miri sucked her pink stained cigarette even harder, refusing to take her eyes from the tv.

'Come on, Miri. Shall I make us a coffee and you can tell me all about it?' said Phil taking her coat off as we walked into the L-shaped kitchen.

Every time we saw each other, there was always some family crisis that had to be dealt with. You could never just open the door and sit like regular people.

'I'll put the coffee on, you go talk,' I offered.

'No. I know what it's about and I'm not taking sides. You go on in and I'll come in with the coffee,' said Phil. I walked back into the room. Phil's strategy was clear. Auntie Miri wasn't about to spill her guts if I was there — friends were friends but this was family business.

I was thinking we would never get round to discussing Lol.

'Is it good, the tele?' I asked evenly.

'Load of rubbish. Haven't seen you for a while, lovey. Phil misses you, you know.'

I nodded. Was there no end to little triggers of guilt?

'Been busy, I expect. Phil said your name was on the television the other day. You're a smart girl, I always knew you'd do well, didn't I say that, Phil?' she shouted. She was off. Given a chance, auntie Miri was an expert at holding conversations with herself. But I was too excited.

'We met an old friend of Phil's in Amigo's today,' I said casually.

'Oh yes?' She leaned towards me and one of her chins shuddered. There was nothing she liked better than a piece of outside world gossip. Especially men's gossip.

'Yeah. A school friend. Lol, I think his name . . .' I trailed off, waiting for the cogs of her memory to get started.

'Lol George? Not that Lol George from up Stoke Newington? Oh yes I remember him. Cheeky bugger.'

'Did you know him, Miri?' I asked eagerly.

'Know him? He heard some words from me I can tell you. Phil was always such a good girl. You see, her trouble's always been she's too kind. I used to say to Tilly, that's the Morris in Phil that is . . . 'Cause I mean Tilly's always had that streak. She's always been hard. A sharp tongue, mummy always said . . .' Miri's eyes were narrowing. Phillipa came in carrying the tray and I leapt up almost knocking it out of her hand. Ma's always saying to me 'slow down, slow down — what you think there is a train to catch?'

I handed round the coffees. 'So what's all this about you and Lol, then?'

'Oh God . . . history,' said Phil looking at the tv.

But she was outvoted.

Miri puffed herself up and turned toward me. 'That's what *she* says,' and moved closer to me, whispering dramatically. 'Morris sent him packing. Told him no daughter of his was going out with goyim. And a pub his father owned. Full of terrible people.'

'Miri, we were barely fifteen, for God's sake.'

'It was the beginning. And then that Mischa. Imagine. Not Jewish, not even English. *Yugoslavian!*' She waited for this to sink in. 'And taking photographs for a living. Tch! Unbalanced mind. Always it's the same with the creative people.'

'Phil, you didn't tell me you knew Lol like that?' I said and it sounded like an accusation.

'There was no like that about it. I was just another one he fancied, you know. Only he a got a bit more than he bargained for. Then. *You* know. It was dirty Jews and all that crap.' Phil shrugged her shoulders like it was meaningless.

'What about . . .'

'Kathi? Can you believe it. Married at eighteen. Same as me. There must've been something in the water.' She laughed. 'And it wasn't like either of us *had* to.'

More. I needed to know more if I was going to avoid feeling sick. Phillipa seemed to be reading my mind as if it was coming up on Teletext.

'Angie, for God's sake,' she turned around. 'Honestly, there was nothing to tell. I went out with him a couple of times. I was fifteen. He was seeing Kathi and she found out and threatened to kill me. Then Dad found out and threatened to kill *him*.'

Auntie Miri cackled into laughter and then into a short coughing fit.

Phil looked at me. 'Ok already,' she said. 'They're separated. He moved out a year ago. Happy now?' She rolled her eyes.

I wagged my finger at her making fun.

In the delicious fug of smoke and warmth we all stared at the tv, gently sipping our coffees. Miri began to lay out her solitaire on the table. Phil undid her hair and kicked off her shoes. I sank deeper into the armchair, my mind racing. What was this girl Kathi like? How come Phillipa wasn't bothered about Lol?

'Hello,' Phillipa's cousin shuffled in. Geoffrey had wiry brown hair that crept around his forehead and he wore corduroy trousers. 'Hello, Geoffrey . . . I must be going actually,' I stammered gathering my bag and coat. Why did shy people always put you on edge?

'I'll drive you back,' Phil volunteered. 'Isn't it new year today?'

'Shit,' I exclaimed. Diwali! I was supposed to have been home hours ago. No wonder the whole day had felt like a slice of still sunshine. As though I had no commitments, no responsibilities. Geoffrey piped up that Phil had drunk too much, so he'd drive me back and Phil agreed reluctantly.

'Again?' she said in her stockinged feet at the door. Her face was tired and sad.

'Yeah.' We kissed goodbye. There never seemed enough time to talk.

'Ma's *vex* up with you, Jelly,' said Rax as soon as I got in.

He was dragging his box of records across the hall, feebly assisted by his friend Kyle, a red paisley kerchief tied around his head.

'All right, Kyle,' I said pushing past them into the dining room.

Ma was standing with her back to me over the other side, slowly lifting the little tv onto the floor. Old film songs were playing on the cassette. She opened the sideboard and took out the little bronze gods and the old Bhagvat Gita, blew the dust away, and started to arrange them.

'You see,' said maama ji behind me, both of us watching ma's delicate, assured movements. 'The western god is replaced by the Indian gods, heh heh.'

Ma, pretending I wasn't there, told maama ji to fetch the candles from the Tesco bag.

'Shall I do something?' I asked. I envied English people their 'pleases' and 'sorries' which smoothed over the biggest wrongs. In this family you had to suffer seriously.

'What is there to do? After all this is a hotel you are visiting. Go, go and have a shower, at least you can do that. And tell Rakesh to ask Kyle if he is hungry,' she said, her back to me. I was about to ask how come Rax couldn't have helped her with the cooking but kept *stumm* as Phillipa would say. At least Rax was shifting his records out to the garage.

Upstairs waiting for the bath to run I stared at Lol's number as though some great truth was going to leap out of it. I copied it out into my filofax and then tucked the serviette inside the leather pouch. It was my first souvenir.

Lying in the hot water I thought about the billboards about AIDS. About Madeleine and Charles. I wondered if Lol was a junkie. I remembered the flat in Dulwich where the bath was in the kitchen because it doubled up as a work top. I had held on for as long as possible before braving the snow to go to the outside toilet. Dad saying he was never going to get used to this ridiculous way of cleaning yourself by lying in a pool of dirty water. According to him you could only be clean under running water. Before we ever got a shower, he would fill up a bucket with hot water and sitting in the bath scoop out jugfuls of it to bathe himself, just like in India. As a matter of fact, he still bathed in this way.

'You'll see,' he said whenever anyone took the piss, 'when the west comes around to realising that it is the best way to bath, then you will come to me and say you have discovered something new. Hah.'

'But it's relaxing with the bubble bath, Dad.'

'Pah! This is what the education of this country has taught you! Instant pleasure, instant gratification, as if results have to be immediate or else they aren't results. What about the chemicals in that stuff? No you don't worry about that,' he challenged.

'No, because I buy the natural kind without additives,' I said.

'Eh! And spend the money you would spend on a week's shopping. When you can make it yourself! And anyway, you see back to the natural things, the Indian way of doing things . . .'

There was no arguing with dad.

It was impossible to think about anything at No. 10, there was too much noise, arguments, cooking, memories. Too much going on.

I put on the crisp starched shalwar khameez that ma had laid out on the bed. Downstairs some people had already arrived and conversations were in full flow. Bowls of snacks were dotted around the living room and the scent of joss sticks filled the air. Maama ji was putting lit candles everywhere. He had already put some outside, but they kept going out and Rax had been delegated to relight them. He was wearing his only pair of non-ripped jeans and a white shirt dad had bought. It was important to wear new clothes on the new year, because it meant you would wear new clothes every day of the year. Supposedly. Rax was scowling at his task and maama ji was explaining to him:

'The goddess Laximi will come to the house tonight and she has to see where she's going.'

Rax was looking at his watch.

'She's the goddess of wealth you see . . .'

Rax started to pay attention.

'But she comes up through the drains so that's why we have to clean every cranny and nook.'

Rax kissed his teeth and walked off as if that was the stupidest story he'd ever heard.

'You look nice,' said maama ji, noticing me on the stairs. 'Come. People are here.'

Ma's two friends were sitting huddled around the sofa while the husbands stood by the dining table talking Indian politics with dad. Maama ji went off to join them.

'*Arrey*, look at her. Why do you wear jeans all the time Ungelliee? You look so nice in shalwar.'

'Yes, yes. Oh, our children they can show the westerners a thing or two about stylishness.'

'Oh yes. But she is learning too much from them. Doesn't even help with cooking.' That was ma.

'*Arrey*, Tara she is a working girl now, she has no time for all of that business. She is after all in television business.' Ma's friend jutted out her bottom lip proudly as if I was blue blooded or something. 'Mine are the same,' she added. 'Going out out out all the time.'

'Out! Don't talk to me about out. Parties all the time. Ungelliee hand around the cashew nuts to auntie Roshni.'

This was Delhi and I was the perfect Indian daughter who passed the snacks around and all of their friends were 'auntie' and 'uncle'. Well. It was only once a year.

Dad and the other men had escaped into the garden and I could see them through the french windows illuminated by the row of flickering candles. Distant fireworks crackled the pitch black sky. Diwali was always around Guy Fawkes night and the neighbours were bewildered at the lit up houses and continuing barrage of fireworks that lasted for a week, yet they were too polite to investigate the ritual.

Maama ji came in to get a tray of samosas. Immediately ma started stabbing her finger at him.

'I'll do it, Maama ji.' I walked over to him with a forced smile on my face.

He let me have the tray and had a go at a genuine smile.

'Arrey, the STVs are too afraid to come out of their houses.' Then he made a 'Wooo' sound and rapped his palm against his mouth. 'The Indians are coming!'

'Shankar!' shouted ma from across the room. Her hearing was twenty-twenty. 'They will hear you.'

Maama ji winked and I laughed. Years ago he had christened the old aloof couple next door the 'Safe Tory Vote' and it had stuck. Outside the air was mild for November. Other back gardens were also full of kids screaming and men drinking. 'Of course, the situation is untenable. But what is there to do? Imagine if Indira ji was here how she would have felt about this boy, how he is carrying on such a prolific dynasty . . .' Dad was in full flow. Maama ji was stuffing his face with samosas and relighting a candle. The other two men were holding glasses and nodding gravely into them. One of them puffed himself up and dived edgeways into a gap in Dad's diatribe.

'It is the Sikhs, yaar. Always the warrior people. Look how long this silly request for Khalistan has gone on. And of course can you imagine? Next it will be Rajasthan, and then Bihar . . .'

'Ah, yes, but you see people do not regard him as a real leader. There is no faith in him, only faith that he is his mother's son.' At this there was a mild ripple of laughter.

Then maama ji stepped in with, '*Arrey*, that woman fooled you all. None of you were reading any facts, only your hopes. She was an autocrat of the highest . . .'

Dad and maama ji were opposed on several points in Indian politics and constantly in debate. Whether it was over the chess game: 'That was the kind of move that Indira Gandhi would make. Vicious!', or on the bus in the front seat, Dad smoking away and shaking his head vigorously.

I walked back into the room toward the women. Rax seemed to have conveniently disappeared, just as food was about to be laid on the table.

'Come, come sit next to me. Ahh you are looking very nice,' said auntie Roshni, shifting the folds of her

shimmering yellow sari. All of them had put fresh red
powder in their partings, and bright red bindis on their
foreheads. Ma was wearing some old gold bracelets
and a peacock coloured sari with fine silver thread
woven through it in stripes. It, like the other two, still
showed the crisp lines where it had been starched and
folded.

'So, when are you going to get married?' said one
auntie, nodding her head at me as though she was
coaxing the meaning of her words into my head.

'Yes, Ungelliee, when are you going to get married?
Auntie Munni wants to know.' This was ma, puffing
herself up because her favourite subject had started.

I sat there smiling for a second and then passed around
the sautéed almonds.

'Nice weather we're having, isn't it?'

'Oh no, Ungelliee. It's not going to work. You cannot
change the subject. Auntie Munni wants an answer.' Ma
wagged her finger at me.

'Arrey, leave her alone, yaar,' said auntie Roshni. It was
funny the way the women never said 'yaar' in front of
men, like it was swearing or something. She leaned across
the folds of her stomach conspiratorially. 'Let me tell you.
I don't say you must get married to anybody. No, no.
You must marry a nice boy, of course. But you see,' and
her face broke into a triumphant knowing smile, 'being
married is very nice. Very nice. *That* is the thing.' Then
she sat back, satisfied.

'Who will want to marry you anyway?' said ma. 'Soon
it will be too late my girl and then you will come running
to me saying Hai, Hai . . . yes, then you will see who was
right.'

Auntie Munni, the undisputed romantic, piped up with,
'*Arrey*, yaar, when you are married everything is easier.
We can find you a nice rich boy in India, educated.
Then you wouldn't have to do any work. You could

sit back and have everything done. You wouldn't have
to be like us, every day work shopping work. Rubbish,
yaar!'

'She already does not do anything, what will be
different?' said ma.

'So marriage is just a deal then? He gets respectability,
you get peace of mind and I get servants?'

This was entirely the wrong thing to say to the trium-
virate, who sighed collectively, like revolutionaries listening to the unpoliticised.

'*Arrey*, what else is marriage? Of course a deal between
families, communities. What is wrong with that?' said
auntie Roshni.

'What about love?' I said, and the women exploded into
laughter.

'What do you know about love?' said ma. 'It is not
this rubbish preached in the West. What, you think
love is flowers and chocolates? You should think for
yourself my girl instead of believing what you read in
this *Cosmopolitans*.'

'Mine also says he only wants to marry for love,'
said auntie Munni benignly, like she was talking about
someone who had some screw loose. 'And I tell him,
where is this love? Is it a thing that someone can give
you? A thing that you will know what it is when you
have it in your hand? No, I say to him. Love it is a
very over-estimated thing. Marriage is not so simple. It
is about hard working. Yes. This generation they want
everything instant.'

'You know, my English friends they come to tell me
all about their problems at the coffee break. They say,
Roshni, you are so calm. You never have any problems
in your marriage. And they tell me about their boyfriends,
and their husbands. They telling me about power struggle
and not being treated as an equal. *Arrey*, I say to them,
don't bother, yaar. I tell them what to do. Make him feel

guilty, instead of trying to talk to him. Then he will come around . . .'

All of them laughed knowingly. Outside, the men were shouting at the top of their voices, thinking they knew it all.

Then Rax bounded in and said 'Hi's' all round. 'Stop running everywhere, sit, sit,' snapped ma patting the cushion next to her.

'When we gonna eat, man, I'm starving,' he said.

The women began to fuss about helping ma to put away the snacks and put out the plates and bowls for dinner. They insisted on helping which I knew didn't please ma, because it was a chance for them all to look around her kitchen and make mental notes of its disarray. She said she didn't care about housework and stuff, but under peer pressure you could tell it mattered.

'Where have you been?' I hissed at Rax soon as we were alone on the sofa.

He put his middle finger and thumb to his lips and sucked noisily.

I rolled my eyes. Rax smoked dope twenty-four hours a day. 'That stuff is gonna replace your brains you know.'

'Go and do some work, woman,' he said and walked out into the garden grinning.

An uncle put his arm around Rax. 'So, Rakesh, everything ok? Yes you know we are thinking of moving. My Bablu tells us the Finchley area is very good.'

'Where d'you live now then uncle?' said Rax.

'*Arrey*, he lives in a hole, yaar,' said maama ji. 'South hole.' Everyone burst out laughing. They made the same jokes every year. 'South hole Fraudway!'

'Before that I was in Ealing with no feeling,' added the uncle.

All through dinner, I was trying to think how to escape. Every Diwali it was the same. At the beginning I would think it was ok and I'd sit through the 'get married' suggestions, then I'd hang around while everyone took their blessing from the gods, then we'd eat and then the night would go on till two, three in the morning with the men and women finally together, though still talking to their own sex. They'd all laugh and reminisce over old times, argue about which kind of mangoes were the best ones. The men would be bullied into making the coffee for once in their lives. Then they would all eat paan that turned their saliva orange. There was always someone who would sing and someone who would recite poetry and everyone would shout 'Wah', 'Wah'. More people would come to visit and I'd sit there like a lemon telling the same things to all of them. Yes, I would try to wear shalwar more often, yes, I was working for Channel 4 and no, I wasn't thinking of getting married.

This time, I thought, enough is enough.

By the time the third couple had arrived and people began settling down for songs and poetry, the party was in full swing. It was past eleven. The pubs were shut. There was a slim chance he might be home. I crept into the hall unnoticed, and dialled Lol's number. I had to open the front door to diffuse the raucous laughter and backslapping going on in the house.

One candle was still burning, a breeze wafted through the trees. The sound of fireworks still kept bursting the sky and distant merrymaking was whistling along with the trees. My heart was beating fast. I had one finger near the rest button, ready to cut myself off if my courage failed at the last minute; my other hand cradling the phone as close as possible to my mouth so I could speak softly; one eye kept darting toward the door leading to the dining room; mouth smiling automatically as people kept coming out to use the loo.

'Hello,' he said.

All my senses became jelly.

'Hi, it's Angie.'

'Hi, what you up to?' he said like it was the most natural thing in the world.

'Listen, you want to meet for a drink?' I whispered.

An auntie I didn't know came out of the room, smoothing down her sari. I smiled encouragingly at her.

'Now?'

'Yeah.' It's ok if he says no. It's ok if he says no. It's late and it's a stupid idea and ma's going to have a fit if I leave anyway . . .

'Ok.' Then he laughed. 'What shall we do?'

'I'll pick you up . . . outside the Trumpet. Half an hour?' I felt dizzy thinking he'd said yes, and ma was going to have a fit and what was I going to wear and how I felt sick and excited at the same time.

'Yes, ma'am,' he said in an American accent, and laughed.

I put the phone down and looked at my watch. Ma was in the kitchen arranging more Indian sweetmeats on a plate. Three empty boxes of 'Ambala-Indian sweet centre' lay on the floor already. No. 10 was like a bottomless pit tonight, of guzzling and laughing. Old Laximi, the goddess of wealth, would have a pretty hard time reconciling herself with giving this lot even more dosh to buy even more grub with.

'Ma, I never told you. They gave me the job on the spot. I was so excited I went to tell Phil all about it. That's why I didn't phone about maama ji. He's ok, isn't he?'

'Oh, fine, fine. We got through. He was asking after you. But,' she beamed for the first time, 'you got it? I knew you would.'

'Yeah, but I know this sounds funny, but they want me to meet them for a couple of hours . . . tonight. The researcher and the director. They can't do it another time and we're starting on Monday . . .' I waited for a response.

Ma wrinkled up her face and then said, 'Achha, ok. But make sure you just slip away, I will tell them you have gone later.'

Hurray. I raced upstairs to change. I knew ma would be ok about it and after all it was only a half-lie. I did want to talk to Lol about the film. Whatever she said, I knew ma was all for me having a career and was well proud that I worked so hard. Sometimes I thought I'd hate to tell her I could take it or leave it.

I threw off the shalwar and pulled on the Levis. Lipstick. I started scraping my hair back into a bun and then put some gel on it. Rax was roaming around outside, a roach between his fingers.

'Where you going?'

'Mind your own,' I said and he laughed.

It was beginning to rain slightly. Candles would be going out. Laximi would have given it up for a bad job. Lol was waiting on the corner of Stoke Newington Church Street in the rain. His collar up, looking more cool than protected.

'Jump in,' I said, opening the door.

'Where we going, gorgeous?' His hair was wet and ruffled up, and steam came out of his mouth as he spoke. The temperature had obviously dropped, I thought as I wiggled my toes at the heater. He was all wet and denim and flushed from standing in the cold.

'You'll see . . .' I said and smiled. He settled back into the seat as though girls always picked him up in the night. He did up his seat belt, stretched his legs and began to thaw out. I was driving faster than normal but then I liked driving fast. He started to tell me about his day at Amigo's and what he had done to the garden. It was infectious, and I found myself telling him anecdotes about my time there. He laughed and I drove.

The West End was bristling with energy. It had started to rain in sheets and people were scurrying around, cars screeching, looking for places to park where they wouldn't get clamped. I knew a place, just minutes from where I was taking him.

'We have to go downstairs,' I explained, as we crossed to the other side of Shaftesbury Avenue, where it intersected Denmark Street. Horns were screaming and groups of clubbers dressed in black swished past us. The theatre shift making its way home was giving way to the throng of late night people looking for a rave.

'What is this place?'

'Come on!' I pulled him down the iron steps to Derrida.

The matt-black double doors had two round windows like portholes and we saw the bar in silent animation for a second. Then I pushed the door, and like sync-sound noise burst upon us.

Inside there were tables either side of what could only be described as a catwalk. It was where everyone looked when there was a gust of outside air, or a break in their conversation. I had heard about this place in different conversations at work, and also I had seen it mentioned in *i-D* magazine.

Pallid faces turned to cast a moment's desultory interest in us, then looked away. The walls were plastered and varnished, with stark black and white drawings studded in frames against the glossy terracotta. The floor was bare grey stone. We found a free table and I sat down, looking around.

'What do you want?' said Lol. He didn't seem very impressed with the place. But then he obviously didn't know that it was The Place to be seen. Everyone seemed to be perfectly groomed without rough edges or split ends, wiry hair or smudged complexions.

'A margarita, please,' I said.

He came back from the bar and put his bottle of Beck's to one side. I went for my cigarettes. His head was looking at the floor but his eyes were averted to a corner of the wall. Like it was Clint Eastwood about to deliver his best line amid the dusty trail of a spaghetti Western. There was a patch of silence on the table between us. The vibes had changed. He was angry with me. He looked impatient. I suddenly thought what the hell are you doing here?

I opened my mouth and said the wrong thing.

'I quite like it here.'

'So?' he said without moving his head or his eyes.

'It's not heavy,' I said evenly. What the hell did I mean by that?

He laughed. Then he folded his arms, and the soft leather gathered inside his elbows. Then he looked at me. He carried on looking as though he was finished with conversation.

I shifted in my seat and took a long drag of the cigarette. My mind had drawn a blank again. How to broach the subject? Which subject? About the film? About his eyes? About his indifference? Why wasn't it simple?

Like an answer, somebody suddenly touched me on the shoulder.

'Hey, Hi . . . Hi.' It was Charles, steel Armani briefcase in hand, a strand escaping from the ponytail. He was with a group of people. The women had on bright red lipstick and black hats.

'Hi,' I couldn't help breaking into a grin.

Charles looked at Lol for a second. He put his hand on the table, between Lol and me.

'Hey, listen, it's good to see you. Looking forward to starting on Monday?'

I nodded.

'Yeah, right. I've just finished working on the outline with Maddy.' He rolled his eyes and put the strand behind his ear, 'God.'

'Is it ok?' No way was I going to introduce them. Lol could just sit there and sweat.

'Uh-huh. Well *you* know . . .' He shrugged. I didn't know but he was being friendly and charming and that's what mattered. 'Listen gotta go. See you Monday. Ten is fine, you know, don't kill yourself getting there.' He sauntered over to the bar.

Lol was drinking out of the bottle. I noticed a couple of women at the next table looking him over, looking us over.

'That guy's the director of the new film I'm working on,' I said flatly, finally, after he had shown no sign of interest.

Lol just nodded, his face a blank screen.

'I'm a television researcher,' I added. This is the world I move in, I wanted to shout. Why don't you show some enthusiasm? I wanted to scream.

'Well hey, high,' he said. Then he laughed and this time it was ok to laugh back.

'Shall I explain what we're doing here?' I said smiling, feeling accommodated into his grin.

'You want my body,' he said looking at my face. Maggie says white people blush but black people glow. Then she cackles. I think I went purple. But I liked it. I kicked him under the table. He caught my foot for a second and then let go.

'All right. Go on. I can see you want to be serious. Serious,' he said, pulling his closed mouth downwards in a mock serious expression.

I put my elbows on the table and propped up my chin. I fixed him with my 'I deserve a good tip' look and dived in. 'You know what you said in the pub last night?'

He nodded. We were staring straight across at each other and there was no room for bullshit.

'Was it true?'

'Yes,' he said.

For a moment, Derrida's carried on talking and being around us ignoring the silence that watched me swallow his word.

'You look like you could do with another drink,' he said and walked over to the bar.

I carried on staring in the space where he had been. The empty chair sat there with no clues to offer.

'They're not doing cocktails anymore, I got you a Beck's,' he said and placed the two bottles on the table. Then he touched my arm gently. 'Are you ok?' He sat down.

I was frozen scared. The ground had turned to sand and the tide was washing it away. 'I don't understand. Are you . . .'

'I'm not queer and I wouldn't touch smack if you paid me. I was just unlucky.'

'But . . .'

Lol looked down into the bottle of Beck's. It was my turn. I reached over to the gathers of the leather inside his elbow and slid my fingers into it.

'Don't say if you don't want to. I just want to . . . I don't know.'

He looked up, shook his head smiling faintly, as though he didn't believe a joke someone had just told him.

'I don't know what made me say that to you in the pub you know. You just looked so bloody proud of yourself, I just wanted to . . . I don't know. I wanted to get to you.'

'You thought I was feisty. You thought feisty bitch.' I laughed, using one of Maggie's phrases.

'Yeah,' he said and we both laughed.

'I was married to this girl. Nine years. Anyway it was a bit of a joke. Well she went with this bloke, her boss actually. I didn't even care much . . .'

'When did it happen?'

'About eighteen months ago. Then he gave her the sack. Told her to get herself down the clinic. They told her she was HIV.' He laughed, still looking at his bottle. 'Can you believe it? Just like that.'

'What happened?'

'Well it took her a few weeks to tell me. Thought I was gonna kill her. I nearly did.' He was moving the bottle around the table making a watery figure of eight.

'What?'

'Well, I shouted and screamed at her. Called her a dirty bitch. Other things. She broke everything in the kitchen. We were like a couple of animals that night. Next morning I went down the clinic and when I found out I still couldn't believe it.'

'But you seem so sort of all right about it, Lol. I mean . . .'

'Yeah. I dunno, after a while we just sort of didn't talk about it anymore. There were no signs. That's the worst thing, I mean it's like you've got it but you can't see it.'

'Did you go to any like groups or anything? Well are there any groups?'

'Yeah. The worker at the clinic gave us all the information. Kathi went to a couple of these groups for women but she said they got on her nerves. It was her really that made me think it was all right. Well . . .' He laughed, 'Not all right, but you know, like nothing was different really. One night she came in blind drunk. She'd been down to the club she used to work at. They had some hen night on or something. You know, all birds and a dozen blokes in underpants sticking it under their noses . . .'

'You're joking,' I said. I'd never heard of anything like that.

'Yeah well. She came in and I was watching the tele. She said I was a miserable bastard. I told her to fuck off. Then she said, fuck off yourself. I'm not sitting round feeling sorry for myself. I'm having the time of my life.

Great, I said. Listen, she said, listen to what I did. Well, she'd gone up to him, Eddie the boss you know, and started flirting with him. Really badly. All her mates were shouting and screaming. She was really laying it on, saying you'd like to do it to me wouldn't you, Eddie? Well of course, Eddie was having a fit and also he was shitting himself that she was gonna say something about it. But she never. That was the crack she said. She just went on and on for him to buy her drinks and he just kept buying them. Then she said to him, I'll get you, you bastard. I said you're dreaming, but she said that was the point. She said if I'd gone up there and kicked his head in like I wanted to, then it would have meant trouble, but *this* way she felt good because she was letting him know she wasn't . . . you know in the gutter or something.'

'God,' I said.

'Well anyway, I thought she's right. What's the point of thinking about it all the time. It only fucks your head up. She just started to enjoy herself. She said that you had to use durex and that was it. She didn't give a fuck. I said I was gonna move out and she said she didn't give a toss what I did because I hadn't never been any use to her anyway, so I moved back to my old man's for a while. Above the Trumpet. Then I got myself a flat just across the road.'

'Do you still see her?' I was intrigued.

'Now and again. She rings me up sometimes, but she seems all right, you know. I just . . . I just thought I've gotta be by myself, on my own. Sort it out. I had to think about myself, you know.'

'So, who knows then?' I asked.

'Christ, you really are a researcher, aren't you?' he laughed. 'You want to know everything.'

'I'm sorry. I'm just nosey,' I said. But I couldn't help it. An idea was forming in my mind and I couldn't stop it.

'No one apart from the clinic, her sister and Eddie . . . and now you.' He looked at me.

'Listen. I'm safe. I'm not a big mouth, all right?' I said.

'Do you want to hear a joke?' he said.

'What?'

'There's this Englishman, Scotsman and Irishman, right.'

'What?' I felt off balance.

'It's a joke. Listen. So they've all been condemned to die, right. But they're allowed to choose. So they can choose how to die.'

'What's funny about that?'

'Well, wait. So the Englishman says, ok I want to be shot in the head with a gun that's got one bullet. Like Russian roulette. The Scottish bloke says he wants to be run over in a busy street. Well the Irishman says he wants to be injected by the AIDS virus, and he wants to go first. Why Paddy? the others ask and Paddy says, "Oi fooled them awl 'cos oi was wearing a durex".'

'That's not funny . . . that's sick,' I said, sounding like 'Morally Outraged of Finchley'.

Lol stopped laughing and poked me in the arm. 'No sense of humour.'

'Who told you that one?' I said.

'Kath. She's got a whole load of them.'

Kath.

'Your mate in the Trumpet thought it was funny, what's his name, Hugh.'

God, was there anyone in my life this guy didn't know.

'How do you know *him*?' I demanded. I was surprised that Hugh would have laughed. I would have expected him to say it was ideologically unsound.

'He's all right. He has a pint in there after his meetings sometimes.'

I curled up my lip. 'Oh, yeah. Branch meetings. What do you think of him?'

'He's a good bloke, quite interesting.'

I looked at my watch. Nearly one. Derrida's would be closing soon and people would be drifting into Soho to queue at nightclubs. 'Anyway, so what club did Kathi work at then?' I said.

'Oh, you wouldn't know it. It's not the sort of place you'd go,' he replied.

'How do you know what sort of places I go to?' I said

'Well, let's see . . .' Lol wiped his mouth with the back of his hand. 'I reckon you probably go to places like The Wag, Freds. And then I bet you stand there and slag off all the people in there, because they're just like you, or they're like people you want to be.'

I immediately went hot. He had named two of my favourite clubs.

'I can just see you in two years' time. Golf GTI, a flat in Highgate . . .' he started to chuckle.

'Fuck off,' I said.

'Listen,' he said lowering his voice, 'there's nothing wrong with it. What's wrong with doing well. Your lot do well coz they stick together.'

'Pakis, you mean,' I said viciously. Who was this guy anyway?

'Immigrants,' he said.

'Did you use to be a skinhead?' I sat back in my chair and folded my arms.

He looked at the table and looked up at me.

'Yeah, sort of. I liked the style . . .' he mumbled looking away to the door.

'What, the style of beating up pakis?' I said.

'Listen, right. I never beat up anybody. What do you know about it anyway?'

I thought about it for a second. Nothing. I didn't know anything about it. And I couldn't have cared less whether this man was an imperialist in the Raj, or a skinhead in the seventies.

I laughed. 'Nothing,' I shrugged.

We looked at each other for moments, letting it pass.

'So, anyway, tell me about this club that Kathi used to work at. The one you think I'm too trendy to be interested in.'

'That's not what I said. You're too classy for it.'

I rolled my eyes. 'Leave it out, Lol,' I said.

He sat back in his chair and stared at me as though I was a hundred miles away.

'Do you want me to go, Angie?' he said.

'I want you to stay. I want you to talk to me. Please.'

He bit his lip and looked at the ceiling.

'I can't handle this. What's going on?' he said.

I held on to his jacket as though he was about to fall off a cliff.

'Listen. Listen to me. I'm working on a film about AIDS. And I want you to help me. I don't know the first thing about it, right? They want to make it about real people, you know, not the usual sort of thing. Not gays and stuff . . .' I wasn't putting it very well. Lol started sniggering.

'And you thought, let's see, who have I met recently that's real?'

'Oh, forget it. It was a bad idea all right.'

'What? What's a bad idea? I don't know what your idea is yet.'

'All right. Are you going to shut up and listen?' I asked. He nodded. 'Well. After what you've told me tonight . . . do you think there's a chance of Kathi, I mean she sounds a bit of a character . . .' Shit. That was the wrong word. '. . . well, she sounds like a tough woman, I mean. Do you think she would be prepared to give an interview? I mean it'll be in silhouette and all that. What do you think?'

What the hell was there to lose anyway?

'Kathi?' He seemed genuinely surprised. 'I thought you were going to say me . . . and I was going to say, no way José.'

'Nah . . . You're not ordinary enough,' I said laughing. Then: 'Well?'

He was thinking. 'I don't know. I'd have to ask her I suppose. She's a madwoman sometimes . . . she'd probably do it.'

'I don't know about the cash situation, obviously . . . but can I talk to them about it? The director and the producer? There'll be some money in it, I mean . . .' I was embarrassed.

'That's ok. Don't look so shy. She could do with the money, all right?'

Suddenly, against my better judgement I was desperate to see this woman. To see how she talked, how she spoke, what she looked like . . .

'I don't want anything to do with it, all right?' he said and a serious almost threatening look came across his face.

'Deal,' I said. I didn't even want them to know who he was. But I wanted to know about her . . .

'Shall we leave it like that then? I'll get back to you when I've spoken to them.'

He shrugged.

I looked at my watch. It was nearly two. God, the place must have had a late, late licence. I had to go. I was going to get a lecture anyway. I couldn't drive him back. He'd have to get a night bus.

'The night shift is waiting for you,' said dad sarcastically, opening the door before I had a chance to put the key in.

'Sorry,' I said. He turned around and went back in the front room. The house was quiet and smelt of spices and cigarette smoke. I stood for a moment checking myself in the mirror in the hall.

'Raaas claat, man. Give us the keys. I'm late.' Rax was running down the stairs.

I threw the keys and he caught them neatly. Flash bastard. Yet again I had to face the music while he went off to dance to it.

'Why don't you go out at normal times like everybody else?'

'I'd never have any wheels for one thing,' he smirked, pushing his hair back in front of the mirror. 'I look well hard tonight man. And the club is gonna be kickin'.'

I snorted. 'You better be careful, you know,' I warned.

'Chaaa, man. There's more important things in life than girls,' he said contemptuously.

'Oh yeah?'

'You wouldn't understand. You're hold, man . . .' He broke into a laughing fit. '*Hold!!*' Rax was another one who was expert at having conversations with himself. Just as well. No one other than his mates could understand what he was saying half the time. I opened my mouth but he was out of the door. Ma had gone to bed. Dad and maama ji were bent over the chess game. I yawned dramatically and ran upstairs before they had a chance to lecture.

'Ungelliee,' ma wailed. Why couldn't I have had the upstairs room instead of maama ji? He had the loft conversion all to himself.

I opened her door a crack.

'Goodnight then,' she sighed and turned over. I crept out and shut the door of my room.

CHAPTER FOUR

'Hey, wow!' said Charles, opening his takeaway cappuccino. 'You've really got on the case, haven't you?'

'I don't hang about, you know,' I said beaming.

We heard Madeleine's stilettoes climbing the steps up to the first floor. We exchanged smiles. Charles winked at me.

'Hey, Maddy, guess what?'

Madeleine smiled weakly and reached for Charles's coffee. Her eyes were behind dark glasses.

'Give me a minute, you guys, slow down. I gotta get my head around Monday morning,' she said taking big gulps of the coffee.

I was excited. I swivelled around in my chair taking in the empty shelves, the word processor, the push button telephone, the vase of yellow tulips. Outside, traffic was blaring, people shouting. A faint smell of soya sauce made its pungent journey up through the open window. Traffic was building up around the bottleneck in Wardour Street. I looked across to the first floor of the Chinese restaurant and saw through net curtains a whole tableful of Chinese people laughing and eating quickly with chopsticks. Through another window was the kitchen, full of smoke and chefs running around and arguing.

'They're having breakfast before the lunch rush,' Charles had followed my gaze. We smiled at each other. In the corner was a pile of folders and papers neatly packed away in cardboard boxes on the floor. The company who had hired the office before us would be back sometime to pick up their stuff. I thought of all the sweat and time and trouble that must have gone into some production — now all was left was an empty room. After living breathing and talking about it for several weeks, all of the people involved on that film were now on to another project filled again with the same enthusiasm. They would miss it on tv because they were working late . . .

'Ok, you guys, what's all the excitement about?' Madeleine said finally, having made two calls, one to check on her sick childminder and another to a tv company.

'Jeeze!' she said. 'It's crazy the way you always have to keep an eye on the next job.' She sighed dramatically. 'And Ilaana's sick again. Jeeze, that girl gets paid for having fun sitting around with my kids while I'm out busting a gut,' she said cheerfully. 'Don't have kids, you guys. Forget it. You never get to see them anyway . . .'

Charles playing with his pen, looked faintly irritated. 'Ok,' he said finally. 'Listen, Angie's got a contact for the film and I think it's just what we're looking for.'

'Yeah?' Madeleine was now all ears, ready to start the day. 'Tell me about it,' she said, but Charles continued to talk, frustrated at having had to wait so long.

'Well, she's got a contact whose wife, well they're separated, is HIV. Now, this guy is going to talk with her and ask her if she's interested. Madeleine, I think we've got something.'

Madeleine nodded her head at me appreciatively, but there was no sign of anything else on her face.

'Ok. Wait. Tell me about her,' she looked pointedly at me.

'Well . . . I don't know too much yet or if she's willing to do it.' I was covering myself as I'd learnt to do. 'Don't count your interviewees before they're hatched,' Lindsay'd always said. 'And never work with children, animals or "Real people".'

'But, from what I gather she's pretty fierce,' I laughed, and related the incident that Lol had told me about the club and how Kathi had led on the boss.

'It's perfect. She's perfect. She's as ordinary as. . .' Charles searched around for a word, '. . . as Mother's Pride!' he laughed. Then: 'She's a tough working class woman, she doesn't give a damn.'

Madeleine nodded and then said thoughtfully, 'Ok so what's the story here?'

Charles looked at her for a moment. I thought he was annoyed but when he spoke his voice was lower, less excited, a little distant — he sounded very professional.

'Well, we do an interview asking her about her life. Shoot some GV's around her flat. Stoke Newington's really atmospheric, lots of noise and colour . . . Maybe we shoot the club, sounds tacky enough to work. I mean they have hen nights in there, male strippers . . .'

'That's not a story,' Madeleine interjected, cutting him off in mid flow, 'that's an impressionist piece. I want a hard story.'

My heart sank and I didn't dare to look at Charles. He didn't seem phased though because he put the cap back on his pen, relaxed back into his chair, crossed his legs and said, 'Ok, maybe you're right.' We all sat in silence for minutes. Madeleine was scribbling on her pad.

Then she looked up and her mouth curled into a smile. 'This guy. This guy that gave her the virus. What do we know about him?'

I shrugged.

'Ok. What about this? I'm just gonna shoot my mouth off here so bear with me. We find out about this guy, about the club — do some sexy shots in there, as you said.' She looked at Charles, 'That's good. Then we check out this woman. Questions about how many of his staff he was sleeping with, what kind of boss etcetera. Ok. You with me?' She looked at both of us. 'Then, we say to this woman: listen you wanna get this guy, we're gonna help you. We say we'll provide the solicitor, pay the legal fees, all that. We say we'll help you prosecute him on the grounds that he didn't tell you he had the virus. There's gotta be some legal term for it. He slept with her in the knowledge that he was endangering her life, right . . .?'

I sat for a few seconds bowled over by Madeleine's torrent of ideas. I was impressed. Charles threw up his hands and clapped. 'Madeleine, that's brilliant!'

'I suppose he must have known beforehand . . .' I started to say but Madeleine waved me off with: 'Of course he knew. All men are bastards.' She laughed cheerfully. I gazed in admiration at this tough, fast talking woman who I was sure had never been left with an unpaid restaurant bill, let alone a deadly virus.

She gulped some more coffee. 'Maybe . . . just maybe, it could even be a two hander,' she mused. 'Part one about her lifestyle and part two about revenge — moving in on the guy.'

'Can you do it though?' I asked.

'Sure,' she said. 'In the States people are prosecuting all over the place. And not just for AIDS, for herpes, for any kind of disease they've contracted without being warned. It's right, don't you think?' she asked me.

I was confused. I'd never thought about it.

'Yeah, I suppose . . .' I wavered.

'Yeah!' said Charles emphatically. 'Get the bastard!' Then seeing my uncertainty he exchanged glances with Madeleine and went on: 'Listen, if some guy sold you a car with bad brakes — a fact that say he had hidden from you, and then you drive the goddamn car and break your neck, well wouldn't you want to prosecute if you could?'

I started chewing the side of my thumb nail. I felt uncomfortable but I didn't know why. I tried to imagine what Lol would think of the idea but I didn't have a clue. I didn't even know him, I realised suddenly. Suddenly that sinking feeling came rushing back. This man, who was a stranger, this man in a pub . . . he and his ex wife were becoming a subject for discussion in an empty room in Soho. Up till now I had been watching a movie and suddenly had got up out of the seat and walked right into the screen.

Madeleine reached out to me from her chair as though she had intuited something. 'Listen, think about it, Angie. We don't even know that anything is gonna come off. Your contact has to tell us that Kathi's agreed to it first,' she said placatingly. 'And,' she added, 'I need my best researcher to be one hundred per cent on this or else we look for a different angle. Ok?' She smiled and I thought she understood.

'Yeah,' said Charles turning towards me. 'Hey it's your story after all. You found the contact, I mean we wouldn't even have a story if it wasn't for you . . .' He smiled at me.

'Sure,' said Madeleine, 'and anyway, it's just an idea. Like I said, I'm talking off the top of my head.' She laughed and I felt much better. Reassured. I felt important. They were right. It was me after all who had found Lol and Kathi.

'Who is this guy anyway, the contact?' asked Charles casually.

I stiffened inwardly. I wanted Lol out of this. Also, he had said he didn't want anything to do with it. But I just wanted him out of it for some reason.

'I don't really want to say . . . he's just a guy,' I said. After all journalists didn't have to reveal their sources, I thought smugly.

'Sure, cool,' said Charles and shrugged.

'I just met him in a pub and he doesn't want . . .' I started to explain in case they thought I was being a bit too big for my boots.

'No, listen, I understand,' said Madeleine. 'It's a good thing for us that you have an ear to the ground. We need more people in the business who are streetwise. Too many of them spend their lives in Grouchos, writing screen plays on serviettes . . .' She trailed off and we all laughed.

'Well shall we have a chat about crews etcetera today? Also we need to discuss what questions if any we're going to ask the Terrence Higgins Trust, AIDSline and the rest of them,' Charles said standing up.

'Yeah,' said Madeleine, 'we have to get the party line as it were, or else we'll be accused of it not being well researched enough.' She smiled wryly at me. I knew what she meant. There were so many experts on everything these days that if you missed out the main ones your programme was deemed inauthentic. Not that the three films on regional cooking I had researched for Direct had been accused of being anything except mediocre . . . This was a real chance to establish myself as a serious researcher and I knew it. Also it was important that Madeleine approved of me because it would get me jobs in the future.

Madeleine and Charles went off to discuss crews in the editing suite next door while I drew up a list of relevant institutions to make preliminary enquiries.

By five o'clock I was exhausted and frustrated. Most of the AIDSlines didn't operate till evening and the Gay Switchboard was jammed all day. Still a few organisations had promised to send me information sheets on HIV and

AIDS. I would have to stay late on my first day in order
to get through to the evening shifts!

The neon lights of Soho had come on. Madeleine and
Charles had shouted 'Ciao' at six. I had a set of keys to
the office in my hand. I was officially in employment,
I thought joyfully and grinned at the empty shelves
that would soon be piled up with photocopied sheets,
newspaper cuttings and other information. By tomorrow
at least I would understand the rudiments of what AIDS
was, how it was being dealt with in different countries
and all that. Madeleine's idea had been flitting across
my mind all day like a weather forecast saying rain
for sure. I knew we would go with it. It was a great
idea. And after all people loved law suits, I thought
gleefully. People liked to hear about other people's
misery but also they liked to hear about the little man
or in this case the little woman winning. We couldn't
lose. I started thinking about Kathi and a little fear
started gnawing into me. What if she didn't like the
idea?

I dialled Lol's number. This time I was measured and
calm.

'Hi!' I said, 'How are you?' When the formalities
were over he said: 'First of all she went mad saying I
shouldn't have said nothing. But I explained it was in
strict confidence and when I mentioned the money she
shut up and listened.'

'And . . .?' My heart was beating fast.

'Well do you want to talk to her? She's just gone down
the shops, she'll be back in a minute . . .'

An arrow of jealousy shot through me. She was there.
Why was she there? What had he told her about me? I
started to feel a little nervous.

'Yeah, I'll call back. Save your telephone bill. Fifteen minutes?' I spoke into the phone trying my best to sound professional.

'Ok. Er . . . I only asked her to come up because I couldn't really say it over the phone, you know what I mean?' Then: 'You didn't say anything about me, did you?' He sounded distant.

I smiled to myself.

'Your secret's safe with me Lol,' I said and meant it. 'Shall I ring you again, you know, after I've spoken to Kathi?'

'Yeah,' he said.

'You all right?'

'Yeah,' he said flatly.

'It's a bit weird isn't it?' I said and laughed.

He laughed back but it sounded a bit strained.

'It'll be all right. Don't worry about it. I'm sure from what you've told me she can look after herself. Nothing she doesn't want is going to happen, all right?' Christ I was so good at this job.

'Oh yes. She can look after herself all right,' he said and laughed. 'Yeah, give us a ring later. Late.'

I went to the loo, checked myself in the mirror, looked out the window at the Chinese restaurant which was even busier than at lunchtime, walked around the office touching the Apple Mac, smelling the flowers and it was still only five minutes since I'd called. Then I made myself sit down and try to write some questions but the pen just kept making doodles on the page. I smoked three cigarettes and phoned home to say I was going to be late. Then I stared into space listening to my heartbeat.

She picked up the phone on the third ring.

'Hello,' I said, 'it's Angie.'

'So,' she said flatly.

I could feel myself leaving off my aitches.

'Well, I suppose Lol's told you a bit about why I wanted to have a chat . . .'

'Yeah.'

She sounded as if she would have punched me simply because she didn't like the look of me, let alone if she thought I was interested in her man.

'Listen, what do you feel about meeting up and having a chat . . . I mean, if you want to,' I ventured.

'What d'you want to talk about?'

She was being cagey. Fair enough.

'Whatever you want to tell me really. Listen, right, let me tell you a bit about myself, ok?'

She grunted.

'Well, I work for Channel 4 and we're making a film about AIDS and people who are HIV, and their experiences.'

It was best to take the line of least resistance initially.

'So?' She wasn't going to make it easy for me.

'I want to tell you straight away, you know, that whatever you tell me is in strictest confidence. I mean, I just want to have a chat and, you know, if you don't feel all right about it then that's ok . . .'

'When?' she said and this took me by surprise. She seemed to behave as if the phone was bugged. And then I found myself wondering if Lol was there while she was on the phone, what the room looked like . . .

'You say. Whatever's convenient to you really . . .'

'All right. Do you want to come tomorrow? You can come to my flat if you want. Got a pen. It's 123A Brodia Road. Stoke Newington.'

I knew it. It was five minutes from where Maggie lived. And it was down the road from the Dog and Trumpet. God, Lol might have moved out but they probably bumped into each other at the supermarket.

'Great. Thanks, Kathi.' I used her name for the first time. 'I really appreciate it. About three o'clock?'

'Yeah, all right. You ain't bringing a camera or anything, are you?'

'God, no. This is just a chat. Just you and me. I won't even bring a tape recorder. We'll just have a chat and see how you feel, yeah?'

'Oh,' she said. 'Yeah. See you tomorrow then ... Angie, yeah?'

I nearly threw all the papers on my desk up in the air shouting 'Whoopee!!' as though I were in a cartoon strip. I couldn't wait.

It was nine-thirty by the time I'd finished getting through to the other helplines. None of them sounded very helpful although most of them said that they would see if someone was available and willing to be filmed. First they wanted to see an outline of the film, of our intentions, our politics. One man said I was wasting his valuable time because he had a hundred callers on hold with more urgent problems than mine. One man on the AIDSline sounded sympathetic so I decided to run Madeleine's idea past him. I generalised it.

'I've heard that in the States people have sued for not being told about a disease that a sexual partner has transmitted to them. Do you think that's something that's a trend here?'

'No,' he said, 'as far as I know I haven't heard of it happening here.'

Brilliant, I thought.

'But I think, good on them if they do it,' he continued.

'Oh. So you think it's a good idea then?' I asked pointedly. It was important after all that people like him approved of the line that the film would take.

'You mean me? Me personally? Then yes. I'm not speaking in any way for the Line.' He was even sharper than me. I supposed that these people had become adept at handling the media which was why they were so cautious.

But, I reasoned, who wanted to see another film about statistics and men in wards. Boring. What did I know about AIDS and HIV? There must be lots of people around who, like me, had switched channels at the start of yet another documentary about AIDS.

'I'm glad you're doing it about straights because it's time. Straight people are only going to sit up and take notice when they start dying from it,' said one counsellor matter of factly.

That's a good quote, I thought. I started to make mental notes of one liners that could come at the beginning of the programme as teases.

CHAPTER FIVE

Next morning Charles bounded up the stairs two at a time and slapped his cappuccino down on the table. I had just got in myself and was taking my jacket off. He seemed very excited and hassled.

'God, I hate the tube. Another strike. Brain damage. I thought this woman was going to pass out. I had to wait half an hour this morning . . .' He rattled on good humouredly winding off his scarf, jacket and dumping them along with his briefcase on the chair.

'Which line are you on then?' I asked, because for once there had been no trouble on the Northern Line.

'Victoria. I live in Finsbury Park. You?'

'Finchley,' I said making a face.

'Oh God!' He rolled his eyes dramatically. 'You know that's the worst one. Largest suicide rate.'

'Huh,' I said deadpan, 'doesn't surprise me. It's all those people who've got fed up waiting.'

Charles laughed. Charles and Hugh must have come from similar backgrounds but Charles wasn't trying to be anything other than what he was. Everything about him was charming, polite and professional. Not to mention extremely attractive.

'Listen, Angie, I've got this crazy idea.' He started

to scrabble about in his briefcase and pulled out two video tapes. 'I saw a friend last night who worked on a series on sexually transmitted diseases.' He rolled his eyes. 'Flavour of the month, right?'

I laughed and leaned back expansively on my swivel chair. 'Anyway. He was telling me they visited some factory in Billericay. No, oh well somewhere, nowhere. The main industry there is the condom factory.' He started to laugh. 'Anyway, so the majority of the girls in employment there work on the assembly line. A condom assembly line!'

We both cracked up laughing. It was too ridiculous.

'It's true. And apparently a pack of three is like legal tender there. People have been known to pay their bus fare with condoms!!'

'Come *on*!'

'This is what the guy told me. Seriously.' Charles had the biggest grin on his face. 'Anyway, anyway. These tapes are their rushes of the factory which they didn't use. I watched them last night and we can definitely use some of it. Watch this,' he said grinning, as he slotted the tape into the machine. It could have been any factory producing car parts. Grey walls, metallic buzzing, all the women wearing little white hats for hygiene. Then the camera zoomed in and Charles and I let out a whoop of laughter. There was a moving row of cylinders flanked by the women. All the cylinders were bullet shaped and had condoms stretched over them like stockings. On their journey they expanded to twice their width and some of the sub-standard condoms burst like balloons. The women picked off the torn latex from the line desultorily.

Charles and I screeched with laughter. 'Someone's gotta do it,' he said.

The camera moved on to the next testing procedure. The condom clad cylinders were now travelling along a runway with holes. Then, like demented disembodied mechanical penises they began thrusting into the holes. 'It's like an orchestra, isn't it?' said Charles. He paused the tape and some twenty 'penises' stopped to attention (mid swing).

'That's the shot we could use,' he said. 'That close up. Right at the top of our film. With music.' He turned round to me triumphantly. ' "Love Hurts". Boz Scaggs, not Roy Orbison.'

'You're joking,' I said wiping my eye.

'No. Watch.' He hit the play button and started singing the tune in time to the rythm.

'Love hurts (thrust), Love scars (thrust), Love wounds and mars (Thrust, thrust thrust . . .).'

I threw back my head and laughed.

'It's perfect, isn't it?' he said grinning. I looked at him. This guy could talk you into buying a paper bag. What could I say?

'Perfect,' I said and nodded.

'Yeah, I've got to have music, you know. I mean Madeleine's all for the hard story and I am too but you've got to *get* the audience. My background's pop promos and there you learn about telling stories real fast.' He leaned toward me: 'You know that's why Madeleine's got us on the case,' he smiled wryly. 'She knows she hasn't got a handle on what's happening, where young people are at.'

I nodded. Madeleine and Charles weren't as much in cahoots as I'd thought.

'Did you do any interesting bands,' I asked. 'Famous' wouldn't have been cool.

'Oh sure. The best. Never Boz Scaggs, though.'

'Look, I've set up a meeting with Kathi HIV today.' I didn't know her last name after all.

'Great. Is she into it?'

'Well, initial chat.'

'Fine. What do you think of Madeleine's idea, now you've had a chance to think it over?'

He was serious. Someone was interested in my opinion. At Direct there was only so much you could do with regional cooking after all.

'It's a great idea,' I shrugged. 'Let's hope Kathi thinks so too.'

'Yeah, I'm glad you said that.' He smiled at me, 'I think this is going to be fun.' He carried on smiling and I felt a little embarrassed.

'I spoke to most of the AIDSlines,' I said opening up the folder I had made last night with notes and phone numbers. 'There's a few quotes that might work as stings, maybe intercut with the . . .' I nodded at the still penises, and grinned.

'Excellent!' said Charles.

The 73 was taking its time. I was sitting on the top deck, smoking one cigarette after another. My leg was shaking nervously. At the back were a group of black teenagers with a huge ghetto blaster, smoking a joint. A couple of pensioners were sitting up front tutting at the loud House music. I looked out the window and saw our driver chatting to another 73 going the other way. A minor jam was imminent but he had jokes to tell. I should have taken the car.

As I stepped off on to Stoke Newington Church Street it started to rain. I looked across at the Dog and Trumpet and it was just an ordinary pub in another inner city street. As I turned into Brodia Road an old black man leaning against a brick wall eyed me sleepily.

'Y'aaright,' he said without changing his expression.

123A Brodia Road was in the middle of a row of council

houses, similar to the one that Hugh and Chloe squatted in. I pressed the bell.

She had bleached hair. The roots were showing and the perm had gone frizzy. She was white not pink, pale as if every time the sun came out she went inside. She was wearing a light blue t-shirt and a white mini skirt. Her bare legs were goosepimpled.

'Hi, I'm Angie.'

She was looking, getting used to the fact that I was a paki or as she would say 'coloured'.

'Come in then. It's freezing,' she said rubbing the sides of her arms.

'Thanks.' I shut the door behind me. The hallway was narrow. Woodchip wallpaper painted white, the kind you used to cover up uneven walls. I was searching furtively for signs of Lol — dirty size 10 sneakers kicked off in the hall; his leather jacket hanging over a chair. He must have painted the hall, shifted the furniture, taken out the rubbish . . .

The tv in the front room was on. *Neighbours.* There was a brown dralon three piece suite, and the sort of radiator that was boiling hot for five months of the year and dead for the rest because it was on a grid system or something. You didn't pay for it, so you couldn't turn it up or down. It was fairly cold today and she had rigged up a little gas heater so at least the front room was warm.

Women's magazines lay scattered on the floor. Apart from that the rest of the floor seemed to be covered with cosmetics. Two zip-up make-up bags on the floor with eyeshadows, foundation creams and lipsticks spilling out around them. On a little stool there were two books propping up a small mirror. Across the middle of the room stood an ironing board. Slinky black material was flung over the arm of one of the chairs. There was nothing of Lol to see.

'Sorry,' she said, hurriedly clearing things away. 'I'm going out later.'

I glanced at my watch and she laughed.

'Takes me a long time to get ready, boy,' she said looking at me.

Boy? She must have black friends I thought.

She stopped clearing up and put her hands on her hips, surveying the mess.

'Sod it. Let's have a cuppa in the kitchen. You don't mind, do ya?' she asked, leading the way out of the front room and further down the hall. All the rooms led off the hallway. She seemed completely at ease and unabashed. I liked it.

The kitchen was small but large enough for a square table covered with a plastic tablecloth printed with poppies. There was a faint smell of washing-up liquid and the dishes draining upside down, soapy bubbles making a trail into the sink.

'English people washing up!' Maggie and I had chanted at university when Chloe had started to wash up after our first meal together.

'What?' she had said, embarrassed.

'English people never rinse,' I'd explained.

'That's why their head too full up with Fairy Liquid,' Maggie had added and everyone giggled.

The kitchen was the warmest place. Near the oven. I sat on the chair while Kathi put the kettle on. She put the mugs on the table and sat down. She was half smiling. It felt rather cosy and I liked her. I hadn't wanted to but I liked her.

'Where you going tonight then?' I asked.

'Down the Robey. Then there's a party later. Do you know it? It's a laugh in there.'

'It's in Finsbury Park, isn't it?' It was a pub with live music.

She nodded. She leaned over to look at my reporter's notebook.

'You work for Channel 4, then?' she asked without taking her eyes off my pad, trying to read my questions upside down.

'Well, I'm freelance. I'm working for this company that's making this film for Channel 4,' I said.

'That's brilliant. How d'you get into it then?' She folded her arms on the table. Most of her eyebrows were plucked off and she had no make-up on, but she had a face that was essentially beautiful. You couldn't have a debate about that. Her eyes were hazel and her complexion pale, with natural freckles across the top of her nose.

'Did you go to college for it?' she asked.

God! Who was doing the interview? I laughed and told her the story about meeting Lindsay at Amigo's.

She startled me by banging the table with her palm and laughing out loud. It was a really raucous laugh from deep inside her chest.

'Wickedness, man,' she said. Her accent was pure East End with no Jamaican accent despite the fact that she used the same words as the black girls in Stoke Newington.

I couldn't help grinning. I had come to interview her but it was she who had put me at ease. She got up and made the coffee. 'Hope you don't have sugar because I haven't got any,' she said putting my mug down before me.

'I've got some sachets in my bag,' I said smiling.

'Me mum used to say if you never have sugar in your coffee you'll never put on weight. That's about the best bit of advice she ever gave me,' she said wryly. 'Oh yes and,' Kathi started to smile and remember, 'when I was going out she used to sit in front of the tele and shout out: Be Good and if you can't be good be careful and if you can't be careful remember the date ...' Kathi trailed off and bit her lip. She was looking at space past my shoulder.

I was touched by her honesty. And by the irony which she too seemed to have seen. I looked into my mug and when I looked up again she had got herself together and was smiling with her mouth closed.

'Silly cow. Mind you, brings us round to the subject, doesn't it?' Then she laughed her laugh.

'When did she pass away?' I said solemnly.

'What?' said Kathi and let out a peal of laughter. 'She's not dead. She lives in Milton Keynes with some bloke. Ten years now. Tough as old boots, my mum. Like me.'

I was so embarrassed I put my fingers to my mouth like a little girl. 'Oh sorry . . .'

'That's all right. She may as well be dead. Do you want some cake?' She walked over by the window, looked curiously behind the net curtain at the neighbourhood kids playing football and then lifted a tent made of fine white mesh. Underneath it was a cake on a little board. She cut two slices and brought them over.

'Wow!' I said 'Marble cake, my favourite!' It was Maggie's mum's speciality.

'Come on then,' she said.

'Oh yeah. I'm supposed to be working, aren't I?' I said, wiping cake crumbs from my mouth. She was sitting back in her chair.

'Well, like I said, this film. It's part of a series called *Contemporary Dilemmas*.' I rolled my eyes to show what a pretentious title I thought it was but it seemed to skim past her. She was concentrating.

'Well, the producer and director think you'd be perfect. I just told them, you know, that you were a friend of a friend . . .' I added hurriedly. She nodded ok.

'They want someone who's just . . . normal, you know. Who's just getting on with their life.' I wasn't about to say 'real' or 'ordinary' after Lol's retort. She nodded again. So far so good.

'Ok. Now listen to this and see what you think, right? Did you know that in America a lot of people are suing because someone gave them a disease, and didn't tell them. And that's with herpes, hepatitis and now even HIV.'

'You're joking!'

'That's what I thought. But apparently you know Rock Hudson? You know he was gay and he died of AIDS? Well his lover, boyfriend, sued him because he never told him about it and carried on sleeping with him. He got 21 million dollars in damages,' I said looking straight at her.

'No.' Her eyes were wide.

'Yes,' I said and nodded. Then: 'I mean that *is* America,' I added in case she started thinking about getting 21 million dollars for appearing on a little tv film. 'But,' and I leant back in my chair, 'the point is that people are suing all over the place. Apparently no one's done it here. Now we thought if you thought it was a good idea that maybe you could get that guy. The guy that gave it to you. We'd pay for the solicitor, the legal fees and all that. He did know he had it before you slept with him, didn't he?'

'Yep. He knew all right. He must've done,' said Kathi. She was thinking it over. 'He's the sort of bloke that thinks he can do what he likes. And he's got plenty of money as well,' she said bitterly.

'Where's the club?' I remembered that Lol hadn't told me.

'Highballs, it's off Oxford Street. In Soho Square.'

'What did you do there?' I asked. It was so easy to talk now.

'I used to work behind the bar. He just had to pick on me. Bastard!'

'Did he used to go with anyone else?'

'Not that I know of . . .' Kathi smiled. 'I was special see . . . No, but he used to go up St Anne's Court most days. Filthy pig. I shouldn't have done it, but . . . Well what's the point of going on about it now?'

St Anne's Court was a street that connected up Wardour Street and Dean Street. It looked like an alleyway and was full of doorways saying Model 2nd floor.

'He does scag as well. I've seen him jacking up. God, there's a million ways he could have got it.'

'What was the clinic like?'

'They were all right, you know. They were all right. There's some nice women in there. But I mean they can't be with you all the time, can they? It's not like you're in a wheelchair or anything, is it? I mean, you're no different really.'

'Right,' I said. I'd run out of questions. She had made no reference to Lol so my curiosity would just have to wait.

'What would it be like then? You'd come round here to film it?'

'Yes. We'd probably take a day shooting you. Your interview, I mean, then we might film the club, a bit around Stoke Newington. I mean you'd be in silhouette and all that. You know blacked out so no one would know who you were. And then . . .' I trailed off.

There was no way she could be in silhouette if a solicitor was going to represent her, surely? Damn I hadn't bothered to check it out! But I was desperate that she agree in principle.

'We could take him to court because he gave it to me?' she said slowly.

'We could take him to the cleaner's, man.'

She was smiling and nodding her head.

'Didn't you say you wanted to get him? Well you can get him all right.' I was driving the point home. I felt like I was in Amigo's and she was about to order the most expensive cappuccino and all she needed was a push.

She looked serious. 'I don't know . . .'

'Listen, think about it. Here's my number at work. Give me a ring.' I scribbled on my pad, in case she said a flat no.

She took the number silently.

'Listen. You've got to get ready, I'd better go,' I said. 'Thanks for the coffee and cake.'

She sat thinking. I was putting my coat on. It was nearly six. Then suddenly she called out 'Angie'. I turned around. She was grinning. 'I'll do it,' she said.

'Well, think about it, Kathi, I mean . . .'

'Nah. I'll do it. You're all right. You'll be on my side, won't you? Yeah, I'll do it.' She was nodding her head vigorously.

I wasn't sure who she meant by 'You'. Me or the company.

'Well, don't you want to ask anyone's advice . . .?' Why was I trying to talk her out of it, for God's sake?

'Who am I going to ask? Lol said it was up to me anyway. I'm not asking any of them lot at the clinic. You're going to do the filming, aren't you?'

'Um . . . yeah. I'll probably ask the questions. You should meet the director and the producer as well. Give me a ring tomorrow, all right.'

'Bye then.' She was standing at the door, rubbing her shoulders again.

'Bye. Thanks, Kathi. I'll speak to you tomorrow.'

I was so close to Maggie's I thought I'd drop in. They wouldn't expect me back at the office anyway. Maggie's studio flat was one of the recently converted Victorian houses in Foulden Road. She had a steep mortgage and was forever moaning about it.

She opened the door and her face lit up.

'*Yeah!*' she ushered me in.

Her flat was on the ground floor and she had decorated it bit by bit over the last year.

The whole place was done out in white — Maggie insisted it was Ivory Satin but it looked white to me. The front room had very little furniture. There was a grey flecked sofabed, tv, hi-fi and a table with two director's chairs. On the walls were a couple of African masks and the shelves were lined with books by Frantz Fanon, James Baldwin and Maya Angelou. A maddening smell of rice and peas cooking in the kitchen had filled up the front room.

'I was on a research trip in bushland so I thought I'd pop in,' I said deadpan and she ribbed me. It was Maggie who had initially christened Stoke Newington 'bushland' when we used to struggle up from Finchley and Wood Green to see Chloe and Hugh, only months after finishing university.

'No tube!' Maggie had said aghast. 'This is bushland.' Now I always threw it back at her.

'I'm off sick.' She settled herself on the floor leaning against the sofabed. She was a residential social worker for Hackney Council.

'Skiving,' I laughed, and threw my shoes off, crossing my legs on the floor opposite her. She had spent a small fortune on the thick-pile grey carpet and we always liked to sit on it.

'No. I'm really run down. You just don't know what's happening in Hackney at the moment. The social services have been slashed. We've got half the staff we need. It's crazy. Everyone's doing twice the work.'

'Oh yeah, I know all about you lot in the social services. Having meetings all the time . . .' I started.

'No, Angie, it's serious. I've been doing fourteen hour days and it just doesn't stop. Clients have become more violent, staff are getting attacked weekly. I just don't know how long I can go on for,' she said rolling a joint.

'You should get danger money,' I said.

'Oh yeah,' she mocked. 'You don't know the half of it. This country's cracking up and we're the people that have to deal with it. This government's got a lot to answer for. People aren't interested in taking any kind of personal responsibility any more. They just want their own garden to be all right, never mind about the backyard.'

'I'm starving.' I changed the subject.

Maggie laughed. 'What a surprise!' I followed her into the kitchen and stirred the pot of goat curry next to the rice and peas on the hob.

'Mmmm . . .' I put a spoon in and had a taste. 'Perfect,' I said licking my lips. 'Oh, Maggie, I wish I had a bachelor pad like you.'

'Rubbish, cut up the cucumber,' she said, her face inside the fridge, sniffing. 'Something smells off in here.'

'I *do*!!' I insisted.

'You love living at home, your family's a bit mad but no bills at least. Do you know what? It's a bill every day. Sometimes I think I'm too young for all of this. Can't your folks arrange a nice marriage for me. Nice Indian boy, lots of money . . .' We both started laughing.

'You think I'm joking. I mean it,' she said.

'Shut up, you fool. Listen I've got loads to tell you.'

We walked back into the front room with the bottle of Sasparilla and a jug of water. As she poured I told her everything. About Lol, about the job, Phillipa and Kathi. I had to tell *someone* the whole story.

'Brodia Road, really?' was all she could come up with.

'She seemed to really trust me you know. She seemed to like me,' I said in wonder.

Maggie laughed. 'Of course she did. That's the kind of person you are.'

'What do you mean?'

'Look, Angie. People like you. How could they ignore you. My God, with that mouth!' she laughed, 'and you've got front. People like that too. You're open. Not bitter and twisted like me.'

I laughed. Most people were plain awed by Maggie because of her politics and her intelligence. She just liked running herself down occasionally — after all no one else would dare do it.

'What do you mean, front?' I asked innocently.

'Please! She rings up the man, takes him for a drink, gets a story out of him . . . if that's not front,' Maggie kissed her teeth.

'This bloke at work I must tell you, Charles his name is. Really nice looking, right? But he's a bit, "Tarkers and I were leggers on the champers", you know what I mean?'

Maggie laughed. I started rolling another joint.

'What about Lol then?' she said.

'I quite like him . . .'

'Well, he sounds all right, but you've got nothing in common apart from the story, have you?'

'Oh so what?' I said suddenly irritated.

'Well, I mean. He sounds a bit of a bastard, leaving her when she needed him. Anyway, you need to have a few things in common to have a relationship with someone, don't you?'

'You sound like my mum.'

'Sorry.' She looked at me for a moment. 'Just be careful, Angie. I mean, I don't have to tell you. You're doing a film about it but . . .'

'Yeah, yeah, yeah . . .' I didn't want to talk about it any more.

She went into the kitchen. I didn't want to smoke the joint now. She came back with two plates of rice and curry on a tray.

'I went to this warehouse party last week in Vauxhall, and it was Rax. Rax had organised it'

'It's all kids, isn't it? Acid house or whatever they're into,' I said bored.

'Yeah. It was all right. Lots of good dance music and Red Stripe. Good atmosphere,' she said between mouthfuls. 'It was quite funny. He was standing by the door checking people with the bouncers and he said "Maggie dreadlock". He let us in free. I thought, eh, eh, Angie's lickle brother. All grown up boy.'

'She reminded me of those girls at school, you know. The kind of girls that were out to get you,' I said. Maggie had known me for ten years. She didn't need signposts to know what I was talking about.

'You mean like Pauline Metcalf and that lot,' she said.

We had always referred to those girls using their full names, the way you did when you talked about pop stars or important people. Even now. When we were a hundred miles away from being fourteen. Even now I had said Kathi HIV . . .

'Do you remember that night we went to the school disco?'

Maggie nodded.

We had spent all Saturday in Brent Cross looking for a top. Up till then ma had always taken me shopping and we ended up with clothes that were reasonably priced, but never right: the platform just one inch too small, the skirt always one inch too long, the blouse too sensible — even if after leaving the house I opened two more buttons. Pauline Metcalf and her mates wore clothes with flair. They would take off their ties and knot up the white shirt just above their stomach. And with the make-up and jewellery it would look great . . .

The school disco was a chance to prove yourself and I managed to persuade ma that I was old enough to buy my own clothes now. Maggie and I bought the same top — a cap sleeved t-shirt with blue stripes. It didn't matter then that we were going to the same disco wearing the same top. It would go with my skin tight jeans that I had already washed and left instructions for maama ji to iron. Maggie was going to wear hers with her white skirt.

Maama ji had ironed the jeans with a crease down the front, the way he did his trousers. I'd sat down and cried — it wasn't cool to have lines down the middle of your jeans. They should have been ironed flat. I was inconsolable. He volunteered to wash them again and rush down to the launderette to dry them in the dryer. It was five o'clock and I was resigned to having nothing to wear and looking like a frump. My life was over, he could just forget it. All dad could say was: 'You spent £10.99 on a t-shirt? You could have bought a whole outfit for that much money.' — I hadn't learned to halve the prices then. Ma had said, 'No one will notice the creases,' but what did they know? Trevor Fairweather would notice. In the commotion maama ji had slipped away and by seven o'clock the jeans were pressed and ready.

Inside the disco in the community hall, it was dark and there were already a few people dancing. No drink was allowed but I knew a lot of the fifth formers had smuggled in bottles of Cinzano or cider even though teachers were about. Trevor Fairweather was standing in a corner surrounded by his friends. We went over to a set of seats at the other side of the room, where I could see him. Maggie wanted to dance but I told her to sit while I smoked my cigarette. I had bought ten Rothmans for the occasion.

'Want a light?' said a familiar voice and I looked up in terror to see Pauline Metcalf. She had on frosted eyeshadow and a tight black top that showed off her figure. It was in a different league to our lame cap sleeves. She stood in front of me and struck a match, her face was illuminated for a second. I leaned forward and she dropped the lit match. It skimmed past my jean clad knee onto the floor. I jumped and held on to my cigarette, looked up at her.

'Sorry, try again,' she said and struck another. This time she threw it between my legs and I had to jump up to avoid it. She struck another and laughed. This one she aimed further up and I had to swat it away like a fly or else it would have burnt my t-shirt.

'Come on, let's go and dance,' said Maggie taking my arm but I couldn't budge. Maggie was annoyed and walked off.

Pauline looked at me and struck another match. This time she held it. Then she let it drop like a stone and it rested on my knee for a slit second before I brushed it off. I was scared. Two of her friends came over and one of them said, 'I'll give the paki a light,' taking the matches.

The three of them just stood there laughing, smoking and throwing lit matches for hour-long minutes. Trevor Fairweather saw it all. I was sitting with a circle of dead matches around me on the floor when Maggie came back with a glass of Coke. I couldn't open my mouth. Everyone was laughing. We sat in silence waiting till dad came to pick us up hours later.

'I shouldn't have gone off like that. I should have stayed.' Maggie poured the Sasparilla.

'You were pissed off with me for not standing up for myself . . .' I said looking at the window.

'No. I was scared like anyone else would have been.'

'Really?' I had always thought Maggie looked down at me because she thought I was a wimp.

'Yeah,' she said, then started to laugh. 'Those t-shirts though! At least you wore your jeans. I had to wear Cynthia's nasty hand-me-down skirt.'

We laughed. 'Why did this Kathi remind you of them, though? I thought you said she liked you?'

I shrugged. I didn't know. 'I just felt that like because I was working in television that she was impressed . . .' I trailed off and screwed up my face because I thought I was talking nonsense, but Maggie just nodded and said, 'Go on'.

'And I played up to it. You know pretending I was streetwise but at the same time removed from her life, professional. And then, when I saw that cake and everything, I liked her. It was such a nice gesture. But I thought: Is this all a disguise? I mean because she thinks I can do something for her and also she can do something for me. I mean, I'm still me inside. If I was in the playground wearing that shapeless skirt and she was there she would still have contempt for me and put me in the bin.'

None of this seemed to be making any sense but I carried on.

'And I thought: Perhaps that's why I like Lol. Because he's hers. And I can take him . . .'

Maggie interrupted. 'But you're not in the playground, Angie. And you liked him before you knew about her anyway. And the reason they put you in the bin wasn't because there was anything wrong about you. It was because they were ignorant and stupid . . . and powerless.'

I smiled. How many times had Maggie made the sun come out?

'You're so grown up, Maggie,' I laughed. 'So what's the lesson then?'

Maggie shrugged. 'I don't know. Do your job as well as you can and don't let the past bother you? I don't know. Anyway, he's not hers. He left, didn't he?'

'All's fair, you mean,' I said looking at her.

She smiled at me. 'I can't remember a single time that you didn't do what you wanted to do, Angie. Why stop now?'

'Hey,' I said suddenly remembering, 'do you want to go out tonight?'

'Not the Trumpet. Can't you just ring him.' Maggie closed the curtains. Shit! I was supposed to have rung him but I'd got so involved making notes from the Helplines that I'd forgotten. I rang the number, but there was no answer. I felt a bit put out.

'No, not the Trumpet. This club Highballs that Kathi used to work at. We might do some filming in there so it's sort of a reccie.'

'A what?'

'Reconnaissance. You know, checking out the place to see what it's like before you go in there.'

'A club?' Maggie was considering it.

'Oh go on. It'll be a laugh. The drinks are on me. And we can get the night bus home. Can I stay the night?' I was bubbling over with enthusiasm. She had to say yes.

'All right, but I'll have to find something to wear. Maybe . . .' said Maggie tapping her lip, and looking at my cowboy shirt, 'I'm sure I've got a cowboy shirt somewhere.'

We burst out laughing.

'Don't you dare,' I said wagging my finger at her. 'I'll do the washing up if you promise to get ready in under an hour.'

Just off Oxford Street we saw a sign in pink neon saying 'Highballs' signed with a flourish onto the starless sky. A large bouncer in a monkey suit barred our way.

'Good evening, ladies. Are you members?'

Maggie began to worry, but I knew it was the usual line they used to stop people getting in.

'We aren't members but we'll join,' I said holding my ground as the bouncer unashamedly looked us over. A man in a suit appeared and said something in his ear and then to us, 'All right, ladies, come in.'

That must be Eddie, the boss. I smiled memorising what he looked like. He was middle aged with brylcreamed brown hair and stank of Kouros.

'Mr Medallion man ten years too late,' Maggie whispered to me as we made our way downstairs.

The dancehall was pulsating with light and loud disco music. There were little multicoloured lightbulbs along the walls that came on one after another like traffic lights. The dancefloor area was shimmering under a mirrored ball that rotated on the ceiling. There were a number of square columns that separated the dancefloor from the bar area and built into the middle of them were aquariums. The fish just swam round and round, oblivious to the vibrations of the music. About fifty young women sat in bunches or bravely danced around handbags. They all wore too much make-up and mini skirts. Most of them were eating crisps and watching the near empty dancefloor expectantly. A couple of men in leather trousers leaned against the columns looking bored.

Maggie kissed her teeth and hauled herself up on a stool at the bar.

'It must be a girl's night,' I hissed at her. I'd seen a poster on the way down proclaiming 'Twenty hunks tonight' with pictures of men flexing their muscles.

'This place is unbelievable,' she said.

I was staring at the bar staff. There were four barmaids behind the bar either chatting or wiping glasses. One of them noticed the ten pound note in my hand and made her way over to us, bringing with her an overpowering smell of floral perfume.

'Can I get you something, ladies?' she said in her best telephone voice, deliberately sounding her 't's' and 's's'.

I ordered two margaritas. Like the other barmaids, she was wearing a low cut black swimsuit with fishnet tights and high heels. A mane of synthetic hair trailed down her back. At the front there was a perfect Cleopatra fringe. As she shook the cocktail shaker, nodding her head to the music, her earrings crashed against the sides of her neck.

She had made the margaritas as I liked them. Go with the tequila, hold the lime juice, as we used to say in Amigo's. She smiled as she delivered the cocktails and you could see sincerity trying to fight through the make-up, three shades deeper than the colour on her neck.

One of her colleagues walked over. She was wearing the same outfit, but she was short. Her wig was bright red and it matched her lipstick.

'Were you all right getting in, ladies?' she asked.

I was in the middle of passing a cigarette to Maggie so I naturally offered her one. She accepted with a smile.

'Yeah, sort of,' I managed to mumble. Maggie was still in shock.

'Oh, that's all right then,' she said, sucking in the cigarette deeply, like it was a joint. You could always tell people who smoked dope.

'Because the gorilla on the door's got a thing about coloured people. He's usually all right with girls but with blokes . . .' she rolled her eyes. 'I said to him: But, Gary, how am I going to meet a nice big black man if you don't let any of them in? Winds him right up.' She started to laugh and we couldn't help but join in. Even Maggie, who I thought was going to have a fit.

'Yeah, he did give us a bit of attitude at the door,' said Maggie nodding.

The red wig hadn't bothered to put on any kind of voice with us. She was playing it straight as though we were waiting for a bus and passing the time of day chatting.

The mane came back with my change and put it on a little tray along with our bill. At Amigo's we'd personalised our own tip trays so that customers would be persuaded to leave tips, even though it wasn't custom to tip barstaff in London. I hadn't forgotten and I left some change for her. She smiled and said, 'Enjoy your drinks, ladies.'

'The show's about to start in a minute, if you want to go closer,' she said nodding toward the dancefloor which was now filled up. All you could see were heads craning to look at the stage. A lot of giggling and excited screaming was going on.

'No thanks, I think it'll put me off my drink,' I said.

Both the barmaids laughed.

'They're all poofs anyway,' said the mane.

These must have been Kathi's workmates. I wondered how Kathi must have looked dressed like this. I could imagine her hating every minute of it, and I could see them all having the time of their lives when Kathi had embarrassed the owner Eddie that night.

'Do you know a girl called Kathi . . .?' I *still* didn't know her full name. 'She used to work here . . .'

'I knew her,' said the red wig, although the taller one drew a blank. 'Yeah, she was all right but she had a mouth on her. Eddie gave her the sack because he said she was trouble. Rude to customers and having a go at him all the time about what we had to wear. How d'you know her then?'

'Oh, just around. She said to come in here for a laugh,' I said casually.

So, I thought. So he had told them all she was no good at the job. Bastard.

'What's he like your boss?' I asked carefully and added, 'a mate of mine's looking for a job, you see.'

'He's slime,' she said candidly. I would have laid bets that the smarter ones were on a fiddle but of course I couldn't ask that.

'But, it's all right working here. It's a good job and the other girls are all right.' She shrugged. She wasn't going to tell me anything else. 'Tell your mate to say she's a friend of mine. I'm Sandra,' she said smiling. 'Got to go now, look the show's starting.' She disappeared behind the bar.

'*Such* a researcher,' Maggie whispered and I dug her in the ribs. Suddenly there was a great whoop of girls screaming and waving their arms. A man with muscles and a leather G-string had appeared on stage. He had a microphone and was singing and dancing to a backing track with complete abandon. Arms were reaching out to touch him but he kept coyly dodging away as if he was a pop star. The lyric was 'Now we're solid. Solid as a rock . . .' but when he sang it, he changed the last word to 'cock'. At this there was a huge burst of laughter and shouting. Then he began to let the outstretched arms touch him and to gyrate to the music.

I started to laugh.

'Chloe would *kill* us if she was here,' said Maggie. We laughed even more.

'It's so . . . gross, ridiculous . . .'

'I'll never be able to listen to that record again,' Maggie spluttered.

Another record came on and there were more cheers. Three more men had appeared all of them thrusting themselves in the air singing, 'If you're in love with a beautiful woman it's hard . . .' The barmaids were deep in conversation, busy arranging bottles. Occasionally they looked toward the stage. They'd seen it all before. Charles's idea of the opening shot seemed tame compared to this. But somehow there was a bitter taste in my mouth.

'I don't like it here,' I said to Maggie.

'My sentiments exactly. Let's go.'

We fought through the now hysterical crowd, praying that the performers wouldn't decide on audience participation just as we passed the stage.

The cold air outside felt sweet and fresh. Cars purred through empty, lit up Oxford Street. We made our way to the bus stop in silence.

'I don't know what to think about it really,' said Maggie looking at the pavement.

'No,' I mumbled, deep in thought.

'I can't imagine working there . . .' she said.

'No,' I said.

She linked her arm through mine and we started checking the bus times.

'It's cold,' I said.

I was glad to be out of there. Highballs seemed like another planet — sticky, desperate and full of dirt that looked like tinsel, the barmaids like trapped animals, smiling, watching, being of use.

By the time we got to Maggie's I was desperate to phone Lol. I told him Kathi had decided to do it. I told him we'd been to Highballs. He laughed. I said it upset me and I didn't know why. 'Because it's ugly,' he said. 'It's ugly and rotten.' I said I wanted to see him. He said was it a good idea and I said it was the best idea. 'I'll meet you in the Trumpet at nine tomorrow,' he said. 'Not tomorrow,' I said, 'the night after that.'

CHAPTER SIX

'*Arrey*, turn the rolling pin around as you roll. What are you making, dumplings?' Ma was sitting on a stool behind me as I made chapattis on the counter.

'Thinner, thinner. What you want everyone to get indigestion?' She reached out from behind me to press one side of the rolling pin. 'That's it. Good,' she said and settled back to watch.

I had to concentrate on rolling out one chapatti while the other one cooked on the skillet. Just as I'd finished rolling, the cooked one was ready. I picked it up with the tongs and held it over the open flame next to the skillet. It darkened and puffed up like a ball. Perfection! I turned to look at ma and raised my eyebrows three times to indicate the tour de force. She was always expecting it to sink.

'*Arrey*, get on with it. You want a round of applause. In the time you have made five I will have finished.' She was smiling, putting ghee on the finished chapatti, and stacking it on the pile in the stainless steel bowl.

'Yeah, but you just chuck them on, I'm giving them TLC,' I said smugly, rolling out another carefully. It had gone into a triangular shape.

'TLC, PLC . . . Pah!! Turn it round, round. It looks

more like a samosa,' she said, pressing one end of the rolling pin again.

She started clicking her bare heels together. Her feet were dangling six inches off the ground. The apron she had wrapped around her sari was spotless. Twice a week we'd gone through this ritual, ever since I had returned from university. Every time she would be itching to do it herself in half the time, but if I was going to learn then she had to content herself with directing and criticising the proceedings.

'At your age! Taking ten years to make chapattis. Who will want to . . .?' she started.

'I know,' I said solemnly and put on a tragic face. '*Who* will want to marry me . . .?' Then I burst out laughing.

She pursed her lip and then laughed along with me. She knew when she was beaten.

After thirty chapattis I had to have a rest. I left ma in the kitchen to finish off. She still had two vegetable curries, rice and salad to prepare . . .

I was lying on the settee with my feet up in the tv room. Dad was sitting on the chair engrossed in *India Today* but he insisted he was watching a documentary so I couldn't turn it over to *Top of the Pops*.

Timing I thought. Families were all about timing. If I'd gone out tonight then it would have been just that one night too many in a row. There would have been huffing and puffing, comments about hotels, and then it wouldn't have made any difference if I'd stayed in for a week. This way, there was an illusion that I was still a productive member of the family. I was exhausted anyway. With a satisfied smile on my face, I stretched my legs and watched the tv pictures getting hazy. My eyes started to close as the scent of onions and garlic frying in ghee wafted in from the kitchen.

Just as I was drifting off, I heard the familiar 'Ungellieee!' I groaned and got up slowly, started to set out the plates and jug of water, happy in the knowledge that Rax was going to get the silent treatment when he got in. He hadn't worked out the Strategic Timing factor yet and I wasn't about to tell him.

We were all sitting at the table in the dining room about to start, the black and white tv was on the nine o'clock news, when Rax put his key in the door. From the hall to the dining room, he left a trail of coat, Adidas bag, two plastic bags of records and his baseball hat. 'Shh,' said dad looking at the tv, his hand deftly collecting up some potato curry with a piece of chapatti. More news on the unrest in India. We all turned toward the screen obediently. No one except maama ji was talking to Rax because he treated the house like a hotel. Who was I to go against the majority?

After dinner I flopped on the settee and watched Rax collect up the plates and pots and help ma to stack them in the dishwasher. Dad went back in the tv room to read, and maama ji sat down in the chair opposite, having put on a cassette of *gazals*, Indian love songs.

Having paid his dues Rax escaped to his bedroom. Ma was still clanking about in the kitchen. Only the two wall lights were on in the dining room, blurring the browns and beiges of the furniture and carpet. Maama ji's eyes were half closed as he listened to the sitar music. Occasionally he would catch up with the drumming of the tabla, rapping his fingers against the side of the armchair. As usual the house was a flood of noises — distant reports from *News at Ten* in the next room were filtering into the dining room, and I could hear Rax moving around his room above my head like an elephant. I lit a cigarette and aimed the smoke at the dusty lampshade. Ma came into the dining room to put something away in the sideboard, glanced over at my cigarette and clicked her tongue. I ignored it.

'Kahaani, Maama ji?' I said suddenly, tearing my eyes away from the lampshade.

'Now?' he asked opening his eyes.

I nodded, smiling.

Ever since I was seven or eight years old, maama ji had told me stories, *kahaanis* in Hindi — after school; when I was angry; when I had wanted to be white; when I had come home from university for fleeting excited weekends; when I had smoked cigarettes into the night wondering if all the world had to offer me was a career in waitressing. . . Always in Hindi. Over the years the storytelling had taken shape. When I was nine I would hit him and plead 'in English, in English' because I couldn't understand a lot of the words and because I didn't want to hear them if they weren't in English. He continued regardless. Then at twelve I'd listened disdainfully about village life because it wasn't as exciting as the Famous Five. At sixteen I thought I was a bit too grown up for stories although I had begun to understand them now and didn't have to keep asking for translation. During the weekends from university I would ask him questions about how come the girls in the stories never went to the towns, and how come there were no lessons, no morals to be learnt? Wasn't Indian culture all about superstition and tradition and morality?

'Arrey, *what* lessons, yaar,' maama ji would wave off my questions with his hand. '*Stories*, yaar. They're just stories. To absorb.'

Tonight I wanted to listen to 'just stories'.

We hadn't had a session for months. Not since I'd started at Direct Vision. I was too busy working or going out and Rax had no interest. He could understand only a few words of Hindi.

The last time, maama ji and I had started discussing how we would put a particular word in a story into English. I had leafed through the dictionary and we had begun to explore the nuances and bridges between the two languages. Maama ji had brought out his *Hobson*

Jobson to prove an English word had come originally from Hindi. Abandoning the story, we sat up till three in the morning, poring over the thick book.

Hobson Jobson was an exhaustive catalogue of ordinary English words derived from Indian languages. We knew about 'pukka' and 'wallah' but those were actual Indian words. The book told of words like 'jodhpurs' coming from the city of Jodhpur where the style of dress had been copied by the British.

'Where did all those stories come from, Maama ji?' I asked. He was turning the music down.

'From long ago. Most of them were written by your father.'

'What?' I sat up, amazed.

'Oh yes. When he was at university he would write them. You don't know, Nirmal could have been a great writer. He would come and visit the house. He and your other maama ji, uncle Anand da were great friends at the university and of course he came also to see Tara di . . .' Maama ji giggled behind his hand.

'Oh yes!' I said, sitting up now. 'You never told me you went out with Dad before you got married,' I called out to ma. 'Shock. Horror.'

Ma poked her head round the door, one hand holding an aubergine with a slit down the middle. With the other hand she was stuffing it full of a mixture of spices.

'What nonsense. He is telling all rubbish now. Shankar, what rubbish are you talking?' she said, waving her aubergine at him.

Maama ji started to laugh and cough at the same time.

I got up and patted his back. 'Not an arranged marriage! Disgusting!!' I said in my best impersonation of a public school accent.

Ma clicked her tongue and returned to the kitchen with her aubergine.

'No, yaar. It wasn't like that. They were friends, your

father and Anand da. Tara di was around and about, you know. Bringing tea and what not. One time he bought her a fine shawl for Diwali. Then we all got talking as to what a good match it was. Same caste . . .'

Ma came into the front room and poked maama ji's shoulder with her elbow. 'What *rubbish* you are talking! Why can't you talk about sensible things?' she said and opened up the fridge door. 'Ungelliee, why don't you clear up the things Rakesh has left around the place? He is a fine one. Calls himself "black British" and carries on like a nawab who has servants to do his businesses for him . . .'

'He can pick up his own stuff, and *anyway* don't change the subject, Ma,' I said, laughing at her embarrassment. 'Have you still got it then? The shawl? Ahh, how romantic.' I clasped my hands together looking upwards to the lampshade.

'Romantic, pomantic,' she mumbled.

'Don't tell me you haven't *got* it,' I said aghast.

'Arrey, it is somewhere around. Probably in some trunk in Delhi,' she said going back into the kitchen.

'God!' I was disappointed at her lack of interest. 'Go on Maama ji,' I urged.

'Huh? Oh yes. So Nirmal would come over in the evenings and he and Anand da would go to the coffee bar to have coffee and samosa after dinner. I had to stay back and of course so did Tara di. Anyway. They would come back and sit outside the house for hours and your father would read out his stories. Anand da would listen and criticise. Later on I begged him to show them to me, when I was older. I would read them all but never dare to criticise of course. But then . . .' Maama ji trailed off.

'Yeah, go on,' I urged.

'Well, it was marriage and all of that. He had to get a job and the writing was finished. Everybody had to get a job. Everybody had to live. I had read them so often, I knew them all off by heart, yes.'

I nodded.

'When I came to this country thinking all about Shakespeare and Wordsworth and found myself among philistines eating fish and chips, I sat in Dulwich in that room and I remembered the stories. They were all about the village where your Dad came from. About scarcity and railway stations, about mangoes and loyalties . . .' Maama ji started to smile.

'He wrote them when he was at the university. Oh everyone was proud in his village that he had gone to Delhi, such a big town. And he wrote them because he did not want to forget, could not forget . . .' Maama ji was searching for words.

'Because it was his roots, you mean?' I asked.

'No, no. More than that. It was who he was, it was a way of looking at the world that could be transported, transmitted from village to town, from town to a metropolis. Do you see?' said maama ji.

'Like religion or something like that?' I asked feebly. I wasn't sure what he was driving at.

'No, yaar. Faith perhaps. But . . .' he jutted out his bottom lip. Then he pointed to the kitchen. 'Stuffed aubergines. It is about stuffed aubergines.' Then he started to laugh.

I 'ooked at him patiently. Was he losing it?

'Anyway,' he said wiping his eyes, 'when I started to tell you the stories, I began to corrupt them. I added my own little bits for the things I had forgotten. I changed things.'

'So they aren't the original truth, then? They're a mish mash?' I ashed.

'What is original truth? They are stories and they have been carried by different people. That's all. What's original is only other people's ignorance,' he laughed.

'Tell the one about the earrings again, Maama ji.' I sank back into the settee and shut my eyes.

'You tell it, Tara di, that was your favourite. Go on, you tell it,' I heard maama ji say. I smiled and listened to ma protesting.

'*Arrey*, I don't remember it. The one about earrings? "Baali aur Bunndey"?'

Finally she agreed and although my eyes were closed I knew she was wiping her hands, taking off the apron. Maama ji would be relaxing, listening to the cassette, his eyes closing. This was a first and I suddenly wished I could read them in Hindi.

She raced through it as if she were reciting a Key Facts sheet. Her story telling was useless. Especially since she had decided to tell it in English.

'What?' There was a rich family and a poor family. Each of them had a son who went off to university. Then the poor boy's mother was cleaning for the rich woman and she heard them talking. The rich woman was saying to her friend how good it was that her boy had entered the university and how he must have this that and the other. How he must have this thing, the Parker pen, to write his exams with. Well the poor woman went home and thought I must send my son one and two things.'

I started to laugh. 'One and two things . . .' She sounded like Peter Sellers doing the Indian doctor. Any minute she would say, 'thanking you verry much.'

'What is funny?' she demanded.

'Nothing. Carry on.'

'Anyway. This son of course he respected his mother and did not laugh at her. He was. . .'

'Yeah, all right, Ma. We don't need the morality. Get on with it.'

'Ok. So then she started to think how will I get him these things because I have no money? But every time she went to the rich house she would hear them talking so she does this thing and she sends him the Parker pen. Well, when the boy returned he bought them all presents because he was a good son. He was always thinking about his family not going out all the time . . .'

'Ma!'

'Yes. Yes. So he comes back and says to her, why are you buying me this rubbish? I don't need the Parker pen, you cannot afford to spend this money. So what he had done was sell the Parker pen and buy his sister these earrings. And that is it. Now goodnight it is past twelve o'clock.'

'Eh?' I opened my eyes. 'You've completely messed it up, Ma.'

'What? Oh yes, yes. That's right. Because the mother had first of all sold her own earrings to buy the Parker pen. That's right. I forgot,' she said and started to laugh.

She could never remember jokes either, especially the punchlines.

'Honestly,' I rolled my eyes, '*that's* the whole point of the story!'

I got up to go to bed and as I climbed the stairs looked into the tv room where dad was reading. The chess game as usual was sitting on the coffee table waiting to be finished. They didn't play on Wednesdays because that's when *India Today* came through the letterbox and it took dad the whole of the evening to read the lead stories. My dad the civil servant. My dad the writer . . . I stopped on the stairs and a picture formed in my mind. A picture that was a collage of old photographs, stories, memories, programmes about India I had seen on tv, trashy Indian films . . .

. . . the smell of burning fires. There was mauve and copper and rust in the sky. Lush trees swaying in the breeze. On the verandah dad and Anand maama sat on two armchairs. Dad was thin and had a moustache like Clark Gable. He was reading from a handwritten manuscript. Inside the house ma was sitting against a whitewashed wall, reading a book by an electric light; maama ji fixing his bicycle. Crows were collecting on top of the roof and one swooped down to sit on the head of a cow that was lazing in a dirt track nearby . . .

Their lives.

They had lives, and stories and two shirts and earrings. I smiled. *Obviously*, I told myself. And the picture I had conjured up was probably unreal, a mish mash for sure. But it belonged to me.

That night I lay in bed wondering if those 'philistines eating fish and chips' were people like Lol and Kathi. And I smiled because I knew that maama ji had been wrong, because he had thought there was nothing to be learnt.

CHAPTER SEVEN

Thursday morning I ran up the stairs. I was late. I had spent some time choosing what to wear. We were going to see Kathi today. I wanted to look smart. There was a message from Charles (stuck on the phone):

> Angie, I've got an appointment with my accountant this morning but I spoke to Madeleine last night and she can make the meeting with Kathi for two as arranged. We're meeting up in the Dome at the Angel around twelve. We need to discuss questions etc. Can you bring the file with you? See you there. Get cabs. C.

I looked at my watch. It was ten-thirty. I smiled. People always seemed to get their appointments over and done with at the beginning of a film. The dentist, optician, childminder, accountant were dispensed with in the first week because as soon as we started filming and then editing there would be no time. I made myself a coffee then looked at the file that Charles had marked 'Love Hurts — HIV'. I photocopied all the notes and information that had arrived from the various agencies and, having stapled the separate piles together, wrote Madeleine on one, Charles on the other. Then I watched the Chinese restaurant for a while, got up and shut the window because of the smell of diesel mixed with fat. I was going to see Lol tonight and I had to make sure we didn't work late so I could go home, have a bath, get changed. I wondered how Kathi was going to react to Madeleine and Charles. I felt we were winning. She wasn't going to back out now.

The Dome brasserie was warm and half empty. Waiters in crisp white aprons were wiping glasses. Most of the seats were still arranged from morning and there were newspapers and magazines by the coat stand. Edith Piaf was imploring 'Je ne regrette rien'. Madeleine was sitting at the far end, poring over her filofax. I made my way over, feeling a little daunted, because Charles wasn't here yet.

She looked up and smiled immediately.

'Hi, wonder girl,' she said.

She ordered more coffee and I began to take out my file.

'So, you think Kathi will be good?' she said glancing through my notes. 'Hey, this is all very efficient.'

I nodded. I hadn't met that many Americans but all of them seemed to have this ability to make you think you were really important. They seemed so open and receptive or maybe it was just that they weren't subject to classification by class and so you couldn't tell where they had been educated and how they felt about people. Or maybe it was just that they were American and everything about America was bigger, bolder, more ahead than it was over here.

I drank my cappuccino while Madeleine made notes. Then she put down her pen and sighed.

'I'm sorry I wasn't around yesterday. I had a lot of stuff you know. I'm really glad both of you are on this, I think it's going to work. I talked to the commissioning editor yesterday and he seemed to like the idea of a two hander so it looks like we'll get the money. Also I talked to some lawyer friends who gave me a few names to contact. There's a lot of people who are going to start making big money out of this kind of thing. Already in some states in the US there's a legal precedent called Sexual Liability Law. I think we may just have a real scoop out of this.'

At that moment Charles walked in saying the traffic had been unbearable and we all nodded in agreement. I was surprised at how fast Madeleine had moved on this. I felt a bit peeved that she had contacted lawyers already. I was the researcher after all. Still, I consoled myself, if she had more contacts than I did then that was fair enough.

We decided to have just one more coffee before we set off.

'Well, I think we should just get to know her a bit today, put her at ease. Make the shoot as painless as possible. What exactly did you tell her, Angie?' Charles was tying his hair back into a ponytail.

'I told her about the series and how we all thought she would be really good.' They were both nodding. 'And I said, was she sure he had known about it, and she said, yes. And, as I told Charles, I went to Highballs and saw Eddie. He really looked like a nasty piece of work. I said she would be in silhouette and all that, you know we would, I mean the company would pay the legal fees for. . .'

'You did what?' Madeleine looked up at me and her voice had changed.

'Er . . . I said the legal fees . . .' I started but she stopped me in mid sentence.

'Why did you say she would be in silhouette? We didn't discuss that. Did she say she would only do it if that was the case?'

'No. No it wasn't like that. I mean she didn't seem to be bothered about it. I just wanted her to trust me. I mean she just seemed to like the idea about prosecuting the guy. No, there was no deal about the silhouette.' I was

speaking quickly but I was thinking faster. It was true
that Kathi hadn't made it a condition. Damn, I shouldn't
have mentioned it.

Charles looked at his coffee and then at Madeleine.

'It's fine. We'll check out the situation when we get
there. I think Angie was right to get an overall yes,' he
said to Madeleine. 'We can deal with details.'

I was so relieved I could have hugged him.

I didn't say much on the journey except give directions
to Brodia Road. Madeleine and Charles discussed some
project that a mutual friend had started. By the time we
arrived at Kathi's I had talked myself into a better mood.
I had to be professional. No point in being sensitive. It was
no big deal. This was my story.

'Y'aaright?' said the old black man standing against the
brick wall.

'All right,' I replied. Madeleine and Charles must have
thought I was au fait with the area. That's what I wanted
them to think.

Kathi came to the door and I almost did a double take.

Her hair was a platinum thatch with an inky stream
where dark roots were showing proudly. She had on red
lipstick and pale foundation and her eyes were rimmed
with black. She was wearing a black lycra mini dress.
She stood shifting her weight from one foot to another
squinting under smudgy daylight. She looked stunning.
The dark roots insolently proclaiming the right of the
bottle blonde; the too-red lipstick bouncing off her white
face. Madeleine and Charles were standing behind me
with smiles on their faces.

'Hi, I'm Madeleine Davis. It's a pleasure to meet you,
Kathi. This is Charles Russell, the director.'

We all made our way inside and into the front room
which Kathi had cleaned up for the occasion. The tv
was off and magazines had been placed in a pile. The
gas heater was on.

Charles and I sat down on the settee and Madeleine and Kathi each took an armchair. We all refused coffee and then Kathi began to fiddle around with her cigarettes. Charles immediately lit one for her with a lighter he produced from his jacket. Madeleine was looking at Kathi and smiling. I was occupying myself with my file notes.

'Did you have a good time the other night?' I started to make some light conversation.

'Yeah. It was ok,' said Kathi, furiously inhaling and exhaling smoke, her eyes on the carpet somewhere near her feet.

'Charles lives in Finsbury Park, don't you?' I said turning toward him.

He nodded.

'Kathi was off to the George Robey the other night . . .' I started to explain.

'Oh right,' he said looking at Kathi who then looked back at him. 'They have some really good music down there, don't they? It's a good atmosphere. Yes I like that place,' he said and she was nodding.

Charles was all right I thought. It was just his accent.

'I did some filming in there once actually. They've got quite a reputation for good bands.'

He had succeeded in engaging Kathi's attention.

'Will you want to film in here then?' she waved her hand indicating the room. 'God, it looks terrible,' she laughed her laugh and Charles laughed along.

'Oh, no. Listen you'd be surprised. I've filmed people before in their place and they've said they didn't even recognise it,' he said.

'Oh sure. The camera can totally change things. This woman I filmed back in the States said she'd wanted to get rid of her curtains for years and once she saw them on the screen she thought, hey, they look great. And you know it was really funny because she spent the whole time looking at her curtains and her room and we're saying, what did you think of the interview, you know all her friends were watching the transmission with her and like she was just too busy looking at all the other stuff,' said Madeleine laughing.

Kathi started to laugh at the story. 'Yeah. I'd be like that. I'd be saying look at the state of my hair, you know.'

'Listen, you'll look terrific,' Charles shrugged his shoulders like it was fact.

'Kathi, let me say a little more about our idea and see what you make of it,' said Madeleine leaning toward her. 'I'm in the middle of negotiating two films right now. We were thinking that perhaps the first one would concentrate entirely on you. We'd do a fairly long interview. It wouldn't be formal, just conversation. We can patch it up in the editing stage, ok? And we'd ask you questions about yourself, about the club you used to work in, maybe you could tell us about this Eddie a bit more? Whatever you want. Then in the second film, we'd introduce a lawyer who would be fighting on your behalf. I mean this kind of thing hasn't been done here although in the States as you know it's becoming more and more frequent . . .'

Kathi was listening intently and nodding. 'Yeah. Ever Ready Eddie. I could tell you about him.'

Madeleine smiled 'Well right. So it depends what kind of fight he puts up but you know, it's a risk. If you're willing to take a chance, and this depends entirely on you, we'll take that chance right along with you.' Madeleine shrugged, 'Put it this way. The guy's done this, what can you do about it? Well you can make him pay for it.'

'Yeah,' said Kathi, 'I want to make him pay.' She looked seriously at Madeleine and her arms were crossed. She looked determined and ready. 'Yeah, I'll take a chance.'

'I think you're right. That side of it will come later. Let's talk about the first film. We'd ask you questions about him, how you feel about things, about other people's attitudes, about how you deal with it . . . you know that kind of stuff. Do you think you can handle that?'

Kathi hadn't moved her position. She was looking resolutely at Madeleine. 'Yeah,' she said unsmilingly, 'I can handle it.'

Madeleine smiled at her. 'Good for you. You're a brave woman Kathi, and I respect that.'

Charles had been taking a back seat during the interchange and I too had been listening attentively.

'When's a good day for us to film you?' he said and I started making notes.

Kathi thought about it. She felt at ease with us and I was glad.

'Well, I don't really mind because I've got this part-time job Monday and Thursday . . .' A cautious look came over her face. 'I don't want them to know I'm doing this because, um . . .' she started to bite her lip. I looked at the floor because this silhouette issue had finally come up. '. . . um, because I'm, well I'm signing on as well and . . .'

I nearly sighed with relief.

'Oh, Kathi, don't worry about that. It'll be fine. What we'll do is we won't shoot you in shadow. We'll shoot you for real and then we have these video effects that make the face into little squares, we can even change the voice. So I mean really, no worries,' said Charles leaning forward.

'Sure, absolutely,' said Madeleine.

'Oh yeah, I've seen that on the tele. Is that how you do it then? You put it on afterwards?'

She looked at him and smiled. He certainly had a manner about him that encouraged confidence. I was pleased that he had found a way out of the silhouette business. We made a tentative agreement to shoot next Tuesday and we said we'd be in touch. Kathi looked at me and said did we want any tea now and she was smiling.

I was glad everything had gone so smoothly. We said yes and she walked off to the kitchen.

We sat in silence. Madeleine turned toward us and winked, 'Mother's Pride, right?' and we grinned.

Kathi came back in with the tray of tea and a plate of biscuits.

'Oh, digestives,' said Charles and eagerly reached out for one. Kathi laughed and took one herself. English people were obsessed with sweet things. That was something I had noticed over the years. Biscuits, chocolate, puddings, they couldn't get enough. Maggie thought it was because English food was so boring that everyone filled up on desserts.

'You know, I just remembered something,' said Kathi sitting down with her mug of tea. 'No, never mind.'

'What?' I said.

'Nah. I just . . . it was just, I don't know why I remembered it.'

'Go on,' I urged, sipping my tea.

'Well, one time my sister was coming round for dinner. And she knows that I'm HIV, right?'

It was the first time the disease had been mentioned and everyone just took it in their stride. There we all were, sipping tea, with a gentle breeze humming outside, making light conversation. About a bloody killer virus!

'Anyway so she rings me up. She lives in Tottenham. With her bloke, Stafford. He doesn't know of course. So anyway, she goes, you know when you chop the onions and, you know when you cry and the tears drop into the onions? She goes, does that mean you can catch it? She thought you could get it from the onions.' Kathi laughed but no one else was laughing.

'God,' said Charles. 'How do you feel when people say things like that?'

'She's thick my sister. I told her, you know, you can't get it like that. But I felt a bit funny, you know. I mean if she thought of the onions, she must be sitting there thinking about everything. Every little thing that I do, and thinking can I get it from that . . .'

'That's a really sad story, Kathi. That's the kind of thing. If you tell us that story on camera, you know a lot of people would listen to that and it would make them think, yeah I'm really uninformed about this subject,' said Charles and Madeleine nodded.

'She's really amazing, isn't she?' said Madeleine when we were driving back. 'Perfect.'

'She's *so* real,' said Charles.

'And brave. Imagine, she's on her own, her man's left her and she carries on regardless. I guess that's your frontier spirit for you,' said Madeleine to the rearview mirror.

I was looking out of the window, scowling. I don't know why she was bothering to include me in the conversation now. As soon as we had left the house the pair of them had been going on and on about how great Kathi was, as if they had discovered her themselves.

'What about that guy, Angie?' said Madeleine. 'What kind of person is he anyway?'

'I dunno. He's just a guy in a pub,' I said flatly, looking out of the window.

CHAPTER EIGHT

For the second time that day I headed for Stoke Newington. We were to have a meeting on Monday to discuss the shoot so I'd spent the afternoon making phone calls, photocopying, compiling questions and crossing them out. I couldn't think straight.

I pushed open the door of the Dog and Trumpet and saw Lol standing by the bar talking to a man with ginger hair. Lol saw me and raised his hand. I took a deep breath and walked over to them.

'All right?' I said to Lol. 'Do you want a drink?'

He smiled. 'Yeah. I'll have a Guinness.'

I turned to his friend, who looked a little embarrassed and said, 'No thanks, darlin'. I'm all right. I'd like to buy *you* a drink but I'm a bit skint you know.'

I could feel a whirlwind of rage mounting and I didn't know why. I drummed the bar with my fingertips. I scowled at a man who was trying to queue jump me at the bar. Hugh was at the far end of the pub playing the pinball machine and I looked the other way thinking if he came over I'd scream. The smoke and conversation seemed to have meshed into a fat snake winding itself around the pub, tangled up with the chairs and feet and pool cues.

'Cheers,' said Lol and turned his attention back to the man who was rolling a cigarette.

I stood with my bottle of Beck's expecting some more conversation but the man was lighting his roll up.

'Well, I mean we were the *real* mods man. We were the real mods. There was me, Mickey Donnen, Andy Bowen from up Holloway and Bowie. You should have seen Bowie then. He used to wear a chalk stripe suit, fly collar, cuban heels, slight flares and his hair was all combed over to one side like this.' He showed Lol the angle of the cuban heel with his fingers; drew imaginary chalk lines down his jacket with his thumb.

Lol was listening intently sipping his Guinness. I was standing there feeling like an uninvited guest.

'You know, I was in Amsterdam last week and I bumped into Bowie in the Milky Way. He had some good toke man, I got wasted. Cleaned him out.'

The man started chuckling and I crossed my arms watching him. There was a hole in his boot and you could see the tartan pattern of his nylon sock. He had clearly done every drug from A to Z and back again.

Sure, I thought, I just bet David Bowie — international rock star — was your mate. I just bet he let you smoke all his dope without realising it.

'Actually,' the man said with a serious expression, 'Bowie's quite an intelligent bloke. I was quite surprised.'

Oh *yeah*, I thought, and *you* should know, Mr Brain of Britain.

'Did you have a scooter?' I asked.

'Nah, man. All that came later. We were the original mods. They were just weekend boys, the scooter boys. This was '62. We had long hair. It was different every week. Mod see. Short for Modern. It was pure fashion. Fashion. We used to go up The Scene in Windmill Street. They wanted to put us on the tele, on *Ready Steady Go*, but then it was dead. We'd move on.'

A woman was pushing past him trying to get to the bar. She had a paper plate in her hand with a half eaten burger on it.

'Sorry, darlin'. You trying to get past?' He shifted out of the way.

'Oh ya,' she said in an impeccable Kensington accent, 'thanks. I'm just like trying to put this plate back.'

He eyed the burger. 'You finished with that darlin'?' She nodded and he unashamedly took the meat from the buns and popped it into his mouth.

'Waste not want not, eh?' he said and winked at her. She looked shocked but kept her smile intact and walked away.

'D'you want another drink mate?' said Lol finishing his Guinness.

'No thanks, man. I've gotta go. See about some business.' He winked at me and Lol and looked at the felt tipped notice above the bar: ANYONE FOUND SELLING, TAKING, EXCHANGING OR SMOKING DRUGS IN THIS BAR WILL BE BANNED. Signed The Guvnor.

'Do you want to sit down?' said Lol looking at me for the first time in the evening.

We walked over to a table by the door. Lundy walked past us heading for the pool tables. 'Yaaright, darlin',' he said. I smiled back.

'Who was that bloke earlier?' I asked Lol.

'Just a guy. He was trying to sell me some drugs but I told him to forget it,' said Lol laughing.

'God,' I said staring into space.

'What?'

'I wish I was in Paris. All those cafés and people sitting on sidestreets watching the cars go by. Drinking wine.'

Lol kissed his teeth.

'I hate that café culture. It makes me sick. That's what they're doing to all the pubs here. Like that bloody Amigo's. It's a joke. It's just a gimmick.'

'Lol!' I felt irritated with him. 'That's not the same at all. That's Americanism. It's different.'

'Look it comes to the same thing. It's all that. Coffee and wine and bloody plastic flowers. All of it is rubbing out pub culture.'

'Well what's so wrong about that?' I challenged. 'Pubs are full of blokes drinking and talking rubbish. And it's all about buying rounds and it's all blokes telling tall stories.'

'Listen. I grew up going to places like that. I'm not saying you shouldn't have no wine bars and all that but they shouldn't get rid of the English pub. That's English culture.'

I started to laugh. 'Oh yeah, blokes drinking and singing "Rule Britannia". Great. Do me a favour.'

Lol looked at me for a moment. 'All right, so what? A lot of blokes I know do that, did that. Every Saturday after the football. I don't slag down your culture. Don't slag down mine, all right?'

'Is that it? Is that all your culture amounts to, Lol?'

He looked into his pint and shrugged.

'I can't *see* anything else. It's all been torn down or forgotten or just made into something else,' he said.

We sat quietly for minutes. I lit a cigarette and blew the smoke straight ahead of me. His hands were around his glass and I saw him move his glass a little closer to mine. I watched that space on the table become less.

'Well it's not *my* fault,' I laughed and dug him in the ribs.

He looked at me and screwed up his face till his eyes were crinkled up.

'Yes it is,' he said. 'It's *all* your fault. Everything. It's all your fault and nothing to do with me. And it's my ball and I'm going home now and taking it with me.'

We both laughed.

I looked at him and he was smiling and looking at my face.

'I bet you used to do that. I bet if you didn't get to kick the ball you'd say it's my ball and I'm going home,' I said mimicking a spoilt brat.

'Nah. I just beat them up,' said Lol with a straight face. 'That solved everything.'

'Yeah, right.'

'Until the next day when they got their big brother on to me. Then I got mashed,' he said still smiling and looking at me.

'Serves you right,' I said.

'Yeah. I agree. Serves me right,' he said.

'Oh,' I said and laughed.

'You see. Thought I was going to disagree, didn't you? You're always looking for an argument you are.'

'No, I'm not,' I said straight away.

'Yes, you are.'

'No, I'm *not*.' I poked my tongue out at him.

'All right then. Have you heard about this thing called Yours?'

'No, what's Yours?'

'I'll have a pint of Guinness please. Haw. Haw.'

'You think you're clever, don't you?' I said grinning.

'No, I don't.'

'Yes, you do.' I rolled my eyes and walked over to the bar.

When I returned a man with straggly brown hair and combat jacket was leaning over our table. Lol was giving him a light with my lighter.

The man looked sideways at me and smiled lazily.

'Are you In-di-an, man?'

'Yes,' I said putting our drinks down.

'I've *been* to India, man. Blew my mind,' he said.

Lol was grinning.

'I'm going back, man. Yeah, India,' he said with a stupid grin on his face.

'Good sunsets, yeah?' I sneered. Lol burst into laughter. The man looked confused for a minute. Then he started grinning.

'Yeah, man. The smack was amazing. Really pure.'

Lol was leaning back on his seat next to me watching the show.

'Is that all you did?' I said full of contempt.

'Yeah, man,' he said. He looked like he had just won the pools.

I folded my arms and exhaled cigarette smoke, noisily. The man looked upset like a kid that had been told off.

'So, how'd you get there, Al?' said Lol leaning toward the hippy.

He slipped his left hand underneath the table to touch my arm. I smiled because no one could see.

Al brightened up. 'Begging man.'

'How much do you make?' asked Lol squeezing my arm. A rush ran through my whole body.

'Fifty, sometimes seventy, a day,' said Al and then nodded smiling away.

'What?' I said. 'That's more than I make. Where d'you do it?' I asked grinning.

Al puffed up proudly. 'Kings Cross Tube station. Finsbury Park. And Leicester Square's good in the evenings.' His face became serious: 'There's a lot of competition.' Then abruptly he got up. 'I'll see you later, man,' he said and shuffled off towards the pool area.

Lol still had hold of my arm. He slid his hand down and laced his fingers through mine. We looked at each other and smiled.

'This place should be called the Dog and Bullshit,' I said.

'Very good,' Lol laughed.

We watched Al, oblivious to the world, bumping into the band dragging the equipment onto the stage.

'I just like stories,' said Lol.

I looked at him. 'Yeah. I like stories too,' I said.

The guitarist plucked a string on his electric guitar. The speakers shuddered and the mixing desk gave off piercing feedback. 'Ouch,' Lol screwed up his eyes. 'Like this is a downer, man. Like let's split this joint, man,' he said, taking off Al's accent.

It was a strangely warm night for the middle of November. There was a full moon. People were laughing in the streets, jackets flung over their shoulders. Windows were open. Greek music was wailing from a kebab shop.

Lol held my hand. I felt as if we had stepped off a space ship.

'Why's it so warm?' I asked.

'I don't know,' he said.

What? The greenhouse effect? Alcohol? Intimacy?

We walked down the street to a wooden bench marked 'In honour of Lady Anson-Williams for her good deeds for the poor'. We sat and watched the street like a movie.

'All we need is some sandwiches,' said Lol.

'And a bottle of whisky. Cheapest brand,' I laughed.

Lol was looking straight ahead at the kebab shop.

'Why did you leave her? Why did you leave Kathi?' I blurted out abruptly.

'That's my business.' His face was set.

'You bastard,' I said bitterly. It wasn't on behalf of Kathi. It was because he wasn't telling me about himself, because he was the kind of man that ignored women in public, because he was the kind of man who was just a guy in a pub.

'Yeah. Right. I'm a bastard,' he said flatly.

Suddenly my anger swam back. He had a life and I had
no access to it. I wished I'd never met Kathi. I wished he
had been just a guy who had chatted me up in a pub. But
it wasn't like that. Everything had happened and here we
were. Caught up.

I pulled my knee up, rested my chin on it and sighed.

He laughed without opening his mouth as though he
was mocking me.

'Everything's so easy for you, isn't it?' he said.

'Yeah. It's all my fault,' I said looking at the traffic.

'Look, you started this. You wanted to meet her. Now
you think she's great and I'm a bastard. It's not as simple
as that.'

'No. Because I like you,' I said simply.

'Don't bother. I'm a bastard.'

'Oh, stop saying that. You sound like a fucking record,'
I shouted in the empty street. I wanted to hit him.

'It was a long time, Angie. I went out with her at school.
School. We were kids. Marriage. Why not? I didn't think
about anything then. We lived in that house. I just carried
on as normal. Out with the lads, screwing around, out for
the crack. She was always there when I came in drunk,
horny, fucked off. She was there. We were just living. It
wasn't working.'

'Maybe she didn't want to always be there. Maybe she
wanted you to treat her better.'

'No, she didn't. It was all her little brain could see. She
doesn't know anything beyond Stoke Newington and a
grope in the dark.' He shook his head.

'One time, I met this bird at a party. She was a student.
I don't know what she was doing there. Anyway we were
talking. I just wanted to fuck her. Kath was up Tottenham
at her sister's for the weekend. So we went back. The bed
broke. We'd just done it and the bed broke. We slid off
toward the wall and started laughing. Then we started

talking. I liked listening to her. She knew a lot. I dunno, she was picking the hair from her face and talking and I was lying back listening. It was nice. And then, it was four in the morning and Kathi was banging on the door. I got scared and told the girl it was my wife and she'd better hide. Kathi must've found her keys or something. She came charging up the stairs and we were in a heap in the corner. She was pissed and she looked ugly. She started screaming the place down saying she was going to kill this girl and all this shit. She said she'd better fuck off out of it and she better not see her again because she was going to kill her if she did. This girl just looked at me like I was shit and said, "I'm not a tart," got dressed and left.'

'But Kathi must've loved you, Lol. To show herself up like that.'

'God. Is that what you think love is? God. Birds. Always going on about love. I was her bloke and that was it. She didn't want me but she just didn't want anyone else to have me. All she wanted was to moan about it with her mates. Afterwards she started on at me. She was saying I was a wanker. She was saying you just can't leave it alone can you. She went on and on. I couldn't bear it. She was insane. I just listened to it and then I went out. Came out and sat on a bench where it was quiet. Next day I told her I was fed up with it. I was going. She just started on again telling me I was treating her bad and I had to change. And I said I was treating her bad because she made me sick.'

He lay back against the bench. I lit a cigarette.

'Then that business with Eddie happened. I wanted to go round and kill him. He'd given it to her all right but she'd given it to me. It wasn't fair. All right, I'd fucked her around but this wasn't fair. I was a fucking innocent bystander. I was scared. I hated her. But something changed. Afterwards we seemed to get on all right. She seemed to calm down. She wasn't worried about it. She didn't have anything to say about me. And I thought it's all right now. Now I can go.'

'It doesn't make sense,' I said.

'None of it made sense. I had to get out, get away from her. Just be by myself.' He shrugged. 'I wanted to be somewhere different. Not Stoke Newington, not the Trumpet . . . all those people talking rubbish.' He looked at the pavement. 'I didn't get very far.'

'But you said you liked it all. You said you liked pubs and . . .'

He looked at me and smiled. 'I know. I do like it. And I hate it. But it's what I know. It's part of me. But I don't know what to do with it either. When I'm in the pub and I'm having a crack I think it's all right. I know who I am. But it's nothing. It means nothing. And I hate it.'

I ground the cigarette out with my foot. It would take a hundred years to understand. I could have sat there and said what do you mean by this and why did you do this and it would still take a hundred years. And I had to be home by one o'clock, or else there'd be lectures.

'Let's have a coffee at your place,' I said.

'All right. We can sit on my roof,' he said.

'Your roof?'

'Yeah. It's only the top of the extension below me, but we can sit there like it's summer. In deck chairs with our coats on.' He laughed. 'You know. Like the song.' Then he started singing. 'Up on the roof, up on the roo-oof . . .'

I looked at him and started to laugh. 'I didn't know you couldn't sing.'

He put his key in the door and we stood in the dark hallway. It was a big house divided into bedsits. There were old fashioned black and white tiles on the floor like a chess board turned sideways. It smelt musty. There was a hatstand with a round mirror with hooks on either side, and a seat covered with letters addressed to different people.

The front door was heavy with three locks. On the top half there was a section of coloured plate glass. The moonlight seeped in, throwing pink and green light on to the mirror. Lol's face flashed by as he bent to check the mail. He picked up a bill and looked in the mirror where my face was, and turned. I bit my lip. He smiled and some of his face was in shadow.

'Show us your roof then,' I said and we ran up the stairs.

The roof was a square piece of tarmac at the top of the house. There really were two deckchairs standing against the wall. The moon lit up the Hackney skyline of satellite dishes and tower blocks. He came upstairs with two mugs of tea and a checked rug which he threw across my knees.

'Probably get a bit cold in a minute,' he said smiling.

'What are the neighbours like?' I asked.

'Oh. I don't see the people in the flats really. Everyone works different hours. But see that infants' school,' he pointed across at a grey playground with swings and white lines painted on the ground. 'In the day time if I'm home I come up and watch the kids. There's hundreds of the little bastards and they sound like a load of birds. Running around and shouting at one another. I have a joint and I watch them. They're weird. Kids.'

We laughed.

'Last week I was sitting here and I got so stoned I sat here for hours. They looked like mini people. And this girl was kicking the shit out of this little boy and she just kept on thumping him. Then this other one came up and started sticking up for him. Then the girls had it out. Slapping each other and pulling their ponytails. It looked like it was all in slow motion. And they're all wearing the same things, little duffel coats.'

'What happened?'

'He got up and legged it,' said Lol and we both burst out laughing.

'Typical man,' I said.

I moved my leg and the mug of tea spilt across my ankles. I jumped. 'Ouch.' I said.

'Serves you right,' he said pulling a face.

'Where's the loo?'

'There's a sink in my room. There's a towel. Wait!' he said catching my arm, the smile draining out of his face.

'What?'

'Don't use that. I'll get you another one. It's not . . . it's not safe.'

'What?' I stared at him. I couldn't move.

'Well maybe it is, I don't know. Look I'll just get you another towel.' He was looking away from me.

'Forget it Lol, it's only tea,' I said reaching out for his hand.

We looked at each other and didn't say anything.

'It's bloody freezing now isn't it,' he said still looking.

I got up and stood in front of him. The breeze blew gently against my ankle where the tea had spilt. I could feel it. I put my hands on the sides of his face and kissed his cheek.

'Is this safe?' I whispered. He nodded.

I kissed his neck. 'Is it safe?' I whispered. He smiled.

He was holding my hand and I brought it up to my mouth and kissed the spaces between his knuckles.

'Is it safe?' I whispered.

'You sound like bleeding Larry Olivier,' he said, his hands touching the sides of my shoulders.

'Eh? What?' I said.

'Is it safe?' he said from his throat.

'Is it safe? Is it safe?' he said again, this time with a menacing edge to the throaty rasp.

I sat back down in my chair and folded my arms, and rolled my eyes.

'No, no. Listen. Haven't you seen it? Brilliant film. *Marathon Man*. Larry Olivier's this mad Nazi dentist and he's drilling Dustin Hoffman's face and he's going "Is it safe? Is it safe?" and Dustin hasn't got a clue, right. "What?" he's saying. "What? What? Get out of my face." It's really funny. But it isn't supposed to be.'

'Are you saying I'm like Laurence Olivier?' I said sharply.

'Well I didn't say you *looked* like him.'

'I was trying to be romantic,' I said quietly.

'I know. I liked it. But I was a bit nervous. Sorry. Dunno why I brought Laurence Olivier into it,' said Lol and we laughed.

'Nervous? I'm terrified,' I said.

'It's just that I haven't . . . not since I left Kath,' said Lol.

I did a quick calculation. 'What? Not for six months?' I blurted out.

'Shh,' he said theatrically putting his finger to his lips. 'Don't *tell* everyone.'

We abandoned the deck chairs and my cigarette butts on the roof, and ran the half set of steps down to Lol's room. The inside smell and warmth made me realise how cold it had been on the roof. I had the rug around my shoulders. He opened the door and shut it behind us.

There was a large wooden bed, a wardrobe, a sink, a chest of drawers and two piles of records leaning against a wall. Everything was neat and tidy. The room was painted white and there was nothing on the walls except a mirror. It could have been anyone's room. There were no magazines or clues lying around.

I sat down gingerly on the bed and Lol started putting a record on, his back to me.

'Just listen to this before you go'

I crossed my legs and looked at the grey t-shirt stretching across his back. I was making a decision. But I knew I had made that decision days ago.

'I'm not going yet,' I said.

He turned his head. 'Maybe you should.' Then he shrugged. 'No big deal.' He went back to putting the record on.

I folded my arms and smiled. 'No chance, mate.'

He sat down cross legged next to the record player and looked at me.

'You sure?'

I threw my shoes off and lay back on the bed.

'You bet,' I said.

He got up and walked around the room, picking up a record sleeve, brushing his teeth at the sink. I watched him. Aretha Franklin shouted 'Respect'. There was a large brown paper bag sitting on the bedside table.

'Oh, sweets. Can I have one?' I said pulling the bag on to the bed. 'No . . . no, hang on,' said Lol, but it was too late.

About ten packets of Durex spilled out. There was Gold, FeatherLite, Gossamer, Nu-form, Raspberry flavour, even ones called Black Trojan.

'Oh God. I'm sorry. They're just . . . I just,' said Lol trying to stuff them back into the bag.

I let out a whoop of laughter.

'No, no. Let's have a look. I've never seen so many,' I said wide eyed and started rifling through them like a kid in a sweet shop. We were laughing.

'Look at this one. Haitch Tee. Extrem reissfest und super elastisch, but Is it zafe? Ja, Ja. Dis ist Das condom für safer sex,' he read the packet in his Laurence Olivier voice.

'German efficiency, man,' I tried to copy Al's accent from the pub.

'Like yeah, man. Like Vorsprung durch Technik, man,' said Lol.

'You're mad.' I pushed his shoulder and he toppled over as if I'd pushed really hard. I collapsed on top of him laughing.

'Help,' he wailed, and reaching out his arms he pulled me toward him till I was so close that a kiss wasn't open to discussion.

'That was a big fat lie earlier. You said you hadn't since Kathi. What's all these then? Christmas decorations?'

He laughed.

'Listen, right. It's ridiculous. After I'd spent weeks getting stoned, drunk, miserable you know, I ran into this chemist and bought the whole lot. The girl must've thought I was a sex maniac or something. I just bought them all like my life depended on it. Like if I *had* them, then it didn't mean I wasn't going to have sex ever again. Mad,' he said shaking his head as if at his stupidity. 'I never even used a single one.'

I narrowed my eyes in mock disbelief.

'You can check them if you like,' he grinned.

'Right!' I said freeing myself and plunging my hands in to the packets, 'I *will*.'

Each contained three neatly sealed rectangles holding a condom.

'You are *so* suspicious,' he said folding his arms.

I giggled. He lay down across the foot of the bed and I sidled up next to him, pushing the multicoloured packets on to the floor.

'Actually, that's exactly what I did when I went on the pill,' I said looking at the ceiling. We were holding hands as if we were standing in a horizontal world.

'Eh?' he said.

'Me and my mate Maggie. As soon as we hit sixteen some blokes at school, older ones than us, said we were "legal lays", right? So we ran down to the Family Planning clinic and made out that we had steady boyfriends, didn't smoke and all that, so that they would give us the pill. Then I hid them in my underwear drawer at home. Didn't even use them till about a year later. But I thought, yes, I've got them. I'm a woman now.' I giggled remembering those days.

Lol's face was buried in my hair and I had just stopped giggling when he said in the best Bogart impersonation. 'Lissen, baby. Ya wanna tark or ya wanna burn rubber?'

I tried to keep a poker face but giggles came tumbling, sniggering out like coins from a fruit machine.

'You have *got* to be the corniest man I have *ever* met.'

Under the light of the lamppost that made his eyes look so blue he had said to me, 'Of all the bars in all the world you hadda walk into mine.' And there had been no piano, just a cat shrieking in Stoke Newington High Street.

The bedside lamp was on. We were propped up on pillows, his arm around me, his hands exploring German engineering. I wasn't allowed to smoke because it was a disgusting habit. I drummed my redundant fingers on the quilt but I was told that it was no good whining, I *still* couldn't smoke.

So I watched him take the rubber out from its sealed packet. We peered at it. He pulled the latex about, put it up to the light, examined it from all angles.

'Test run,' he said with a straight face. 'What do you reckon, Watson?' He handed me an imaginary magnifying glass.

'Safe as North London houses,' I said.

'Check,' he announced and dropped it by the side of the bed and nodded his head jerkily as in a sharp salute.

Then he turned to me and became Lol again and grinned. 'I haven't had so much fun for years.'

'And that's with your clothes on,' I said. His one liners were infectious. It was like a tennis match. A friendly.

'This bloke I slept with once when I had to go off the pill because it was giving me hassle. He went *into* one about it. He said it interfered, he said it killed the romance, he said it was like having a bath with your socks on. God I was so worried that he was going to have a terrible time I just let him do it without one. Then I had a hundred fits before I finally came on.' I rolled my eyes, because he had *still* disappeared off the face of the earth and I had sat drinking, worrying and composing suitable retorts that I *should* have made.

Lol pulled me closer and grinned. I couldn't for the life of me think why I was telling all this to a man I didn't even know.

'We used to fill them up with water and chuck them,' he said.

'I remember that. All the blokes threw them at the girls. And all the girls would scatter in the playground screaming their heads off.'

I was rattling on because the patterns of our past seemed to share similarity. Even though he had been in Hackney and I had been in Finchley, at some intersection of time we were seeing the same scene.

'I used to chuck them at pakis.' Lol's face suddenly went blank. and he was staring into space.

'Oh,' I said. I suppose I was shocked but it seemed so incongruous. Then I wanted to laugh because it was so pathetic. Little big men running around throwing condoms filled with water at people. But I didn't laugh, because I supposed I should have hated him.

'For fuck's sake, Angie!' he shouted but it was a whisper. I looked at him and we remained motionless. There was no space between us.

'There was this bloke in Camden. We'd all been up the Music Machine. We were pissed. There was about ten of us. Some of them were head cases but I liked the style. I was in my two tone suit with the thin lapels. And my crombie over that. Silk lining. A real crombie. And this bloke was walking down the road. And Kathi was going "Go on you haven't got the bottle". I looked at her and then pushed the bloke over in the street. He was so light, like a scarecrow or something. Took his money and emptied the rest of his wallet on the street. It was all flying around in the wind and he was running after it like an idiot as if it was fivers. But it was just stuff. All his stuff. He only had two pounds. Then one of them went over and started kicking his head in because he only had two pounds. I just stood and watched. I couldn't have given a monkey's. I just watched the show. All right?' He spoke to the ceiling as if it had been trying to squeeze a confession out of him. But there was no policeman, no priest, no judge in sight.

He turned and looked at me. I could see him setting his jaw, mouth closed, his teeth pressing together as if he was gathering up anger. Like a trembling sky before a storm. Then his brow furrowed up so much there was a ditch in the middle of his forehead. Like he was thinking so hard that his brain was going to burst out of his head. I just watched him.

'So what?' I said. It didn't frighten me.

'She was going on at me saying I was a poof and I should have done him over. In front of my mates. And I just slapped her. Across the face. She started crying and I hated her. I didn't want to be there. Didn't want to be part of that . . . that pathetic existence they all thought was so great. Just because you looked sharp on a Saturday night and drank cans of Special Brew.' He laughed but he wasn't smiling. 'And I looked the sharpest of all. I was the main man. It was me building that fine wall but all the bricks were rotten. What you gonna do? Start again? Nah, too late. And with what? Everything's still the same. My old man's a bloody crook, still watering down his beer and pretending he can't see them taking drugs under his nose. Still giving the pigs free drinks. Counting his bloody money. What's he gonna tell me that I don't know already and think is a pile of shit anyway?'

He put his hand over his eyes and I bit my bottom lip, still watching him.

'Can you imagine it? That was ten years ago. I knew. But I still thought I was hard. I was Jack the Lad. Everything would come right for me because I was so smart. So smart. So smart that I still got married to a girl because she had nice legs. Still hung round with those boneheads because it was my moment. As if that moment was going to last forever. King of my castle. Yeah.'

'What do you want me to do about it?' I said and I hadn't meant it but there was an edge to my voice.

And I thought: He doesn't want me to forgive him or be frightened of him. He wants to clear the decks. He wants a reason. He's somewhere else now. And he can't even get out of Stoke Newington. And all that's left are stories. Dancing around him like material ghosts.

And I wanted to say: Things can be different. But what did I know? How could words make a difference?

'Say something.' He sounded choked. I watched a tear travel past the dam of his hand, making a wet track on his cheek.

My heart hurt. I clambered through my head for the right thing to say. The word that made pain, regret, go away. But there was nothing. Whisper something . . . anything.

'Paki basher,' I whispered.

'Evil, thick, stupid, moron, cunt, shithead, ignorant . . .'
All this bile came out from Lol's mouth, tumbling into the
half light. It sounded like someone smashing their head
against a brick wall.

I lay next to him staring at the ceiling. I felt cold. We lay
there each cut off in our drowning pools. He'd started, so
he had to finish. There was no sound except the purr of
an occasional car driving past. The record had stopped
and the needle was scratching at the end of the last track.
Night was slowly easing itself into morning, laden with
heavy luggage that had no destination tags. I closed my
eyes and waited.

Then out of the blue, a phone rang upstairs. It rang
again. It rang again. It rang for twelve times before Lol
broke the listening trance we were caught up in, and
shouted 'Answer it!' so loudly that grits of anger seemed
to fall off the words.

We listened together timidly as there was a creak and
a groan and someone bellowed an angry 'What!!' into the
phone. I exhaled as if I was the telephone and had been
holding my breath.

He turned to look at me and the lines of his face had
softened and relaxed, like muscles after a workout. My
head was reeling. 'The birds have started,' he said. Dawn
was creeping in and the room was suspended in a purple
light.

I passed the base of my palm over his cheek and wiped
away the pain. He closed his eyes and the corner of his
eyelashes touched the nail of my little finger. I watched
his face for a moment. It was at peace. At least for now.

'So, are you going to make the earth move or what?' I
asked.

He looked at me, narrowed his eyes. 'Nah.'

'Why not?'

'You won't respect me in the morning,' he said, deadpan.

CHAPTER NINE

All the lights were on in No. 10 as I steered into the drive. Something was up. I checked my watch and cursed. It was five in the morning. Usually when I was this late everyone was fast asleep and given that I had expert knowledge of which stairs creaked, I was able to answer the question 'What time did you get in last night?' with a casual 'Oh just after one.' The door opened before I had a chance to get the keys out.

'Where have you been? Where have you been?' Ma looked like some long suffering mother in an Indian movie. Her hair was dishevelled and her face creased. She hauled me inside and pushed me into the front room, closing the door behind her.

'What's the matter?' I asked.

She started beating her head with her hands. 'Where have you been? You think I don't know what you do? Who do you give our phone number to? Who are these people? Where have you been?' She started shaking my shoulders.

I felt stunned at the volume of accusation flying around the room, but even my mother could not know about my dealings with sex and drugs and rock and roll all in one go.

'Wait, Ma. Wait a minute. I'm sorry I'm so late. The car wouldn't start. What's happened? Come on.'

Then she started to cry and furiously wiped her face with her sari. I felt embarrassed and fearful all at once. Indian adults didn't cry in front of their kids unless someone had died. These were tears of desperation.

'How would you know who is ringing up the house? How would you know what filthy things your friends are saying? You are the lady of the manor. You are never in,' she said bitterly between sobs.

'*Look*! What's happened?' I said. Then I reached out for her hand. She was shaking. Rax was poking his head around the door.

'Oi!' I said to him. 'Get in here. Explain.'

'Chaaa, man. No big deal,' he said quietly, his back to ma, but she heard it.

She slapped him across the head. ' "No big deal", he says. What is the matter with you kids? All you think about is yourself.' She started shaking her head.

I was getting angry and I caught hold of Rax's dressing gown sleeve and pulled him towards me. 'Now!' I ordered.

'All right. All right,' he started swatting my hand away. 'A couple of hours ago someone rang. I picked up the extension in my room and ma picked it up downstairs. She'd got up for a glass of water. I was still half asleep. Anyway this bloke starts giving it over the phone. First of all it's all polite saying is this so and so number. And ma says no and does he realise what time it is. He goes yeah, paki. And because he's said it all quiet she goes "What!" and he says: "You pakis are gonna die. All of you." By this time I've woken up and I'm saying to ma put the phone down but she starts having a fit and saying who is this, who is this. I mean he's really gonna tell her. Then he just carries on all quiet and creepy pakis this and pakis that and how it's the end of the line for the pakis. Then he's saying dirty pakis, smelly cun . . .' Rax looked at ma, 'You know he starts swearing and all that. At this point I slam the phone down and run downstairs and grab the phone out of ma's hand and put that down as well.'

'What?' I couldn't believe it. We weren't poor Indians living in the East End having petrol bombs thrown through the windows. That's something you read about. This was bloody Finchley for God's sake. People round here wouldn't even say boo to a goose. They even sat quietly and tolerated our festivals going on in their back yard. Tesco's even stocked a range of Indian vegetables and delicacies.

'Ma. What do you think? You think it's someone I gave our number to? How can you think that? Ma, I'm safe. I'm safe. I would never give our number to anyone I didn't know. You know my friends. You've met them. You know Phil, and Maggie and Hugh and Chloe. You *know* them . . .' I was sprinting through all of this. Inside I was boiling with rage.

She began to calm down and Rax put his arm around her, patting her back.

'Look, Ma. There's weird people about. They do this sort of thing for fun. It's like people ring up numbers and put the phone down when someone answers because they want to see if someone's home. Maggie says it happens to her all the time.' I was making all of it up because I had to think fast. I had to trivialise it or else the cocoon of wild fear that she was caught up in would tighten around my throat.

'Who are these people?' she wailed. Then she straightened up and touched me on the shoulder. 'I know. You are a good girl. I trust you. But I became very scared. Twenty years in this country and you still have to be scared of the telephone.' She shook her head defeatedly.

I hated this. I hated seeing them scared. These strong people who had held me, been there always. How could they be so affected by some crank on the end of the telephone?

'Ma,' I said sternly, 'there's nothing to be scared of. We're safe. The doors are locked. It's never happened before. Don't let them scare you. That's their victory.'

She was nodding and looking at the floor. Rax rolled his eyes and drew a silent sigh of relief.

'Hey,' I said grinning. 'Remember that time we were on a bus and those skinheads said, "Go home paki?" Remember? When I was still at school, doing my A levels? And you hadn't even heard him? And I started shouting at him to piss off and you told me off for swearing. I thought you were being ridiculous but you said why waste my breath. And then you turned to him and you said ever so politely: "Young man I am from India. Pakistan is another country." You held your head up, Ma. You remember that?' I had mimicked her accent and was prodding her in the arm, urging her to remember.

She looked up and smiled weakly. 'Yes. Yes. They were only boys.' Then she straightened up and became ma again. Ma the back seat driver, ma who had a romantic past stuck in a dusty trunk in Delhi because one didn't splay out one's emotions to everyone.

'Why are you talking like that? You sound like that Peter Sellers? I am not talking like this!' she said mildly affronted, pushing back her sari. 'Now come on. Both of you. Go to bed. And not a word about this to your father or your maama ji, all right?'

We all agreed to keep the secret. They would only have ten fits about it and go into a debate over whether we should ring the police. Dad would say yes because the police should be informed and must be informed. Maama ji would scoff and say the police in this country were only good for telling the time. Both of them would have a go at ma for not putting the phone down earlier. They would go on about it for days. Discussing it, analysing

it, pondering it. Then dad would get paranoid and say I
couldn't go out late and someone may be watching the
house or following the car. Maama ji would join forces
and the house would be put in a state of emergency. We
all knew we didn't want that so it was settled.

Ma crept back to bed. Dad's snores were rivalling the
drone of the world service. I took a mug of tea to my room.
I was wide awake now and although I wanted to climb
into bed and think about Lol, I had things to sort out first.

I pushed Rax's door. He was already in bed, his
dressing gown in a heap on the floor. There was nowhere
to sit in the narrow room except the bed. Every square
inch was filled with plastic boxes of records. Above his
bed on the shelf were two record decks covered with clean
dusters. At the end of the bed and in another corner of
the room were two huge speakers. On top of one of the
speakers was an upturned pink frisbee.

'Don't you dare go to sleep yet. I want a word with you.'
I pushed his feet over the duvet. He kissed his teeth loudly
and reached into the frisbee where he kept his cigarette
papers, took three out and started constructing a joint.

'It's the middle of the night, man,' he said frowning.

'Look. I want to know what's going on. What's all this
about?'

He laughed.

'Boy. I just don't believe youz. "I'm not from Pakistan,
I'm from India".' He mimicked ma's accent thickly. 'Boy,
I bet he was well scared of that.' He kissed his teeth.

'Don't kiss your teeth at me,' I said passing him the
dope.

'It's no wonder we get mashed up you know. Indian
people got too much humbleness. What them people
need is a good hiding . . .'

'Rax! What do you know about this business? And
don't pretend you don't, right? And that's another thing.
Maggie said you'd organised that warehouse party.

What's all that about? I thought you were only DJing at these gigs?'

'Yo. Maggie Dreadlock,' said Rax grinning.

'Her name is not Maggie Dreadlock, right? Now talk or else.'

'Hey, man, Jelly. Chill out. I was gonna tell you about it anyhow. Listen, I'm in business now. Yes, boy. Business.'

I waited patiently as he drew long and hard on the joint.

'Spliff on this, man. Relax,' he said passing the joint.

'Well,' he said lacing his hands behind his head, settling down to tell his story. 'You know I've been DJing at these parties for the last two years, right? Right, well. Warehouse parties have been getting rough lately, man. Over the last year everyone's either got busted or gone legal. I was getting vexed with it, man. Me and Kyle running down to some place somewhere, carting all the records. Then half way through the night the police come and bust the place. They confiscate the drink, clear the people out. Chaa, man. And me and Kyle had to pack away the records and run out of there. Lotsa time we never even got paid. Big fifty pounds for a night that we never got paid. And these pasty white boys who organise them parties were just too untogether anyway. Even if we never got busted you'd have to hassle them for the money and they'd be out of it on their heroin or ecstasy or something. So I said, Kyle, my man, we gotta find a better living than this.'

'You got paid fifty pounds for a few hours of spinning records?' I said amazed.

'All nighter's, man. And it isn't a few hours. I line up my records beforehand. I work out the beats per minute. You have to! For the mix. It's the crucial mix that counts . . .'

It was all getting a bit technical for me. DJs just put one record on after another as far as I was concerned. Rax looked at me pityingly. He could tell it was over my head.

'Anyway. So we decide to get a warehouse ourself and do our own party. That was about six months ago. We check the Art Centre. It's a space just by Vauxhall tube. We go and meet the committee, all wet white people and I'm saying we want to do parties where it's cool for black people to come and not get hassle like in the West End. I'm saying to them black people got nowhere to go and they're going God that's terrible ya. I mean I sussed that they don't know clubs in the West End, not soul clubs or else they'd know it's all black people anyway. We offer them £100 for a night. They can do with the money 'cos the Centre's skint and British Rail who *they* pay rent to don't want to refurbish. And it's cool because it's between exhibitions and they want to do their bit for the "community". So we get tickets printed, get the beer from the cash and carry. The first few ones we did we made over a grand. Fiver entry. Cheaper than the West End. So I say, Kyle, my man, we're in business. Then the Centre says British Rail want to sell the property and they're closing it down till they find a buyer. I'm vexed because there's nothing in there and it's perfect for parties, but I can't tell British Rail that. Then these white boys come up to me and they say they want to hire the place and do a party in there. So I've got a copy of the keys, right, and they think I own it or something. So I say, right you can rent it off me for £500 for the night. I go and open it up at ten and then lock it up again at seven in the morning. If they get busted it's their problem. Perfect.'

'So, hang on,' I said rubbing my eyes. 'You rent them a place that's not even yours to rent. And you have no liability. If they get busted they get busted. And you've got the only set of keys . . .'

'Exactly. So I just sit and make five hundred every week.'

'And . . .'

'Well I think it's one of them that phoned up tonight. They're just feisty, man. I'm gonna say to them next week, sorry but I got different clients now. You'll have to find somewhere else. Get them where it hurts.' He shrugged. 'No big deal. Anyway they try something else and I've got some friends that'll sort them out. I know some serious bouncers. And they hate white people, man. They'll take the chance to mash them.'

'Rax . . .' I was speechless. My brother sounded like a gangster and businessman rolled into one. Making money without getting his hands dirty.

'Look. You just make sure ma doesn't freak out. I've been renting that place for a few months now. I'm gonna do it till Christmas. There's lots of parties in December. I'll probably be able to do it twice a week. Then I'll stop. I know this bloke who works in the City, he's gonna invest it for me. Shares, man. I don't have to work at no Telecom no more and I hire out my decks to Kyle if he wants to play out like I used to.'

'You've got it all planned out, haven't you?' I said.

'Sure,' he said, 'You've got to. Otherwise you just end up like all that lot at Telecom doing nothing with their lives. They sit there talking about this and that and all they do is piss their lives up the wall. They all sit and talk hard but they've got nothing. Go to Butlins for their holiday. They're happy with it all. Not me, boy.'

A chill ran up my spine. The heating must have gone off hours ago but it was a different kind of chill.

'You're nobody unless you're somebody. And you're somebody if you got money. If you control. If you can control you got everything. Simple really,' said Rax yawning.

CHAPTER TEN

'I'd like to use Ross Taylor if possible. He's done a lot of docs. He's very experienced.' Madeleine was spooning the froth from her cappuccino into her mouth. 'Wow. Love that chocolate. Gives me a real high!' she said.

Charles was sitting on the chair, his feet on the table, pad in hand.

'Mmm. Ok. I've got a few other cameramen in mind. But they usually do commercials or features so I should think they'll be pretty busy.' He chewed his pen.

We were discussing crews. I was looking busy because I had no names to contribute. We had used different crews at Direct Vision but it had never occurred to me to remember any of their names. Now I saw why it was important. Different cameramen used different techniques, and depending on your film you had to choose the appropriate one.

'Hmm. Maybe we should get a camerawoman, huh?' said Madeleine. 'I mean if the guy is going to get chauvinistic or if Kathi can't cope with him. What d'you think, you guys?'

'Yeah. It would be good to have a camerawoman,' I piped up. 'It's good to give women jobs anyway.'

Madeleine snorted with laughter. 'Listen, sweetheart, the female technicians in this business don't need the work. They're damn good. The problem is getting hold of them, seeing if they're available. Anyway I never gave anybody a job because they had an excuse. If you're good enough, you work. If not then you don't.'

'Oh,' I said. Well thanks Madeleine, I thought. That put me in my place. However it was a kind of compliment because she was also saying she hadn't hired me in order to do the Commission for Racial Equality a favour. I felt put down and acknowledged at the same time.

'Madeleine, I'm easy. As long as they can take direction. I can't bear it when camera operators start directing the film,' said Charles.

'They gotta be able to do hand held. I'll go crazy if we end up with wobble vision,' said Madeleine and we all laughed. I was assiduously filing away buzz words to use on my next assignment.

'Shall we try that Chinese across the road for lunch?' suggested Madeleine.

'I can't. I've got some things to do.'

'Ok. Me and my researcher will go.' Madeleine winked at me.

I grinned. I was always available for lunch. I was determined to try out all the restaurants in Soho. Anyway, I never had boring things to do at lunchtimes like paying bills or doing the shopping. Chloe had been so shocked when I'd gone back home after university.

'Won't your parents want you to have an arranged marriage?' she'd said wide eyed.

'What like you and Hugh?' I'd replied grinning.

'Eh?' she'd frowned. 'We're not married. It wasn't arranged.'

'Yes it was. By me. Remember?' I'd said and we'd laughed.

'So. How'd you like your second week at Davis Films?' asked Madeleine as she poured the tea.

'Great,' I said.

The huge restaurant was packed out with diners, most of them Chinese. At the front door a Chinese waiter was shouting at customers in broken English as they stopped to look at the menu.

'Hurry, please. Hurry, please,' he said, pushing them towards a table. Steaming dishes kept arriving in the dumb waiter from the kitchen upstairs. Waiters balancing five plates on one arm, circled tables shouting out names of dishes above the hubbub of chopsticks and lunchtime gossip.

'That's us. Cantonese duck and noodles. Over here.' Madeleine shouted across to a waiter who stormed over and dumped the food unceremoniously on our table.

'The food here is as good as the service is rude.' Madeleine dug into her plate of noodles.

'So you're from India?' she said. 'I've been to Bombay. What a fabulous place. But wow, the heat is really something, isn't it? Mind you I didn't step outside the Taj Hotel most days. I was on my honeymoon.'

'I've never been there.' I was surprised to learn Madeleine was married. Divorced obviously.

'Yeah. India. I just loved the food out there too. Everything's so cheap. We had these cute waiters in the hotel and they were dressed up like they were in the Raj or something. But it's difficult to handle the poverty out there. You know like there's these rich Indians living on one side of the road and these shanty towns on the other side. You weren't born in India though. No?'

'Yes. I was. I came here when I was five . . .'

'Oh, but you're British now. I mean that's a real cockney accent you've got.'

'I grew up in North London. Kathi's a cockney. She's from the East End,' I said. Madeleine nodded but she didn't notice the difference. Did she think I was just like Kathi? Or just a little better? Jumped up. Like underneath the designer clothes did she think I was just the same?

'Sure, sure. But you know India has the biggest film industry in the world. Did you know that?'

Did she seriously think she was telling me something new? As if a hundred documentaries hadn't been made on it. As if every Indian grocery shop in Finchley that stocked hundreds of Indian film videos wasn't enough evidence?

'Did you work in the film industry in the States?' I changed the subject.

'No. I was a student. My husband's English. Was. Well still is of course. We're divorced happily,' she said tightly.

'Oh,' I said. 'Right.'

'He's a producer at the BBC.' She rolled her eyes. 'How 'bout you? You involved with someone right now?'

'Um well no. Sort of.' I started fumbling for words.

'Listen, it's just as well. This business kills relationships. You have to work late. He doesn't understand. You fight. You feel guilty. Blah blah.' She was moving her head from side to side as though she were watching a tennis match that was the relationship. 'Does he work in the business too?' she asked. 'I used to think that helped but believe me I'm not so sure now. You have to contend with that male ego.'

I was listening intently and smiling at her diatribe. If she only knew.

'He doesn't work in the industry,' I said and nothing more.

'Ahh, well. 'Cause I'm telling you, this industry's a village. Everyone knows everyone. So! If your guy's screwing around you find out double quick. *Everyone* is into gossip.' She laughed cheerfully.

'Charles seems all right.' I realised the hidden meaning there.

Madeleine picked up on it like a shot.

'Ya like him?' she said smiling lazily.

'*No*! I mean, yes. I mean to work with. I mean he doesn't seem to gossip and all that.' I was getting a bit hot under the collar.

'Are you kidding? He's the worst one. No Charles isn't into people gossip, although he's pretty good on that too. No Charles is into career gossip. He knows who's got what commission, who's working with who. Who hasn't been hired again and why . . .' She started to laugh. 'He's also very good at his job. He'll go far. For sure. He can play those games real well. He's ambitious.'

I was nodding. There was a lot of information here that I should have been collating for future reference but I kept thinking about Lol.

'So. What d'you wanna do? Direct, I guess. Right?'

'Um. I don't know really. Yes I suppose I'd like to direct. More control . . .' I sensed this wasn't the thing to say. 'Yeah. I'd like to move into directing,' I added, trying to sound anxious.

What I really wanted to say was that I liked working in television. I liked going out for two hour lunches and talking endlessly about other films. I loved the idea of this glamorous world. I wanted all the prizes, success, money, power, easy living. Who didn't? And I wanted then to be able to say to people: 'You just don't *realise* how pressured the television industry is. God, sometimes I wish I just worked in Woolworth's.'

But I couldn't say any of those things. It would have been too crass.

'Well, you know. I've worked in this industry for some time now. And what I know is that it's all about ideas. There's a lot of people out there who haven't got the ideas. They've just got the contacts. Ok, you need that too. But like see you came up with a good idea, a good angle. That's the mark of a good researcher. Now if you wanna follow through into directing you gotta learn to *take* direction too. You understand?' She was pouring out more weak tea.

I nodded intelligently although I wasn't sure quite what she was driving at.

'It's all about timing and judgement. You gotta know when your idea is good and then you gotta follow it through. Stick to your guns. But,' she raised her eyebrows, 'but you also gotta know when the idea needs help and you gotta take the help. I mean you can't just stick to it because it's yours and no one else can play, right?'

I laughed. 'Sort of like it's my ball and if I can't play then I'm going home and taking it with me. Right?' If Lol was there he would have laughed. But Madeleine didn't know the reference. She frowned.

'Sorta, yeah. What I'm saying is that a lot of people in this industry get real precious about their ideas. And really what you're doing, all of us, is making a goddamn film that sells. Making a film that's exciting and creative and stimulating television. You know, something that people are gonna want to watch. That's the bottom line, right?' She hunched her shoulders at this fact.

I nodded. It seemed to make sense. Yet I had a strange unresolved feeling of being instructed, told, warned. Forewarned . . . ?

In the afternoon I called Lol. I hadn't seen him over the weekend, deliberately. Friday night had been so intense and then I'd spent all Saturday thinking about what had happened at home and about Rax. I wanted to tell the world and I wanted to tell no one about Lol. It all seemed so fragile that I thought it could just get blown away. And then I thought maybe it was just nothing. And then I thought, my God, how can I feel so involved when we didn't even *do* anything.

But it had felt safer and better than anything else. It had felt better than with other men: worrying when I'd forgotten to take a pill or relied on it being the safe period; or being drunk but not uninhibited enough to say no; frustrated because some man had nothing to say; wondering why someone said I love you between the sheets . . .

Something new had happened and it felt good and warm. And funny. And friendly.

'Hello.' He was out of breath. 'Sorry I just charged down the stairs. How are you?' I could see him smiling even though British Telecom had a wall of wiring and networks between us.

'I just wanted to say. Um. Hello'

'Hello.'

'Hello.'

We both laughed.

'That was it really,' I said and laughed.

'Say it again,' he said.

'Listen. Stop messing around. I'm at work. I just wanted to tell you. I *have* got a phone really. At home, I mean.'

'Oh,' he said.

Then I told him about what had happened. About Rax and his theory about who the caller was. I just wanted to tell him.

'Sounds like he's got the right idea,' Lol said over the phone. 'But you don't want me to say that, do you?'

'He just thinks he can solve everything. By . . . by, I dunno. Violence. Getting someone else to do the violence. He thinks no one can touch him. It scared me.'

'Sometimes you have to look straight ahead. Do you know what I mean? You've got to feel strong. That's the most important thing.'

'I know. I know all that. And yeah, seeing my mum crying made me feel bad. Seeing her scared. Of a bloody phone call.'

'Yeah. You have to believe in the strength of your nature sometimes.' Then he laughed. 'God. That was a bit deep for me. For two o'clock in the afternoon.'

I ignored him playing the dumb working class boy.

'That's what Kathi's doing, isn't it? That's what you're doing. Feeling strong.'

'Let's leave her out of this.'

That stung.

'Aren't we allowed to talk about Kathi now? We're making a bloody film about her for Chrissakes.'

'I know. I'm sorry. I just . . . Forget it.'

'No. Go on.'

'I just thought this was me and you.'

'Oh,' I said.

'Still there?' he said

'Of course.'

'Did I tell you Friday night was the best time I've had. I had a really good time,' he said.

'Yeah, but say it again,' I said and he laughed.

'God,' he said.

'You called,' I said and broke into a giggling fit.

'I thought it was me who was supposed to be corny.'

'It's catching.'

'Long as that's the only thing that *is*! Haw. Haw.' There was a silence. 'Do I keep saying the wrong thing?' he asked seriously.

I laughed out loud. 'No. I like it. I like your attitude.'

There was a silence.

'Still there?' I asked.

'Yeah. I was just thinking.' 'Yeah?' 'You're a career woman.'

I laughed and tried to imagine what the words meant. Career Woman. 'Career girl,' I giggled.

'They say you shouldn't mix business with pleasure.' He laughed but I knew his mouth was closed.

'*That's* not funny, Lol.'

'No?'

'You're a bit more than that, Lol.'

'What do you mean? A bit on the side.' He put on an even stronger cockney accent.

'Why is it that *you're* the only one allowed to be romantic? Everytime *I'm* romantic, you take the piss.'

'That's because I'm so much better at it.'

'You're doing it again.'

'I'm not,' he protested.

'You are. I can feel it.'

'I wish I could feel *you*,' he said quietly.

'Anyway, I must go . . .'

'Someone walked into the room?'

'Yes.'

'Say something. I dare you.'

'No.'

'Go on.'

'I *must* go.' I was trying not to giggle.

'Spell your name out to me then.'

'What? You know my name . . .'

'No. Your real name.'

I rolled my eyes at the street outside but I was smiling at the telephone.

'Angellie.' I spelt it out for him, 'A-N-G-E-L-L-I-E.'

'Angellie . . . Angellie. That's a lovely name.'

'Good *bye*. Call you tomorrow.'

Charles had been walking around the room discreetly waiting for me to finish my call.

'Hi. Shall we go through the questions? The shoot's

booked for Wednesday if you want to call **Kathi** and ok it with her.'

'Sure,' I said getting out my disk from the drawer. 'Let me just print them up for you.'

While the printer was rattling I walked into the edit suite next door to call Kathi. It was a small room with a small window. On a shelf were two tv monitors and on the table underneath two video machines with an editing consul in between them; on another shelf a row of sealed video tapes. Next to the consul was a mug full of pens. I sat down heavily on the large editing chair and bounced on it. Editors sat on their asses all day so they always had good seats. With all that hardware in front of me I felt like I was sitting in a tank, clueless about all the bleeping, all the buttons and knobs.

Behind the door someone had sellotaped a photocopied cartoon of an old man, quill in hand. Behind him were angels and the Pearly Gates. The caption read: 'DEADLINE? NO ONE TOLD ME ABOUT A FUCKING DEADLINE.'

Editing was the last stage of post production and deadlines were invariably met by working late into the last few nights of the schedule.

'She says it's fine. I said I'll try to get there a bit earlier.' It was weird talking to Lol and then Kathi but I was getting used to it.

Charles nodded.

'Did you see the cartoon in the edit suite?' I asked.

'Yeah. Let's do this.' He sighed and tore off the paper from the roll on the printer.

I sat down quietly. He was obviously in a mood about something. It was funny. We had only worked together for a week and already it felt like months.

'Kathi. Could you tell us when you first discovered you were HIV?' He started reading them out.

'Do you have any idea how you got it?'

'How did you feel towards Eddie?'

'How did you feel when you realised Eddie was carrying the virus and had slept with you without telling you?'

'What about how you feel now? How do you carry on as normal?'

'How many people know about it? Are you frightened of people knowing? How do you think they would treat you if they knew?'

'Do you feel angry?'

'What did you know about AIDS and HIV before this happened? Did you think heterosexuals could get it? Were you aware of the Government campaigns? Do you think they are informative enough?'

'Why have you decided to prosecute this man?'

'What advice would you give to other young people?'

'Hmm. Good questions. They should get her going,' said Charles.

'Yeah. I mean obviously if you want to add any more.'

'No. I think they're good. Get her to tell us some anecdotes because we've got to get that laugh,' he said smiling. 'I'll make some copies and hand them to Madeleine.' He sighed and I had a feeling that whatever had happened between them had become fractured.

'We had a nice lunch. You should have come,' I said.

'Yeah. Look, why aren't there any questions about her husband?'

'He's her ex husband,' I said coldly.

'So?'

'All right.' I started scribbling on the page. I felt irritated with him. I had tried to lighten the mood and all he could do was throw Lol in my face. 'How do you feel about your husband?' I read flatly.

Charles sat down on the chair and the phone rang. I picked it up.

'What?' I said into the phone. 'Who? Tatiana?'

I frowned as Charles reached across for the receiver. I turned my back and started collecting up papers, my ears wide open.

'Hi,' he said 'Listen. This isn't a good time. What? Oh, the researcher.'

He was doodling on his pad and listening.

'I don't know. How the hell should I know which is the best hotel in Paris? The George V I suppose. Just call American Express for Christ's sake.' Then he looked up. 'Angie, do you know any good hotels in Paris?'

I turned around and laughed. 'No.'

'I can't. Listen I can't, all right? Take Cassandra's car. Why? I *can't*! I need it, ok? Look. I have to go now. I'm sorry. Yes. Yes. All right. Next week. Bye. Yes. Have a nice time in Paris.'

He put the phone down and sighed.

'Want some coffee?'

'Yes, please. Two sugars.'

'Are you trying to kill yourself?' he said.

I was thinking. Tatiana? Cassandra? I tried to conjure up a picture of Charles at play, croquet lawns or tennis clubs, but there wasn't enough raw material. I followed him into the kitchen area.

'This friend of mine. She's going to Paris for work. So she calls me to ask which is the most expensive hotel. God.' He rolled his eyes spooning the sugar into the mug. 'Are you sure?' Then he turned around and said, 'I thought you were sweet enough already.'

'How come she's going to Paris? Sounds like a good job.' I was fishing wildly.

'No, it isn't. Advertising. Bullshit.'

'Oh, advertising,' I said.

'She wanted to borrow my car to do her shopping in when her flatmate's got a car she never uses.' He handed me the coffee.

'How do you say that? Tatiana?'

'Yeah,' Charles laughed.

'Tatiana.' I rolled the name out. I had never heard of it before.

Charles laughed. 'Very Sloaney. As the name suggests.'

'What *are* Sloanes?'

'Oh, God. You know. They live in Chelsea and Daddy pays off the overdraft and everything's just too tedious.' He rolled his eyes.

I giggled. I could hear a faint embarrassment in his voice. He knew that I didn't know people called Tatiana or Cassandra. But in the street credibility stakes I had more marks out of ten than he did. Even if he did have an accent that counted everywhere like a gold credit card. It was ironic. While Charles and Madeleine thought I was streetwise, Lol classified me as part of the same yuppie army that Charles belonged to. Well. Perhaps not.

'You haven't missed anything. Listen, what kind of mood was Madeleine in today? At lunch.'

'Ok. She was telling me about going to Bombay for her honeymoon.'

Charles rolled his eyes again. 'She wants to come to the shoot. It might be a drag.'

'Why?' I leaned forward. Producers didn't usually come on shoots.

'Oh, nothing sinister. The cameraman's an old friend. You know.'

'Oh, you mean . . .'

'Yes. But that's ok. We'll just ignore it,' he laughed.

'She's nice, I think. Madeleine.'

'Yeah. Very nice. She doesn't take any crap. But she's a bad enemy to have.'

'What do you mean?'

'Oh. Just, you know. She likes things her way,' he shrugged.

Suddenly a familiar voice called out to me: 'Angellie! Are you *very* busy?'

I turned around and broke into a smile.

'Lindsay! How nice to see you!' I got up and kissed her on the cheek. I suddenly saw her as an old friend. 'This is Charles, the director,' I said waving my hand in his direction.

They shook hands.

'So. How's it going? I hear you're hot on the trail . . .' Lindsay raised her eyebrows. Her inherent cheerfulness didn't hide the shadows under her eyes. But I couldn't ask her what was wrong because I didn't know her that well.

'Fine,' I smiled.

'Great. We're just compiling questions,' said Charles smiling at me. He seemed to have abandoned his mood for the sake of politeness.

'Are you well? You look well,' I lied. I knew her mother had cancer and that she was probably not working and supporting her but there was no time to talk about that.

She shrugged. 'Let's just say I'm having an extended rest. I'm in the process of moving down to Gloucester to my mother's house. I was in Soho so I thought I'd come and see how you film people go about your business . . .'

'Don't you believe a word of it,' interjected Madeleine from behind her. They kissed. 'This woman introduced me to this goddamned business. This woman is an old hack. She just can't keep away from it. *That's* why she just happens to be in Soho . . .' The two women laughed and embraced. 'How's Edith?' said Madeleine and it was private and soft.

Lindsay shrugged. 'Well, she hates my cooking.' They laughed again. 'She says she only had to put up with it at the weekends before but now it's going to be full time.'

'Mothers!' said Madeleine.

I wanted to agree but it was their conversation. Charles and I were not invited.

'So you're really going?'

'Sold the flat last week.'

'Let's go for a coffee, Lindsay. See you later. Angie, is everything ok for Wednesday? Good.'

'I'll see you soon. I'm glad you're enjoying it.' Lindsay's eyes creased up in a gentle smile.

We listened to their stilettoes thudding down the stairs. It was a shame she had gone. But we didn't really have anything else to say. I wished I could have let her know I was grateful to her for recommending me for the job.

'How do you know her?' asked Charles.

'Oh, I used to work at Direct Vision.'

'Really? Yes, I heard about that. She just gave it all up apparently. Why?'

'I think her mother was ill and she decided to get out for a while.'

'God. Imagine giving up everything you've built up. Just like that. Amazing.'

'Yeah.'

'Pretty silly. Madeleine had a bit of a row with her last week. About the film.'

'Our film?' I looked up surprised.

'Yeah, well I guess she's under a lot of pressure. That's what Madeleine was saying.'

'What did she say?'

'Oh. She thought it was a crazy idea to prosecute the guy. Accused Madeleine of making sensationalist programmes.'

'It isn't sensationalist . . .'

'Exactly. But you know how these woolly liberals are. Scream at the first sight of blood. Apparently her background is community oriented films. Is that what you worked on?'

'No. Regional cooking,' I said making a face.

'Oh.' Charles shrugged. 'It must've been before your time. Her company won a few awards. She gave

Madeleine her first job. Madeleine was her personal assistant.'

'Really?'

'Long time ago. They go back a long way but I don't think they share the same views about making programmes. Still, sounds like she's retreated in any case. And Madeleine's having to turn work down, she's so busy.'

'Really?' I was lapping up all this information.

The phone rang and I picked it up.

'Tatiana,' I said looking at him but he shook his head. 'I'm sorry, he's in a meeting at the moment. Can I take a message? Right. He's got the number. Ok. Bye.'

'Can you call her at work or at home tonight?'

Charles smiled weakly:

'Thanks, Angie.'

I smiled back.

'God, I'm sorry. We're kind of ex lovers.' He rolled his eyes.

'That's ok,' I said. I *knew* it.

CHAPTER ELEVEN

It was raining on Wednesday. It would have to rain. I couldn't eat any breakfast and sat watching the tv with glazed eyes. Rax came bounding into the kitchen and shouted 'Where's my paki lunch, Ma?' Maama ji looked up from last week's *Sunday Times* magazine and grinned. After all these years he still thought some of Rax's stupid remarks were funny. Dad was buried behind the foreign section of *The Guardian* as usual, drinking his third cup of tea. Ma put the sandwiches into the Tupperware box and added an apple next to them.

'What is this film about that you are filming, Ungee?' asked maama ji, spreading butter on a piece of toast and putting it on my empty plate.

I pushed it away.

'Different lifestyles,' I said vaguely.

Kathi opened the door before I had a chance to ring the bell. She was all dolled up and she'd painted her nails.

'Great isn't it? God I'm really nervous. Do I look all right? Come in. Come in. Great, isn't it? Bleedin' weather.' She was so excited she ushered me in, pausing only for a second to look into the street as if a whole crowd was supposed to appear.

I put my umbrella in the corner and we sat in the kitchen while she made tea.

'I'm so nervous. Do you think it's going to to be all right?' she repeated as I watched her filling the pot.

I had talked myself into being calm and not thinking about Lol. About Lol and Kathi. About Lol and me. I was doing an interview for a film. That was all.

I had just finished reading out the questions and reassuring her that it would be all right when the doorbell rang. Kathi jumped out of her skin. 'That's them. That's them.'

I smiled. 'Calm down. I'll go. And remember. It's not live. Anytime you feel uncomfortable we can stop the cameras. And don't worry about making mistakes. We'll just do it again. All right?'

She nodded.

I opened the door to a bearded man holding a tripod that was covered in rainproof material. 'Hi, you must be Angie. I'm Ross Taylor. This is the soundman, Guy Clegg.' The soundman was short and balding. Both of them trooped into the hallway. I watched while they made another trip to a red Volvo. Ross hurried in carrying his camera underneath a black cloth while Guy carried two sets of lights under each arm.

'Phew,' said Ross wiping the rain off his face. 'It had to be like this today.'

We walked into the front room where Kathi was sitting erect in her chair like a little girl waiting to meet the headmistress. There were introductions all round. The men started setting up their equipment around the settee. Ross took out a length of plastic and laid it out in the hallway but there were already muddy footprints on the carpet.

The bell rang again. It was Madeleine and Charles. We all retired into the kitchen for more tea, while Madeleine went into the front room to say hello to Ross.

'Ok. Could you just come in so I can get a light reading?' said Ross at the kitchen door. He smiled encouragingly at Kathi.

The front room had become extremely crowded. They had moved most of the furniture to the sides of the room and the table was in the hallway. Kathi and I picked our way over fat cables that seemed to trail most of the carpet. We sat down on the settee. Guy was fixing a long pole to a microphone, which he then covered with an oval grey mitt. To the sides of the settee stood two lamps on tripods. They had four little flaps around the bulb. Ross was to the side of us adjusting the tripod legs and looking through the camera. Madeleine and Charles on the other side of the room were peering into a small television monitor which was attached by cables to the camera.

'All right, ladies. Now I'm just going to turn the lights on.' Ross walked up to the lamps and flicked a switch. Kathi's mouth was open as she gawped at the transformation of the room.

The harsh, almost white lights came on from either side and we blinked in their glare.

'Wait a sec. I *do* need that reflector, Guy. Maybe another redhead would do the trick.' Ross and Guy went about their business as though no one else was in the room.

Kathi looked at me and frowned. 'Does he want someone else?'

'Oh. No. No. A redhead is the name of those lamps,' I said pointing.

Madeleine was pacing the small area in front of the monitor. Charles was squatting to our right, squinting at us, making frames with the index finger and thumb of both hands.

'We've got to boom it, Madeleine. The neck mike's broken,' he said.

I looked straight ahead at Madeleine watching the monitor with her arms folded.

'If you give me some nice big close ups and we'll do some wides later. I want some tension. And frame it as tight as you want. Just off centre,' said Charles looking at the monitor.

Without moving his eye from the eyepiece, Ross did a thumbs up. Kathi was staring at the lens as if it was a mirror.

'That's terrific, Ross. Cut some more of the head. That's fine.'

Kathi began to giggle, peering into the camera.

'Ok. Right, Kathi, try not to look at the camera. Just talk to Angie. Now Angie won't be in shot, ok, but we need your eyeline. Angie, can you just start something . . .?' Charles was standing behind Madeleine watching the monitor.

'Right. Kathi. No, don't look at Ross, look at me. So what have you been doing today?'

'Er. I've been getting ready to see you.'

'Yeah, carry on,' I said quickly, looking sideways to see Charles nodding his head at the monitor. Madeleine whispered something to him and he nodded seriously to her. Kathi began to tell me how she'd got ready and how the hot water had run out and I was nodding madly to encourage her flow. Meanwhile Guy was holding the boom above our heads.

'Ok, Guy, just keep it there. That's fine. You're out of shot there. More. Lower. That's it,' Ross was saying from behind the camera.

'Have I got anything to my right?' said Guy moving the pole slowly to his right hand side.

'That's your limit,' said Ross, signalling stop with his other hand.

'It's really hot,' whispered Kathi and I nodded apologetically.

Madeleine was on the floor, leafing through the set of photocopied questions. Charles stood behind her, staring intensely at the monitor.

'Nice lighting, huh?' she said.

'Ok. I just need a level then we can run,' announced Ross.

Kathi looked relaxed and was unselfconsciously checking for dirt underneath her fingernails.

'Ok, running,' said Ross and a faint buzz started.

'And — Action,' said Charles. 'Ok. Now, Kathi, in your own time just answer Angie's questions. Ok, Angie.' Charles nodded at me and then turned his face toward the monitor.

'Right,' I said smiling at Kathi. 'Kathi, if you could tell us when you first discovered you were HIV?'

''Course the test wasn't till May but I suppose it was really . . .'

'Hold on. Cut,' said Charles raising his hand. 'Kathi, if you could just answer the questions with "I realised . . ." or "I discovered I had HIV". Like that, because it helps us when we cut. Great. Ok. Action.'

'Oh. Is that all right? Oh, right. Well I first realised I was HIV when I went down the clinic. They gave me a test and I came up positive.' Kathi looked at me blankly as though she was taking an exam.

'What did they say to you? What kind of counselling did you get?'

During the question Charles motioned Ross to go in close, and Ross turned the zoom on his lens.

'Well, they said um what did I feel like, and what was I going to do if I came up positive. They said was I going to have safe sex and all that even if I came up negative. They were good. They said that either way they would be there if I wanted to talk about it, you know. They gave me a lot of leaflets as well.'

'So, um . . .' I looked at her and abandoned the printed questions on my lap, '. . . so, did you learn, I mean, did you feel like they were telling you how to carry on? Was it helpful to get the information about safe sex? How did you feel about the safe sex side of things?'

'No. I mean . . .' she looked over at Charles 'Well, they were helpful. But the safe sex business. It was a bit late for that. I couldn't really handle all them leaflets you know. I told my mate Pete about it. He's gay, you know. He works in the club. Well, not any more. But there was a lot of them working there on the hen nights. Male strippers, you know. And anyway I didn't get on with them much because I thought, oh they're a bunch of poofs, you know. But one night we got a bit pissed after work and me and Pete were getting on all right and he started telling me about his boyfriend who'd died from AIDS. And I just had a fit about it. I started changing the subject and all that and then I just told him. I started crying and crying and he just held me. Really tight.' Kathi's eyes glazed over and began to fill up with tears.

I looked desperately over at Charles to see if he would say 'cut' but Madeleine was now standing up and she shook her head firmly, and rotated her finger in the air at Ross who was also looking in their direction.

So the cameras kept rolling.

'It's ok, Kathi. Take your time,' I whispered.

She sniffed. 'Well anyway. My mate Pete. He said it was all right and he said there was lots of people in the same boat as me and we had to look after one another. And I said to him, what are you talking about? I mean I always thought it was people like him and drug addicts that got it. I mean they did tell me that wasn't true at the clinic but, well, I could talk to him. I said to him, I mean, I know how you lot carry on. But why me? It wasn't fair.

It wasn't fair. And Eddie. I mean, he's flash and he made me feel like I was something. I don't know. Anyway it just happened. I suppose I was lonely. It wasn't fair. But Pete said it wasn't about fairness, he said he'd slept with loads of blokes but that didn't mean he deserved to get it. He said he was Jewish and it was like his grandparents that had been in the camps. They never deserved to go there. But he said that when they were in the camps, when some of them got fed up and it was too much for them and they just wanted to give up and die. Well then the others said to them: listen if we just give up now, if we don't fight to live, if we don't help each other, then it's like we're animals. And that's what the Nazis think we are anyway. So they said we'll look after one another and we'll carry on like before. We'll still hold our festivals and speak our own language. And if they don't let us have flowers to give one another then we'll give one another leaves and anything. Can you imagine? Anyway, he said it was like that's what they did. They survived. He said: "To die is easy. To live you have to struggle." I mean, I don't know anything about it all. I was no good at history lessons at school and all that but I mean I could see what he meant. He just meant that whatever happens like, you shouldn't give in. You've got to survive.'

'And has Pete been supportive to you all along, Kathi? Do you see him.'

'He died about six weeks after. He was *I-positive*, that's what he called it, you know. He was really healthy — and he had a heart attack. In front of the telly on a Saturday night. He was twenty-nine years old.'

'Oh. God. Um . . . um, so do you think about that, about death.' I could feel my skin begin to crawl.

'No,' she said resolutely. 'I don't because he was right. I don't go round worrying about it all the time. I mean I'm not like that. When I found out, yeah I did freak out. But there's plenty of people who are HIV and have good lives. I don't feel any worse. I'm all right on my own. I do miss him sometimes, though. He said that it was like a family. People like us who had it. He said you didn't get to choose your family in real life anyway if you know what I mean. But. Well, I've never really had a family that I got on with so in the end it didn't mean much. It was a nice idea though.'

I was looking at her trying to understand the strands of her bravery, her rationality.

'And so, Kathi, how did you feel about Lol, about your husband, when he left you?' I wanted to ask her because I wanted to know, to understand the mess, the confusion that I had seen in Lol.

'You know, it's funny. It was on the cards for a long time. When I told Pete, he said you've got to tell him. Because I'd been, you know, I'd been sleeping with Lol during, well after Eddie. He said he had to know and it was a chance in a million that he'd got it anyway. He said it would be all right. But, boy, he didn't know Lol. When it all came out we fought and shouted. It was horrible. And I thought this isn't a life. He called me a lot of names and that. And I thought he just doesn't give two fucks about me. Never did. We weren't no family. Pete was more my friend than Lol. And then suddenly it seemed so simple. I just thought, I don't care. I don't care what he does or thinks. I just had to look after myself. He wasn't going to do it.'

'Do you miss him, Kathi? Do you miss Lol?' I asked quietly.

'Miss what? No, I don't miss shouting and screaming at him. I don't know what I think about him anymore. When I think about Eddie I hate him but I remember how much he turned me on.'

Kathi moved a piece of hair from her eyes and laughed.

'Listen to me. Can you believe it? I hate him, I feel like killing him, but I remember how he turned me on. Not just that. I remember believing in him. But they're all the same, aren't they?'

'And do you think of yourself as a survivor? Like Pete said. How have you survived?'

Suddenly the phone rang and Charles shouted, 'Cut'.

Ross moved his eye away from the camera and Guy brought the pole down to rest on the arm of the settee.

'Sorry, Kathi. Where's the phone? I'll have to take it off the hook,' said Charles.

'In the bedroom,' said Kathi gesturing over her shoulder. She looked at me shyly because suddenly it was apparent that we were being filmed and everything had been monitored on a television set in the corner.

'Can I go to the loo?' she whispered.

Ross and Guy were busy talking. Madeleine walked over to me. She watched Charles and Kathi leave the room. Then she kneeled down in front of me.

'Listen. Move it on. Ok?' she said flatly.

'What do you mean?' I asked.

'Listen. I'm not interested in some half assed analysis of how AIDS victims are like survivors of the Holocaust, ok? Get some stuff about the guy. I want some details.' She was looking at me with no expression on her face.

I looked at her.

'Kathi's not an AIDS victim. She's HIV positive. And anyway they don't say that. They say PWA. People with AIDS,' I said drily.

Madeleine arched an eyebrow and shrugged.

'Whatever,' she said. 'Just move on, ok?'

'Why? I think it's an interesting analogy. I'd like to follow it . . .'

'Hey. Listen, sweetheart. It's a ridiculous analogy. Those people didn't choose to go to the camps. You simply can't compare it . . .'

'But Kathi was talking about spirit, the spirit of

resistance. I think she meant it as a strategy, a symbol of
hope.' I was looking steadily at Madeleine.

'Look. I'm not going to argue with you about it here.
We have a film to shoot. If you don't feel able to
continue this interview then fine . . .' Madeleine's face
was set.

'What? Look, Madeleine, I know exactly what . . .'
I started to say but Charles had come back into the
room and Madeleine was already moving back towards
him. She said something to him but I didn't catch
it. Then Kathi came in pushing her hair back and
pulling her dress down to her knees. I could feel a
throb of anger racing to my temples but I kept my
eyes on her, smiled and ignored everything else in the
room.

'Ok, Angie. You ready to go?' said Madeleine looking
across at me.

I nodded but I didn't take my eyes off Kathi. Kathi was
smiling at me.

'So, Kathi. Would you say that Pete helped you to sort
of understand, to deal with what had happened?' I said
and my arms were folded over the questions.

Kathi was nodding and about to speak when suddenly
Madeleine was standing beside me, her hand on my
shoulder. There was no pressure. It just looked like a
friendly hand on a shoulder.

'Yeah, Kathi. Talking about what happened. Tell us
about it. In your own words. What happened between
you and Eddie?' said Madeleine over my head. I looked
up at her but she was smiling encouragingly at Kathi.

'Well. I slept with him. I mean there's nothing much
to tell,' said Kathi looking at Madeleine and then at me
unsurely. Her eye line must have been all over the place.
Charles was staring intently at the monitor.

'Yeah, right.' Madeleine had now eased herself on
the settee next to me. 'Yeah, but I mean you're a

very attractive woman, Kathi. Had anything happened between you before? I mean had he tried anything on with you?' Madeleine was engaging with Kathi's eyes and there was a sense of two women of the world having a conversation.

'Well,' Kathi laughed, 'yeah. I suppose. He fancied me for ages.'

I looked down at my notes to avoid looking at her, to avoid breaking up the eye line. The camera was rolling and Kathi was in full flow.

'He was always after me. Yeah, I suppose I always knew that.'

'Where did it happen, I mean, when you finally got together?' said Madeleine nodding.

'One night after the club had finished. I mean there were still a few people hanging around but the lights had come on and the DJ was still playing records. Most of the other waitresses were clearing up the tables or finishing off the bar. Anyway I went to the toilet. I was putting on some lipstick and he came in. He came in and started saying I'd always turned him on. You know.' Kathi looked at Madeleine and shrugged, but Madeleine just said, 'Go on.'

'Oh, well, he just started touching me and saying he hadn't had it for so long, and he really wanted me.'

'And how did you feel? Did you like it?' said Madeleine smiling.

Kathi shrugged. 'Yeah, no well. I wasn't fighting him off if that's what you mean. Bastard.'

'Get angry if you want, Kathi. Let it out,' said Madeleine.

'Well, I mean. I was sort of laughing and screaming because anyone could have come in, couldn't they? And he was saying that just made it better. Exciting. We were both laughing and he kept saying my name. I fancied him like mad.' She was nodding at Madeleine but her face was set.

'I felt like a piece of shit when he told me. It was weeks later. I mean I sort of had this idea. Well, anyway, I had this idea that he really liked me. But he didn't. He was just using me. He looks so healthy and everything, I still can't believe it.'

'And he shouldn't get away with it?' Madeleine tilted her head and arched an eyebrow, as if she were daring Kathi to continue.

'Nah. He shouldn't get away with it. He can't get away with doing that to me. You know when I told him I'd tested positive he said "sorry". I mean, "sorry" can't help me now can it? Then he sacked me. That's how sorry he was. Bastard. Yeah I hate him now. And I want to get him. I don't want him to get away with it.' Kathi's face was determined and she was staring at Madeleine.

'How many sexual partners have you had, Kathi?'

I looked at Charles but he was nodding at the monitor. It was clear that I was not going to get to ask any more questions so I silently got up and moved over towards him.

Madeleine immediately moved closer to Kathi and started embellishing the question.

'I mean, would you say you were a sexually experienced woman?' Madeleine was leaning towards Kathi.

I was standing next to Charles looking at the monitor. It was filled up with Kathi's face. She laughed.

'Well, I've been round the block a few times if that's what you mean.' She shrugged and tilted her head to one side.

'Right. And plenty of guys do it but without thinking of the consequences. Would you agree with that?'

While Madeleine was posing the question I watched the shot change, so that Kathi's next answer would be in mid shot not a closeup. She was sitting with her arms crossed, listening intently. For a second my eyes flitted across to where she was really sitting. And there was Madeleine and the microphone and the cables. I looked at Charles who winked at me. I didn't react. He put his hand lightly on my arm, both of us watching the screen. We couldn't talk because the tape recorder would have picked up our murmuring. I was feeling hot with anger so I dumped the pile of questions into the wastepaper basket by my feet. 'I may as well not have bothered compiling any questions,' I wanted to shout. Charles looked at the bin and then at me for a moment. Then he turned his head towards the monitor and took his hand away from my arm.

'. . . and because all he can say is sorry. He should have thought about it before. Now I've got a chance to make him pay for it.'

'Is this why you want to prosecute him, Kathi? Because it's the only way?' The screen was full of Kathi's face again.

'Yeah,' she said.

'If you could just say . . . just say something like, "I want to prosecute him because it's the only road open to me. Because I'm on my own and and I'm fighting back." Something like that . . .'

I turned to look at Charles but he continued to look at the monitor. Something Lindsay had once said to me came to mind like a flash. 'Make sure they tell their own story. Let them speak. It's their life we're making films about.'

'Well, Kathi. Some people may say, you know, life's tough in the big city. I mean some people would say you've contracted this disease, it's your own fault. Form a group or something. Don't tell us about it. How would you answer that?'

Kathi bit her bottom lip.

'Life's tough, yeah. Well I'm gonna make his life tough. I've been to groups. That doesn't do anything to him, does it? He's still all right. It doesn't harm him, does it?'

'You want justice, right? And you want revenge? There's nothing wrong with that. He owes you, right? Can you say . . .' prompted Madeleine, but Kathi didn't need any encouragement now.

'Yeah, he does owe me. I want revenge. I want justice. I want to make him pay.'

'And why are you prepared to let us film you? Do you think people out there will learn from your experience? Do you think your decision to come out and say, no, I'm just not taking this, will give people in similar positions hope? And do you think it will make men out there think twice?'

'Yeah. I hope people will learn from my experience. Because it's not like I've got a lot of money or anything. I mean if it wasn't for you then I couldn't even consider it. But, yeah, definitely, if it stops men doing it without thinking then it's worth it just for that,' said Kathi and laughed.

'Great. Kathi, would you mind just saying the last bit again? Without talking about the money. Thanks.'

I started looking out of the window as Kathi repeated what Madeleine wanted to hear.

'What you're really saying then is that you're an individual. And you're ready to go to court to get justice. And as individuals we all have that right. To use the system. To make sure we get what we can, because you can't rely on anyone else to fight your battle. Is that what you feel?'

I was desperate for a cigarette.

When finally Madeleine looked over at Charles and nodded and the shoot was over, I walked across the cables. Madeleine thanked Kathi and said I would explain the procedure to her. Then she walked over to the monitor where Ross and Guy were standing. They had rewound a tape to see how the recording looked.

Kathi was looking at them and I told her to come and watch herself.

'You look great, Kathi. Told you you would,' said Charles, taking his hair out of his pony tail and re-tying it again.

'Terrific,' said Madeleine nodding.

Kathi was staring at the screen. She started to giggle.

'God. That's the nearest I'll get to being a film star.'

'Mega star!' said Charles and everyone laughed.

'Can I just go over a few details with you, Kathi?' I asked pulling her aside. 'It's really boring but it's just routine. We have to do it.' I could see Madeleine out of the corner of my eye talking to Ross and Charles about the lighting and smoothing down her skirt. I was seething but there was no point in showing it to Kathi.

We sat down on the settee again and I got out the release form as Ross started winding up the cables around us.

'You're very photogenic,' he smiled.

Kathi beamed at him. 'Thanks.'

'Ok, now this is a "release form" that anyone who's been interviewed has to sign. You can read it through if you like but basically it just says that we're going to edit the film and that you allow us to use any bit of the film we want to,' I said mechanically. I felt as though Madeleine had left me with the red tape, the menial administration, having railroaded my position as a researcher.

'I thought that was the whole point. That you were filming me so you could make a film about it,' said Kathi frowning.

'Eh?' I tore my eyes away from Madeleine, 'Yeah, yeah. It's just, you know. You just have to do it. I don't know. It's for your own good really,' I shrugged.

'What for?' said Kathi as she signed her name on two duplicate copies. Her tongue was resting on the inside of her lip as if the task were taking real concentration.

CHAPTER TWELVE

Madeleine and Charles stopped talking as I entered the office. The night before I'd hardly slept, turning over and over the previous day's events. After the shoot Madeleine hadn't explained why she'd taken over. We'd all carried on as though everything had gone according to plan. But I could sense a coldness in the air. By evening, doubt had entered my mind. Perhaps I hadn't been very professional. Perhaps she had been angry with me because I hadn't moved the questions on. After all, Madeleine had been in the business longer than me. But I was angry that she had undercut me. I could feel my face go hot with humiliation, remembering.

'Hi!' said Madeleine 'We're just looking at rushes.'

'Sorry I'm late,' I mumbled, taking my coat off.

'I was just going out to get cappuccinos. Want one?' said Charles getting up.

I nodded.

Once Charles was out of the room, Madeleine pressed play on the remote control and immediately Kathi's face came on the screen.

'She looks great, huh?' said Madeleine.

I nodded.

She pressed stop and then turned towards me.

'Look, Angie, we need to talk about what happened yesterday. I realise you're not very experienced but I think you have a lot of potential. However,' she was looking straight at me, 'however, what you did yesterday was inexcusable. You understand?'

I folded my arms and looked out of the window. I felt as though I had been dragged up in front of the headmistress. Inside, a little Angie was cowering and looking at the floor because she had been told off.

'You lost track of the film. I tried to help you, but you took no notice. That is not the kind of collaboration I expect,' said Madeleine.

'Sack me then,' I wanted to say and storm out of the door. But this wasn't Amigo's and I had a lot riding on this. Apart from the money it was *my* story. She couldn't find people like Kathi even if she searched the world for them. She needed me on the case.

'I spent a lot of time working out those questions, Madeleine,' I said taking out a cigarette and some courage.

'Please don't smoke in here. I don't like it,' she said evenly.

I'm the boss, she means, I thought venomously and put the unlit cigarette on the table between us. Not back in the packet. I supposed this was a power game. The kitchen of the Chinese restaurant opposite was still proving to be more fascinating than her face. Also, to look at her face and see power, experience, pink skin, confidence would almost certainly have made me retreat. And there was no way little Angie was going to be exposed. No way. I wished fleetingly for chewing gum. Inappropriately I remembered a single instance when Pauline Metcalf had reduced a teacher to fury by just brazenly chewing in front of her face.

'Look,' said Madeleine. 'Didn't we agree on this film? Didn't we say we wanted a profile of Kathi? A tough strong

woman. I wanted her to talk about sex and betrayal. You
were taking it down a very dodgy road.' She was half
smiling, tilting her head to one side. As if she were trying
to make amends.

I shrugged.

'And you should know that it's a very bad idea to start
an argument on a shoot. Huh? You know that. That's why
I had to take over. Angie, I *have* been doing this for some
time now. Trust me, huh? I know what I'm doing.' She
smiled and leant back in her chair.

I felt embarrassed, as though I had made a mountain
out of a molehill. It's my ball and I'm taking it home . . .

I laughed and we smiled at each other. It had been a
civilised conversation. Full of information and warnings
couched in smiles and gestures. Decks had been cleared.
She was the boss. But she needed me. I was not
dispensable.

'Coffee's up!' shouted Charles from the stairs.

'Great!' said Madeleine, 'I'm dying for one.'

Charles was standing in the doorway with a corrugated
cardboard box containing four polystyrene cups with lids.
Behind him stood a tall man with a ruddy face and glasses
looking sheepishly around the room. Charles set the box
down on the table.

'This is Derek, our editor,' said Charles.

We all shook hands. Derek had a deep growling voice,
and short brown hair cut to the scalp. His bright blue
eyes were surrounded by puffed, pale pink skin and as he
leaned forward to shake my hand a familiar acrid smell
escaped his mouth. It was the unmistakable reminder of
a night on the piss.

We all settled down to watch the rushes. Charles and
Derek took notes on the quality of the shots and which
take was the best. Derek gave no opinion on the material
apart from frequently commenting that the technical
quality was abysmal on video. Madeleine left for a

meeting at lunchtime and the three of us decided to get in sandwiches. There was a lot to do. We took the rushes and paperwork through to the edit suite and Charles and Derek sat on the two chairs in front of the editing equipment. I dragged a chair in from the main office and sat behind them. The edit suite was cool and reassuringly dark. Kathi's voice boomed out over and over, her face filling both the screens. Frequently, Derek fast forwarded the tape to find a piece of sync that Charles wanted to hear and Kathi sounded like Minnie Mouse on speed. To my delight I discovered that Derek smoked, but he smoked cigars and promised us he only smoked one a day. By the end of the day the room was full of smoke. Charles said he didn't mind because he smoked too, but only in the evenings.

At exactly five to six, Derek stretched his arms in the air and leant back in his chair.

'Shall we call it a day, then?' he said pressing stop on the editing machine.

After he had left, Charles made us both a coffee. Neither of us wanted to stop viewing. I was excited. Here was all this raw material — pictures of the condom factory, shots of the club to come, AIDS and HIV advertisements to photograph, music to lay down, ideas, structures, pictures . . . And all of them to be weaved together into a coherent, understandable film that was going to be exciting, stimulating, sexy. Impossible, I was thinking. But eminently *possible*, I was thinking. It was a question of methodical sorting out, picking out the best bits, making them say things.

Charles winked at me as he came back into the room. I was reticent about using the editing machine in case I wiped anything, so Kathi was stuck on the same frozen frame, mouth open, a finger on her chin as though she were waiting for us to accelerate her to life.

'Ready for anything,' said Charles looking at the frame and we laughed. We left her suspended while we sipped our coffee. I had warmed to Charles. He didn't expect me to make the coffee all the time.

'Derek's an old film hack. Did you guess? Lunchtimes down the pub, tools down at six. Technician,' Charles said good humouredly. 'Still, the film industry isn't exactly thriving so they have to work in video. You wait. He'll moan constantly about the sound guy, the cameraman.'

There was a distant rumbling in the background and I noticed Kathi's face slowly sliding up the screen, frame by frame. Charles reached out and pressed pause, and a new frame stood still. The roaring stopped. It had evidently been her voice in slow motion.

'After a while the machine gets tired on pause and gives up,' explained Charles, as though there was a little man inside holding the picture up and his hands had got tired.

'Never touch the machine in front of the editor. He'll probably report you to the ACTT,' said Charles. He produced a packet of ten Silk Cut and we sat and smoked for a while. I was sitting in Derek's chair. It had started to rain outside and the small window had become smeared. It suddenly seemed to be very dark. Then there was a chilling crack of thunder and I jumped. 'Frightened?' said Charles softly, putting a hand on my shoulder. I smiled, embarrased.

'No, I like thunder. It's so dramatic,' I said. The room seemed even more cosy and warm and dark. We hadn't bothered to switch the light on and our faces were illuminated by the twin blue beams of the television monitors.

'Hey, you want some food? We could hit the new Thai place and wait for the thunder to become less dramatic.' Charles winked. 'We could talk about the film. And gossip.'

I had been toying with the idea of going to Stoke Newington but what with the rain and all.

'Let me make a call first,' I said and Charles nodded and politely left the room.

'It's me,' I said, grinning at Lol's voice out of breath again.

'Hello, you,' he said.

'Not on the roof in this weather, I hope.' I was aware my voice was carrying so Charles could hear that I was talking to A Man.

'No. Just Breathless.' Lol sang the word.

I burst into laughter. 'I've seen *that* one. It's a terrible film. Mind you Richard Gere's in it. But the best bit's . . .'

'It's rubbish. The French version's much better.'

'Subtitles?' I said amazed.

'Yeah,' he said mockingly. 'I can read and write.'

'Can't *sing*, though,' I said and he laughed.

'You're really into films, aren't you?' I said wonderingly. 'It's supposed to be me. I'm supposed to be into films.'

'Yeah. I always go to the pictures. It's cheap at the Rio. Anyway, I've got this mate Toulouse. She's an usherette. Lets me in for nothing sometimes.'

'Oh yeah,' I said suspiciously.

Lol laughed. 'Toulouse don't mess with blokes.'

I was shocked at the extent of his repertoire. French films, lesbians, sexually transmitted diseases . . . I giggled because it wasn't funny.

'What?' he said.

'We interviewed Kathi today,' I said.

'Oh,' he said flatly. Charles was standing at the door.

'I've got to go. I'll see you tomorrow, yeah?'

'I might be *busy*, you know,' he said and immediately I crumpled. Oh God, don't let him think I'm taking him for granted. Why didn't I ever *think* before opening my mouth?

'Oh. I'm sorry. I didn't mean, I mean . . .'

'No, I want you to, I . . .'

'No, I mean if you don't want . . .'

'Yeah, I mean, no . . . Look, for *fuck's* sake,' said Lol and we both started laughing.

'Yes?' I said.

'Camden Town. Eight-thirty. Right?'

'Ok, boss,' I said smiling. 'You'd better not be late.'

'Ok, boss,' he said.

Charles ordered for both of us because I'd never been to a good Thai restaurant before and anyway I was too busy looking at the diners, waitresses and decor. I was digging into a chicken marinated in coriander and lime thinking it tasted very much like Indian food when Charles poured some wine into my glass.

'How was it with Madeleine earlier?'

I shrugged. 'Ok, I suppose.'

'I'm sorry about the shoot. Your questions were fine. But . . . well, I thought it went ok in the end, didn't you?' he said leaning over his fork.

Madeleine was more experienced than me, however many faces I pulled, however much chewing gum I chewed. I wanted him to be on my side, though.

'She gave me a bit of a telling off about it,' I said looking at my plate. I was baring. Insecurity and all.

'Forget it, Angie. Madeleine's a tough cookie. She likes you. I know that. It's just that we've got a lot riding on this pilot. The commissioning editor wants to see this film finished before he decides to give money for the other one. I mean, can you imagine what a disaster it would be if he didn't fund the second one? The first one would mean nothing.'

I was nodding over the chicken. I could see his point. Inexplicably I felt relieved to hear from an outside source

that she *liked* me. Why did it matter? Because she was in
control?

'When she asked Kathi that question about how many
sexual partners, I nearly died,' I said suddenly, trying
perhaps to diminish that sense of power through trivia.

Charles hooted with laughter. 'God. But Kathi held her
own, didn't she? She really got into it. I got it all in close
up. Given a chance people love talking about sex, don't
you think?'

'Oh yeah,' I said. We were talking about someone else,
a subject, so it was ok to be blasé.

'It's amazing. You know, do you remember me saying
how I wanted to talk about sex minus the kid gloves? Well,
God, Kathi's stories do that and more. I mean it's all there:
groping in the dark, toilets, pain, desire . . .' He started to
chuckle. 'The real thing.'

'Mmmm. Kathi's no busy professional woman. All
work and no time to play, if you know what I mean,' I
said.

'God. Yeah. I've met so many women like that. You
know the ones? Oh my career's so important to me
because I want to be taken *seriously*. And they're all
seriously fucked up. They don't fuck,' said Charles as if
he were talking at length about the weather.

I averted my embarrassment by laughing. This must
be the new New Man, I thought, if Hugh was the old
New Man. Charles was into sex not washing up! But,
somehow I didn't get any feeling of passion, or warmth.
Was this because these were all old fashioned clichés?
Where did Lol fit into it? What kind of man was he? At
the thought of Lol suddenly my stomach began to burble
inside. Alarmed, I drank some wine.

'Are you ok? You look like you're about to throw up,'
said Charles concerned.

'Excuse me a minute.' I ran into the loo and sat down
on the toilet, looking at the floor. Like a chant I wished

Lol slowly out of my head. What the hell was going on?
I looked in the mirror over the sink and it was still my
face there. In the yellow hard light I remembered Lol's
face flashing past the mirror in his hallway and I was
smiling and couldn't stop. Weird!

'Hey,' said Charles when I returned, 'I hope the prawns
were ok. One time I had these prawns and you know they
just came out. Both ends. I thought I was dying.'

I started to laugh.

Charles was smiling at me, shifting a strand of hair from
his forehead.

'It's not that funny. God I thought I had salmonella!'
he said indignantly.

For some reason this just made me laugh even more.
Perhaps I was being hysterical. It just seemed so incongruous to think of Charles so slick and mannered, sitting
on the toilet, his face contorted with agony. Totally
uncool.

'Charles, Madeleine's Jewish, isn't she?' I asked forking
the prawns nervously next to the chicken.

'Uh — don't know,' he said.

'What did you think about that concentration camp
thing?' I asked suddenly.

It was as though a freeze had set in. I wished I hadn't
been so bold.

He shrugged his shoulders.

His reaction made me feel uncomfortable. He was on
my side to a degree. But not if it meant putting himself
out. Sometimes I felt as though I just spent my whole life
wanting to be liked by people. Maggie had once told me
I hadn't grown up.

'. . . best Thai restaurant I've ever been to. But we
should try the Spanish in Bateman Street sometime . . .'
Charles was chatting away.

Suddenly something Maggie had said the other day
came into my head. 'You're not in the playground now,

Angie. The reason they put you in the bin wasn't because there was anything wrong with you.'

'Charles, I'm sorry, could we get the bill? I must go soon,' I said suddenly. I wanted to go home. I wanted to call Phillipa. I wanted to see maama ji and Dad playing chess.

CHAPTER THIRTEEN

Nobody was in. Ma had left a note saying they had all gone to the Royal Albert Hall to see Ustaad Ali Khan and there was a cauliflower curry on the stove and I should cook the rice for myself because they would eat later. And that Rax was supposed to write a letter to Anand maama in Delhi tonight and she wanted to see it when they got back.

What the hell were they doing going to the Albert Hall? They must have got free tickets. Dad would have a heart attack before he agreed to pay out that kind of money.

Every couple of months, Rax and I were coerced into writing a letter to Delhi telling them what we had been doing. Usually we just copied the last one and changed a few things so the letters were always about the weather, the television and how we missed them. It was protocol, that was all.

I was smiling at the silence of the house and I walked around the front room picking up newspapers and putting them in a pile. It was only nine o'clock so there was plenty of time to have a long conversation with Phil. I checked the curry and wished I hadn't eaten already. I put on a jazz cassette that Phillipa had lent me at

Amigo's. Must give it back, I thought as I walked into the kitchen.

I was ensconced on the settee, my feet up. There was a steaming cup of coffee and my cigarettes next to it on the small table at my side. A bowl of toasted cashew nuts were balanced on my stomach and I had kicked my shoes off. I tied the 'Cool pack' around my eyes and blew smoke. All I could see was the blue of the pack as it relaxed my eyes. The saxophone was playing in the background. I dialled the number.

'Hello,' said a little voice on the other end.

'Hello,' I shouted. It sounded like auntie Miri but I couldn't be sure.

'Yes?' Her voice was croaking more than usual.

'Miri? Hello it's Angie. Can I speak . . .'

There was a rustling on the other end and I could hear some voices. Low, men's voices. Then I thought I heard sobbing. Alarmed, I spoke deeper into the phone, 'Hello? Hello?'

Then Geoffrey came on the phone.

I was hugging the second pillow to my chest and staring into the darkness of my room. The duvet was wrapped around me like a cocoon, but I was still cold because my teeth had been chattering uncontrollably. My eyes frozen open, I heard the key in the door downstairs.

They were padding about the dining room, and dad and maama ji's voices were raised, intoxicated with excitement. They were discussing the concert and presently the voices reduced to a low mush. The stairs creaked. I turned to the wall, regulating my breathing because I had read somewhere that people breathed slowly when asleep. Or was it faster? She pushed the door open slightly and even though it was on my back, the shard of hallway light seemed to slice into me like a paper cut.

'Oh, asleep. Ok,' said ma to no one in particular and went back downstairs.

I touched the wall with my hand and it felt brittle and cold. A lorry trundled past in the street beyond and left the treadmarks of its echo in the wind. Still my heart was beating and I listened, expecting it to stop, but that factory inside just kept running.

And still Phillipa wasn't here. Wasn't part of it. Not anywhere.

I sat still in my dressing gown the next morning at breakfast, staring at the tv with red eyes. Dad was in the toilet and maama ji had gone to the shops to get some bread. Rax was late for work and shouting he didn't have time to wait for the sandwiches.

'Ten minutes out of your life. It will save you ten years,' ma was saying slapping together the last pieces of bread.

'Now what are you going on about?' said Rax walking into the kitchen and patting her on the shoulder.

'You will eat in the canteen. Frozen processed rubbish. Do you know there is cancer in chickens now? Ask your sister. Ungelliee, tell him about the cancer that is in the chickens. On the television.'

'It's got cancer of the brain this morning. Look at the state of it,' Rax spluttered with laughter.

Ma slapped him across the shoulder but he dodged it and stepped behind her.

'*Arrey*, Rakesh. Chee, cheee. You must not even say such things. All right, now go, here is your lunch. And the letter, what about . . .'

But Rax was already out of the door.

'And what is the matter with you? Sitting like a lady of the manor. What is it, holiday? Why aren't you ready?' Ma looked me over and began to tut. 'Look at your

skin. It is full of spots. It is the smoking that causes
it.'

'Leave me alone, Ma, I'm not going to work today,' I
said without taking my eyes from the tv.

'Oh, and what is so special about today?' she asked
folding her arms, rocking from side to side like a tubby
general.

'Phillipa got run over yesterday. In Brent Street. Drunk
driver.'

Ma was making scrambled eggs and squeezing fresh
orange juice even though I said all I wanted was a coffee.
Dad had emerged from the loo, newspaper clamped
underneath his pyjama sleeve.

He sat down, folding his arms on the table next to me.

'She was the one in Hendon, yes?' he said gravely.

Suddenly it wasn't a standing joke that dad thought
all my English friends looked the same and couldn't
remember their names.

'*Arrey*, what is the matter with you? Phillipa. That one
who was living with her family after her marriage broke
up. Where is your mind?' shouted ma at him, depositing
the plate of eggs in front of me.

He nodded again, his face was full of sadness as if she
were *his* friend. I looked at the eggs.

He touched my arm. 'Shall I ring up your work for you?'
he asked quietly. I nodded. It sounded like getting him to
write a sick note to get me off sports at school, but I didn't
care.

Maama ji came in and heard the news at the door from
dad who was dialling the number.

'*Arrey*, leave her alone, yaar,' said dad when ma heaped
slices of toast beside the untouched eggs and started
telling me to eat.

Maama ji had disappeared somewhere. Dad hadn't
picked up the paper once. He turned the tv off and sat
next to me.

'What a terrible thing,' he said shaking his head and sighing.

'I wish I'd . . . I wish I'd *seen* her more often, do you know what I mean?' I said.

'I know I . . . know. You wish as if the sum total of your friendship, your nearness had been more,' he said nodding and understanding perfectly. It was strange to think that it was dad here and not maama ji. Or Phillipa. How perverse, I thought, that I wished she was here to understand how I felt about her death.

He sighed again. 'You are too young. It is very young for someone to die that is your friend.'

I stared at the blank television. I felt as though I was too young for everything.

Then I remembered. 'Didn't granma die when you were really little?' I said.

He nodded.

'I was thirteen. But . . . many people died, you know. We knew she was dying. It was cancer probably. Nobody knew. There was no real medical care, or treatment, or hygiene.'

I couldn't even imagine it, that time. It was the stuff of history lessons. It wasn't anything to do with how I was feeling.

'Was that why you had to do well? To get an education. To escape the fact that death was an everyday thing?'

He shrugged.

'Many things,' he said and was quiet again.

And me, I thought. Where am I to go? A faceless drunken driver runs over a woman in the street. It happens all the time. And where am I to go? How do I set about crying?

'What do you mean, you are going out?' demanded ma.

'I'm going out. Out,' I said. 'Just get off my back!' She had come in from work at the Nat West only ten minutes ago and already she'd started telling me what to do.

'Don't you speak to me like that, young lady,' she said raising her voice.

I started putting lipstick on in front of the mirrror.

'Look at that. No respect. Is that what well brought-up girls do? Go out to parties when someone has died?' said ma, her hands on her hips.

I couldn't believe it. It was like there was a complete code of behaviour, for life, death and marriage and everything in between. I felt as though she was taking over my grief.

I couldn't bear to drive. I took the train.

'You look nice,' Lol greeted me.

I looked at him and said, 'My friend got run over in the street. I don't want to talk about it.'

He put his arm around me in front of the newspaper kiosk inside Camden tube station. I thought I was going to cry, my face in his shoulder in that public place. But no tears came.

He held me by the shoulders. 'Do you want to go to the fair?'

'What fair?'

'In Finsbury Park. We can get a bus.'

The night was inked with colour. There were people jostling past laughing and shouting, the usual stalls and rides. Different strains of music played out into the night — old fashioned hurdy gurdy music (Welcome! Welcome! All the Fun of the Fair!) mixed with the dance remix of Madonna's 'Holiday'. The big wheel, a sequined ball of squealing faces and white knuckles holding on tight; candy floss and popcorn, kids and teenagers running around crashing into one another like dodgems on an aimless road to nowhere.

'Wanna burn rubber?' he said and I laughed.

We grabbed a car each. I wanted to drive my own. Soon I was relentlessly charging into any car. Spying and singling them out from the far corners of the rink.

I had done two full turns on the wheel and the car was still stuck stubbornly to the side. Over my shoulder I could see advancing vicious buggies.

'Come on, come on!' I was screaming when I saw Lol's car come tearing towards me. I let go of the steering wheel for a moment, hunched my shoulders, bracing myself for the crash. He was making a sound from the back of his throat like a car engine. The impact made me jump involuntarily and as I landed back in my seat Lol was turning my steering wheel to dislodge my car. In seconds our cars were side by side.

'Thanks,' I said grinning, holding the wheel with both hands.

He put his left arm around me and we kissed. One hand left my steering wheel and touched his face.

A bloodcurdling scream rang out as a fat boy hammered into the side of Lol's car, but with a flick of the wrist, Lol sent the invader skimming across the rink. A couple of teenagers banged into my car and I screamed. Lol held me even tighter. Our cars seemed locked together while all hell was breaking loose on the open motorway.

'Oi, you two. Can you break it up? Bleedin' hell. Go and make love somewhere else, willya?' barked a voice in front of us. The session had finished and two spotty boys with distaste on their faces, arms folded, were standing next to their champion, and our traffic cop.

We walked off the wooden rink shamefaced as the new riders in town sat poised at their wheels.

Lol kissed my hair and said, 'That was pretty bad taste after your mate and everything, wasn't it?'

I looked at him, my eyes suddenly wide, my bottom lip under my teeth. I hadn't even thought of it. Christ, I was a heartless bitch. Lol saw my expression and pulled me closer.

'Hey it's ok. It's ok. It's the fair. Everything's all right at the fair. It's pretend.'

A sinister laugh rang out and my head jerked up to see a purple monster with rolling bloodshot eyes, poking out of a tent marked 'Horror Train'. The grass under my feet seemed to have taken on an unearthly luminescence.

'What do you see in me?' I said quietly.

Lol took my face in his hands and pulled it towards him, his face serious.

'Don't say that. Kathi always used to say that,' he said looking straight into my eyes.

'Fucking hell. Everything's a minefield. I can't say anything. Can't do anything. It's wrong to go out. It's wrong to go on the dodgems. It's wrong to say what I think. Everything *means* something. I can't bear it. Why can't everything just *be*? Why does it *all* have to have bloody meaning!'

'Shh. Shhhh . . .' said Lol. 'It's all right.'

'No it isn't all right! My friend's not here and I'm not allowed to tell you how much I think about you because that's reserved for *her*. Why does the language belong to *her*? Why can't I say it? I thought you were bloody well separated anyway. Why don't you just fucking well go back to Kathi, Lol, seeing as she's so fucking well sacred . . .?' I was screaming in a public place. I was making a scene. People could hear but I didn't care. I wanted to hit something.

'Stop it, will ya! Stop it!' said Lol, shaking me. 'Stop winding yourself up. I'm sorry about your friend, but it happens. Grow up. Handle it. It's not my fault. Don't take it out on me.'

I was crying and he was holding me. People were rushing past us, laughing and yelling.

'Angie. Angie. Haven't I told you everything?' His voice was lower, in my ear. 'I told you things I never told anyone. Don't you trust me? Look, look at me.' He lifted my face by my chin and I looked at him through a glaze of tears and clogged mascara. 'Christ! You're the best thing that's happened to me for ages. You're the business. And you don't mean that, what you said. You're proud of yourself, you don't need me to tell you how brilliant you are. You *know* what I see in you. Don't ya? Well don't you? Come on now, you don't have to cry no more.'

A smile started to creep up behind the tears and as soon as he saw it he piped up with: 'Anyway, you should be on this side, lookin' at your boat. Right mess!' He grinned.

I immediately wiped underneath my eyes and laughed.

'You're *such* a horror. I'm going to sell you to the Horror Train and leave you there,' I said poking him in the shoulder. I was laughing. Lol looked casually across at the Horror Train tent and said evenly, 'Actually, I was thinking the same about you. And I wouldn't even need to put a mask on *you*.'

He had started running before finishing the sentence but I caught him and tried to slap him across the head which he dodged.

'*Baastard!!!*' I laughed, hitting out indiscriminately, searching for any unprotected area.

'Ouch, ouch. All right I take it back. I wouldn't get anything for you anyway. Too damn feisty. *Ouch!* That was my ankle!'

The bus had started moving but Lol gripped my hand and we ran and jumped onto the platform before it gathered too much speed. We bounded up the stairs and bounced onto the back seat panting, exhilarated.

'Jeeezus! You trying to kill me or what?' I said. Then: 'Oh shit!'

Lol winked at me. 'It's ok. Words, it's just words,' he said.

'They change everything,' I said looking out of the window.

'Heavy, man,' he drawled and I elbowed him in the stomach.

'Ouch. I can't take any more of this violence. Help.'

'Stop it. Be serious,' I said.

He sat back and looked serious.

'It was Phillipa. From Amigo's. You knew her didn't you?' I said slowly.

He looked at me. 'Shit.' Then he stared ahead of him. There was silence.

'I think she must've hated me. I was a drongo when I knew her,' he said bitterly.

'No. She didn't,' I said. It was irrelevant to her now, but the lie was important to him.

Suddenly the bus took a corner at the last minute and we slid towards the window.

'Jesus Christ!' I said.

Lol took my hand and squeezed it. He was looking at the floor.

'Drunk,' he said quietly.

'I know,' I said looking at the same space he was.

'Why Camden Town?'
    'Why not?'
We were lying on his bed, on top of the duvet, fully clothed, our shoes on the floor. Tapping the joint, I looked

at his face. He was staring at the ceiling silently, miles away.

'Yeah, but why did you want to meet in Camden Town? The fair was in Finsbury Park,' I urged.

'Oh, I just wanted to show you something. Nothing important,' he said.

'What? A pub?'

'Do you think that's all I do?'

'No,' I said quietly passing him the joint. Silence. Breathing. Ours.

'There's a row of saplings. Just by the market, on the High Street,' he said to the ceiling.

I frowned and resisted the urge to say something witty like, 'Oh wow, I've never seen that. Trees.'

'I planted them last month. It was just a week's job. For the Council. Thought I'd see how they were doing. No big deal,' he said.

'Oh,' I said. Trees that he'd planted. He was a gardener. I'd forgotten. 'Where are they?'

'Just opposite that antique shop, by the zebra crossing.'

'I'm going to go down there and see them.'

He looked at me, smiled.

We finished the joint in silence and I watched the smoke swirl around the room. Feeling the grass loosen up the limbs in my body, I stretched out, soaking into the bed. The table lamp speckled the grain of the plain wooden headboard; books by Kurt Vonnegut and Lenny Bruce with hairline cracks on the spines; Doc Martens boots on the floor, a layer of moss and dirt on the soles, some of it seeping into the crevices of the leather. Had I, sometime, a long time ago thought it was a room like any other? Phillipa hadn't had a room. For sixteen months she had been sleeping on the settee in the lounge. Geoffrey had moved into her old room and Phillipa wouldn't hear of him moving out. Geoffrey the drip who always made me feel uncomfortable with his shyness had seemed so assured on the phone. So grown up and sad.

Ever since I'd left Amigo's I'd never found the time to see her properly . . . Phillipa home and tired, the family in the front room playing Kallookie and no extension cord on the telephone.

'I'm partnering Miri, I can't talk now. How about next Monday?'

'Oh, damn (I've got half an hour now), I'm busy next week (something better might come up).'

'We haven't talked for ages, it's ridiculous we live so near.' 'I'm sorry. (Who else can I ring up?) Are you ok though?'

'Yes.'

'Good.'

'I miss you.'

'I miss you.'

Phillipa standing in the doorway; driving her car; hair cascading impossibly.

Wait! Stay! I screwed up my eyes till they hurt, till the images faded. Lol was concentrating on the ceiling. Like when you stare at the sea for too long. For a long solid moment I tensed my body, my arms, my legs, my fingers, I even held my breath.

Slowly, like a tear from an ancient wound, slithered junior school and a crate of milkbottles. The first school with white faces. We had milk at eleven-thirty and I hated it. You got a straw and sometimes ma would give me a biscuit wrapped up in paper. She never used foil because it was a waste and the biscuits were bought especially for me. Dad and maama ji didn't eat them. Rax was a baby. I used to fight and stamp my foot for that biscuit wrapped in foil because that's what all the others had. And then one day. Just when I had managed to make them all believe I was just like them, something happened. Just when I thought I had done everything correct to fit in, the regulation v-neck royal blue jumper, the pleated skirt, the knee length white socks . . . Julia Parkinson said that I was a paki and I smelt. Then she had run over to my sort of best friend Lynne (the only one who ever talked to me) and told her the news. Lynne heard the newsflash and I remember her eyes looking uncertainly across at me. And then she turned away as though something had been confirmed.

I remember the sound in that classroom at morning break. It was like someone had unplugged audio as on a tv because all I could hear was my heart thumping. I felt a circle of chalk had been drawn around me. I'd walked home that day and cried and cried to dad, saying why wasn't I white and that everything would be ok if I was white. He had looked at me sternly and said, 'You are from India. It is a great and wonderful place. And you will never be white because India is inside you.' And he had opened an atlas and shown me the map of India.

I smiled and looked across at Lol.

'This bed is so nice,' I said

'I made it,' he said looking away from me.

In a flash I thought that this was another thing that would last once Lol had gone. But that one day Lol would perhaps be gone, was not what I wanted to think about. And then I knew that Lol, his face turned to the wall, was thinking the same thought.

I stared at the vast whiteness of the ceiling.

Then, like a secret, coded answer both of us turned and gripped each other. Hugged so tight that our heads slotted into the other's shoulder. Safe, intact, precious.

In the morning Lol said I could stay as long as I liked and to pull the big door shut when I left. I wanted him to take the day off work, I felt so close to him, but despite all the emotion that had been generated between us, there were still eggshells.

He was getting ready for work and talking over the noise of the radio. I wasn't upset about Phillipa's death any more.

'You going to the funeral today?' He sat down beside me on the bed.

I looked down and shrugged.

'Why don't you come with me?' I knew it was a stupid thing to say but I didn't want to be alone.

Lol laughed, got up, started to put his Levis jacket on, his back to me.

'Why not?' I said still looking at the duvet.

He turned around and there was an expression in his face that I didn't understand. He laughed again and this time it sounded cruel.

'I think it would be taking the piss if I went to her funeral,' he said. 'I'm the last person who could go. I don't think her family would appreciate it somehow.'

Then he was gone, slamming the door as if he was angry with me for rubbing the past in his face.

CHAPTER FOURTEEN

'What was the funeral like?' said ma taking off her coat and dumping her handbag in the hallway, rearranging her sari that had messed up in the rush hour.

I was sitting at the table looking at the garden outside. A rake and wheelbarrow were standing against the wall. In the middle of the garden was a coil of garden hose lying inert in the scruffy uncut grass.

'This house is such a mess. Why is it always such a mess?' I said irritably. What I meant was, why didn't she clean it up.

Ma looked disinterestedly at the garden, and half heartedly collected together a newspaper, bills and their envelopes, a wedding invitation and a recent *India Today* into a pile. She searched for an empty space on the coffee table and not finding one dumped them underneath the sofa.

'That's really going to help,' I said condescendingly.

Ma frowned and walked over to the table.

'You are very good at orders. Why don't you do something about it if you don't like it then?' She moved things around the dinner table. In vain. Then: 'Oh no, too busy with going out.'

I turned away from her. She always said that.

'I am not a machine,' she said pursing her lips and folding her arms, 'and I've got better things to do than clean up this house all the time.'

'Like what for instance?' I spat at her.

She looked at me evenly and then disappeared into the kitchen. I was rocking against the table waiting for a response, but when ma was angry she meted out the silent treatment. I jutted my bottom lip out and stared at the garden.

I heard dad's key in the door.

'What was the funeral like?' he said taking off his tie and draping it over the back of a dining chair.

I sighed loudly.

He walked into the kitchen and asked ma in Hindi what the funeral had been like. She produced a noise from the back of her throat that meant she wasn't talking to me.

'Shankar has gone to visit the Shah's. They are going to America next month and he is filling out their visa forms and what not for them,' she reported.

'Achha, achha. Good, they have finally decided to go. The son will turn out all right if they get him established there. With the sister already resident, they could get the green card for him'.

Dad was picking at some food and putting the kettle on.

I rolled my eyes at the boring conversation.

Dad came in with the tray and set out two cups, adding milk to his.

'What happened, yaar?' he said sitting down at the table.

'I didn't go,' I said, because he would understand.

'What?'

'I just couldn't face it. It would have been too depressing . . .' I stopped, seeing his face drop as though I had let him down. It irritated me. I started again.

'What difference does it make, anyway? It's all over. I couldn't face . . .'

He looked at me sternly and I felt like a little kid.

'You didn't go because you couldn't face it? What do you think, it is for your benefit, the funeral? You. You didn't go because you couldn't face it?' His voice was rising in anger.

'I'll send some flowers . . .'

'Oh yes. Flowers. That will make it all right? Oh yes. This is the culture you have learnt. Nobody likes to go to funerals, young lady. You go to show your respects. Grief is something that has to be shared. You don't have a monopoly on it, you know. Flowers! Pah! Yes you would have felt uncomfortable. But oh no. Your generation wants everything your own way. Synthesised, sanitised, in colour. Nothing bad. Only nice and pretty. Pah!' He left the table in disgust and walked back to the kitchen.

I stormed upstairs to my room. But as the evening wore on, dad's words stung. I should have rung at least, or asked if there was anything I could do. Of course there wouldn't have been and no one would have missed me at the funeral but . . . I had run away from a responsibility because it had felt awkward. Perhaps I would write a letter to Miri. Perhaps I could do that. Tomorrow.

'Hello, love, you all right?' Derek looked up from his chair in the edit room.

I nodded. 'How's it going?'

'Ok. Not bad. They shot the club yesterday. I was just about to have a look at the rushes. Charles is coming in a bit late, he said, so shall we carry on?'

I nodded, relieved to be back at work, to have something to stir my imagination.

We watched pictures of the interior of Highballs and as the camera zoomed into the aquariums, the mirror ball, the waitresses' cleavages, I sipped my coffee thoughtfully.

The place looked even tackier on screen than it had done the night Maggie and I had visited it.

'Apparently it went quite well. They said they were doing a piece on clubs in general so this Eddie character let them shoot everywhere. Made sure he was in most of the shots as well,' chuckled Derek. He was wearing a navy blue jumper over jeans, clutching a glass of what looked like Alka-Seltzer in his hand.

'Little does he know,' I laughed.

'There he is. Flash git, isn't he?' said Derek taking a gulp as the camera panned across the dance floor.

'Can you pause for a minute?' I said suddenly. The picture froze and I peered at the screen. A man in his late twenties wearing a deep blue double breasted suit stood casually at the bar. He had on a silk tie with big red polka dots and a tie pin. His hair was slicked back and in one ear was a gold sleeper. He was tapping a finger at the bar, looking around proprietorially.

'Who's *that*?' I asked. He looked completely at odds with the general style of the club.

Derek looked at me questioningly. 'Eddie. It's the guy. Eddie. I thought you knew.'

My mouth fell open. I had mistaken the doorman. Looking at him, this lounge lizard, his eyes twinkling and confident, I could imagine any number of women falling for him.

'Looks like a pimp, doesn't he?' said Derek, scowling.

I laughed.

'Hey, are the rushes any good?'

We turned around to see Charles and Madeleine behind us. They seemed in high spirits.

'Ross was a bit worried about the light but it looks fine, doesn't it?' continued Charles, dragging in a chair for Madeleine. 'Hi, Angie. Hey, sorry to hear about your friend. Hey, Maddy, look I told you he'd make sure he was in shot. Look at those aquariums. Wild.'

Charles was in an excited mood, bubbling over with enthusiasm.

'Yeah, right. Actually it was a good idea about the early shoot because the emptiness makes it look more dingy,' smiled Madeleine.

'Hey, sure . . .' said Charles turning towards her and grinning. 'We're talking *direction* here.'

Madeleine winked at him. 'Ok, hot shot. So direct already,' she said hunching her shoulders and making her accent even more New York Jewish. 'Gotta go. Meetings,' she said and pushed her chair back.

I felt faintly annoyed that I had missed the shoot at the club. It sounded like fun. I noted apprehensively that the rapport between Madeleine and Charles had come back. She had on a big lumberjack check shirt. I was sure I had seen Charles wearing it one day but I couldn't be certain. Though I had felt wretched on the way to work, I had concocted a little story about the funeral for them, but it was obvious they weren't interested.

At lunchtime I was busy with some notes. Charles and Madeleine went out to eat before some meeting in the afternoon. Charles had given Derek notes on how he wanted the first cut to look and I would be around in the afternoon if any facts needed to be checked. Then we'd all look at it tomorrow.

'Want to come for lunch, love?' said Derek. 'It won't take long to slap this first cut together.'

'Ok. Where do you go?'

'The Coach and Horses.'

The pub was packed with men propping up the bar, pints in hand. Lunchtime buzz. A group of men dressed in jeans and ill fitting shirts called over to Derek. I was introduced all round to appreciative smiles. It looked as though it was to be a liquid lunch because the only food to be seen was a tray of sausage rolls and Cornish pasties wrapped in cellophane. The bar was lined with beer pumps proclaiming 'Old Peculiar' and 'London Pride'.

'You've got a good tan. Been on holiday, love?' one of the men guffawed.

I raised an eyebrow at Derek and he shifted uncomfortably.

'Shut up, Brian. Want a drink, love?' he said digging into his jeans.

'Nah, I'll get you one darlin',' said Brian.

'I'll get my own, thanks.' I opened my purse.

'She can look after herself, mate. You got no chance there.' All of them were craning over their pints to take a look at me as though they had never seen a woman before.

From the conversations around me I realised that there were no directors or producers in the pub. These were the 'back room boys'. The projectionists, sound technicians, editors that you never saw — so plain and drab in comparison with Charles and Madeleine.

'You know him,' Brian was saying to Derek, 'John, the coloured geezer.' Then he looked at me and said, 'Oh sorry love,' although what he was apologising for I wasn't sure. Was he sorry because he hadn't said, 'the geezer with parents from more than one country of origin'?

I smiled and sipped my drink. I wasn't particularly interested in fighting off phrases like 'women's libber' and 'coloured' in my lunch hour.

'Anyway, good bloke. He's been my assistant on the last couple of films I've cut,' continued Brian.

'Brian's editing a feature,' explained Derek.

'Oh', I said interested. 'Big screen?'

'Oh yeah. I only do features these days. I can't be bothered with sixteen,' said Brian nodding.

Derek clicked his teeth, 'Yeah, you can't do much on sixteen mill, but at least it's film.'

'What, you're not cutting video, are you? Bleedin' video. All style and no content if you ask me,' said a tall man with glasses.

'Can't cut their way out of a paper bag, and they call themselves video editors,' said a middle-aged man with sandy hair and there was more laughter and nodding of heads.

'I know. Can't wait to get back to film,' said Derek laughing.

'Anyway, so I says to him . . .' Brian had picked up his story again, 'What we gonna do about this director? He's been winding me right up. Hasn't got a clue. Couldn't direct traffic down a one way street. How are we going to get him out of the way for a couple of days, get him out of the cutting room?'

'They're a pain when they sit there all the time looking over your shoulder, getting in the way,' said the tall one.

'But you know in video they sit there all the time. Sorry, Angie, I didn't mean you. But yeah, it's a completely different discipline,' said Derek puffing on his cigar.

'Well, I wouldn't mind a pretty lady like you sitting next to me. You can come and work with me anytime, darlin'.' Sandy hair grinned self consciously.

I had to control my laughter. This guy probably had to pay women to go out with him.

'So, he goes I know just the thing and goes off down the shops. Comes back with this laxative that's colourless, odourless and tasteless,' said Brian laughing.

'You're joking,' said the tall one.

'No. Straight up. So this geezer, Nott-Macair his name is. Snot-Macair, we call him. He's always getting John to make coffee for him which winds John right up anyway. But that afternoon any chance he got, John was saying "Another coffee?" and every time he was putting in about twenty of these tablets. Me and the receptionist were pissing ourselves. Next day he phoned up, said he can't

make it to the office. Said he was feeling in-dis-posed.'
Brian started to laugh with the others.

'John says it was "wicked". "Weeee . . . kid". I can't
do it but you know. He makes that noise with his mouth
when he talks about old Snot-Macair. He keeps trying to
teach me but I just can't do it.' Brian made an attempt to
kiss his teeth but it sounded like an old man clamping his
jaws together having forgotten to put his teeth in.

We all laughed and Brian said, 'Same again, love?'
pointing to my half empty wine glass. I nodded even
though it tasted like vinegar.

Derek was shaking his head. 'That's another thing. No
bloody assistants in video.'

'I'll have to be careful I don't get on the wrong side of
you then. Have to check my coffee,' I said grinning at
Derek and the others laughed.

'Oh no, it's not like that love,' said Brian. 'This bloke
was asking for it. Who's your director then, Del?'

'Some bloke called Charles Russell,' said Derek.

'Never heard of him.'

'Well you wouldn't, Brian. He's only been doing
promos for a year and thinks he's world class. You know
the type,' said Derek.

Brian and the others nodded. They weren't going to say
anything else in front of me, just in case.

'Has he only been directing for a year?' I was aghast. I'd
thought that Charles was much more experienced than
that.

'Yeah. It's all front though. These yuppies with their
designer water and all that. They get on my nerves,' said
Derek bitterly.

'Oh, don't pay attention to him, miserable bastard. He's
always like this when he's cutting video,' said the tall one
winking at me.

'Yeah, he's right. Come on drink up, girl. Better get
back to it,' said Derek.

On the way back Derek pointed out film cutting rooms above hairdresser's and fashion shops on Wardour Street. He waved to Bruno's Sandwich Bar saying they made the best bacon rolls in Soho. I stopped myself from looking into the Ally Cappelino shop as I heard Derek mumble 'Bleedin' designer rubbish' under his breath. Two young men in suits and haircuts, saying, 'two million honestly,' almost bumped into us as they strode along the pavement. Derek rolled his eyes and chuckled at me.

'They don't make 'em like they used to. Now they just get churned out of film schools or advertising and they think they know about film. It's pathetic.'

'But surely isn't that what video is about? More access for the ordinary person?' I asked.

'More access to what? Mediocrity?' said Derek pushing the door open.

Madeleine and Charles were still not back from lunch so I decided to make some coffee and phone calls. There was no sugar left.

'I think there's some sweeteners in the edit suite,' said Derek pulling open a drawer. Over his shoulder I saw inside the drawer a half eaten bar of chocolate, some photographs of a little boy and, tucked away in the corner, a half bottle of whisky. Derek turned his head and shut the drawer. I looked away. It was nothing to do with me if he had alcohol stashed away.

'Can't find them,' he said.

'Don't worry,' I smiled, heading for the door.

Derek sighed heavily.

'Are you ok, Derek?' I asked but there was no answer. The picture of the nightclub had frozen on both monitors.

'Oh yeah. Sorry, love. I was miles away. I was just thinking about my son.'

'Oh, I didn't know you were, um . . . had a son,' I said even though I didn't care much.

'Yeah. But I only get to see him at the weekends. I took him to the Museum of the Moving Image on Saturday. I think I enjoyed it more than he did. Well kids these days, they just watch tv all the time, don't they?'

God, turn the record over I was thinking, but managed to nod politely.

Derek sighed again. 'Everything's so different these days.'

I was looking at the floor. The man was a depressive. I had my own problems. But it would have been too rude to get up and leave.

'I mean the world's just changed. You know when you work with film, it's magic. Pure magic. You can feel it, do you know what I mean? You can hold it in your hand, put it to the light to see if it's the shot you want. Jump up and down on it if you want. Warm it against the pic sync lamp if it's got scrunched up when you've been rewinding.' Derek laughed, easing back in his chair lost in memory.

The tv screens had started their familiar groaning. He hit the pause button.

'That's what I don't like about video the most. You can't *get* at it, can't touch it. It's all buttons.'

Remembering Charles's retort at another time I said, 'Yeah, but isn't video more immediate? More slick?'

'Oh yeah, sure. It's pin sharp. But it's stark, because it's electronic. Film isn't sharp but it has depth.'

I looked at him quizzically. Technical concepts always evaded me. I couldn't understand why such things were important. After all a picture was a picture. Surely it was the ideas that mattered.

'Well, imagine a grey scale. That's a piece of card that looks like the colour bars on the tv. You've seen that, haven't you? Right. Well, to put it at its crudest

level, in video there might be five or six shades of grey
between the black and the white bars. But in film, well
there would be about sixteen. So you see film has depth,
and richness of colour which gives the illusion that it's
real, when actually, technically, video is much sharper,
more contrasty, colder. And then of course there's the
sound.'

He shook his head sadly. 'Sound can *make* a film. Give
it a complete feel. In video you can't do much with sound.
You can't lay tracks or anything . . .'

I started to get up because I was getting lost in the
conversation. I looked at my watch to let him know I
had things to do.

'What's the time?' he said looking up.

'Three twelve,' I said.

'Now you see, there's a good example.'

'What?'

'That's a digital watch, isn't it? See, if I was telling
you the time, I'd say twelve minutes past three or nearly
quarter past.'

'So?' I folded my arms and looked at my watch.

'Do you know about digital and analog systems? It's
computer speak. Ok, well, I'll try and explain what I
mean. In the old days you knew the shape of things, the
volume of things. In the example of time, you knew how
much time had gone before, and how much was to come,
right?'

I nodded, frowning.

'I think of those days, or that attitude, as an analogous
existence. Nowadays, everything's the opposite. Digital. If
you think of our existence as being digital, it also means
that we no longer know the scheme of things, the shape
of things. When you look at a digital watch you see three
twelve. That's it. No more and no less.'

I was nodding my head slowly getting to grips with the
idea. Suddenly I laughed:

'It's like my dad always says that the Americans have . . .' I turned to look at the door but they weren't back yet, '. . . the Americans have reduced everything because they can't deal with complicated concepts. He says, they even have to reduce the language. You know, words like Limo, Demo etcetera.'

Derek was nodding his head: 'Yeah, exactly. First of all the Americans think they know it all, and they know fuck all of course. *Then*, they bloody well stick it down our throats,' he grumbled.

'Well, talking of Americans I'd better get off and do some work before our illustrious producer gets back.' I laughed, getting up and shutting the door firmly behind me. Once I could hear the monitors going in the edit room, I dialled Lol's number.

No answer. I knew he must be at work. Why had I called? I listened to the phone ringing uselessly for a while before replacing it on the rest. I needed to talk to him. Make sure he was still there. Apologise for being selfish. Talk to him . . .

Watching the street below thinking about digital existences I saw Madeleine and Charles on the pavement. They were laughing about something. Hearing footsteps on the stairs I put Kathi's transcripts in front of me and pretended to read.

'Hi, hi hi,' said Charles taking his coat off. 'How's the team?'

I looked up and smiled. Madeleine had disappeared.

'Why are you in such a good mood?' I asked.

'Everything's rolling, that's why. We saw the commisioning editor this afternoon and he's really enthusiastic. Wants to see a rough cut next week. Do you think we can do it? Of course we can do it! How's . . .?' Charles nodded his head towards the edit room.

'Ok. I think he's having a breakdown or something,' I said drily. I wanted to make him laugh too.

Charles came up to my chair, leant down.

'Oh God, I can't bear it. It's a good job the rest of us are sane. Hey, guess what!'

He lowered his voice.

'He's got this bottle of whisky in his drawer. He's a bloody alki.'

He ran his hand through his hair dramatically, rolling his eyes. Then he straightened up laughing and shrugged. 'Well, whatever gets you through the night.'

I watched him, unable to stop smiling. His moods were infectious and if this film was going to turn out to be good then I wanted the credit that was due to me too.

'Hey, Angie, one more thing though. We've decided to go with the pictures as is, without the video effects. It's so much more dramatic. And she looks so great on screen.'

'But, didn't we promise her . . .?' I started to say but Charles waved me aside.

'Oh, come *on*. She looks so great. It'll kill the whole thing if we block it up. No, we've got to go with it. It'll look terrific, I promise you.'

'Well, do you think I should call her?' I said uncertainly. The last person I wanted to talk to at the moment was Kathi. I was happy to see her image on the screen but suddenly the real Kathi had got too close to my life.

'Oh God, forget it. We'll discuss it when the film's finished. By that time she'll see that it looks great too. Anyway, if she's going to prosecute then what difference does it make? It'll make her case stronger if anything. People can't relate to a face that's been blocked out.'

I nodded. He was probably right. And anyway, if the worst came to the worst we could still put the effects on because that would only be done at the end anyway.

*

We all crammed into the edit room. The phone had been taken off the hook and each of us had a pad and pen at the ready. Derek looked around to see that we were all looking at the blank screens then pressed Play.

Pictures of the condom factory flashed into action. 'The song will start here. "Love Hurts". And now, here's a title that hasn't been decided yet. Ok, picture freezes and title off, pictures continue,' Charles explained as the factory sequence unfolded. Madeleine nodded.

The image cut to Kathi full screen. 'I want revenge, I want justice, I want to make him pay.'

A slow track along the bar in Highballs.

'Right, music here too. Refrain "Love Hurts" but maybe echo it. Mix another echo, a synthesised "Whoo", you know. So it gives the shot atmosphere as well as sounding like a record that's playing at the club.' Charles was staring intently at the screen.

Madeleine was nodding slowly, smiling. 'I like,' she said.

Eddie was standing in the shadows; Kathi's voice came in voiceover: 'To die is easy, to live you have to struggle.'

Cut to her face again and it seemed to be a continuation of her voiceover phrase.

'Life's tough, yeah. Well, I'm gonna make his life tough. I've been to groups. That doesn't do anything to him, does it? He's still all right. It doesn't harm him, does it?'

'Nice,' Madeleine said to Charles.

The picture cut back to the club, Eddie in the foreground.

'Ok, well commentary here. Kathi blah blah slept with her employer Mr blah and as a consequence found out that he had transmitted the HIV virus to her. He did not tell her about it. Well something like that. Angie and I will have to work on the wording of the commentary,' said Charles.

I nodded, staring at the pictures. It was turning into a *film*. I marvelled at the power of editing. Derek had culled together bits of her speech and got them to make sense.

Kathi was on screen again saying that she'd been around the block a few times and so what? There was a zoom in and the screen was her face, so close that half her forehead was cut off at the top.

Cut to shots of the street and closeups of billboards saying 'Don't die of ignorance'.

'Ok, now here, more commentary. Kathi isn't a heroin addict. She was just an ordinary woman who . . .' Charles was hitching the air for words.

'Who was fucking anything she saw, when bang!' said Madeleine and let out a whoop of laughter.

'Pause.' Charles looked up: 'Madeleine! That's so sexist!'

'Sorry. Sorry. Carry on,' said Madeleine and straightened up.

Something was definitely going on between them.

'Ok, ordinary woman who was, having a good time . . .' Charles burst into laughter. 'Stop it, Madeleine. Sorry, Derek, could you rewind that bit. Something about . . . ok, stop laughing . . . commentary about taking it out of the bedroom and into the courtroom.'

Madeleine snorted.

Charles started to laugh. 'Christ, Madeleine, you're the end!'

Since Phillipa's death everything seemed to have become a multiple choice, and I felt as though I was in the exam room chewing my pen trying to work out the right answer. An answer will be right or wrong, not because there *is* a right answer but because an answer's got to be chosen. Disturbed, I sat looking at the clock.

'Hey, Angie! Shit, my researcher's so bored that she's miles away,' laughed Charles.

I shook my head and laughed.

'Sorry, what did you say?' Since when had I become *his* researcher?

'I was saying, what do you think of it so far? Rubbish, right? No seriously. You haven't been here for two days so I need some feedback. Also, looks like I'm gonna be tied up on the other one next week so you're gonna have to take over more or less. I think the direction of it, the approach is clear but do you think you can go with it?'

I stared at him. Madeleine turned to me and winked. 'Well, Herr Director?'

I felt nervous all of a sudden. They had decided I was capable.

'Um, sure. Yeah,' I mumbled.

'You can do it, babe,' said Madeleine and I felt a glow rising from the pit of butterflies in my stomach. 'The next one needs more work and Charles is gonna see the solicitor next week. It needs to be handled a certain way. If you press on here then we can all get going after the fine cut of this one. What do you think?'

What did I *think*? I'd just been promoted from mere researcher to director. My head was reeling. She *must* like me, I thought immediately.

'Actually I *have* got one or two ideas,' I ventured slowly, full of new found enthusiasm.

'Oh-Oooo,' said Madeleine grinning. 'You better watch her, Charles, she's way ahead a'you!'

Charles grinned.

'No, no. I really like it, but. But, um, there's nothing in it about Pete. You know the guy, her friend. And that piece about "To die is easy, to live you've got to struggle" — I mean that's out of context. She didn't mean the court case, she meant . . .'

'I know you're really tied to that piece, Angie, but it really doesn't work. There's no place for it in our film,' said Madeleine. 'And it's a downer anyway,' said Charles. The film's not about all that stuff, loving friendships and

all that. I know it's important, of course, but it's been
done! And she's really vulnerable in that piece, she cries.
I mean, we took it anyway because I thought we might
use it, but no. I mean, this is about an individual fighting
the system, even when the subject matter is as intimate as
sex. Let's face it, she said it herself, that all these groups
she's been to were supportive but they don't get *him*, do
they?' Charles leant across Madeleine, using his hands to
explain.

'Lol, what's the matter?' We were in the Dog and Trumpet
but he was somewhere else.

'Nothing. Why?'

'You're, I don't know. Don't be so distant. What's up?
Talk to me.'

'Look, Angie, what's there to say?'

Silence.

'Was it . . .? Is it something to do with Phillipa, I
mean . . .?' I was shooting in the dark because the silence
was weighing heavily on me.

'I don't know. I suppose it knocked me back. I've never
known anyone who died before. I'm lucky, I suppose, but
I haven't.'

'Neither have I,' I said indignantly.

'Oh well, give a prize to that woman in red,' said Lol and
laughed at the pub.

'Oh, I *hate* it when you make fun of me. Why do you
have to be like this.'

'For Christ's sake, Angie. What do you want me to say?
It's not a bloody competition.'

'I never said it was a . . .' I countered immediately.

'All right. All right,' Lol sighed heavily.

'No, come on. You've got something to say. Spit it out,'
I said venomously.

'All right,' he said slowly and turned towards me. 'All right. I think I've got more reason to be thinking about death at the moment, that's all. I've been thinking about it and it scares the hell out of me, all right?'

I closed my eyes. I didn't want to think about it. A dream that I'd had a couple of nights ago came flooding back.

I was driving a car. Madeleine and Charles were sitting in the front next to me talking to each other. I kept seeing them and I'd forgotten their names, and at times they looked like one person. Charles said, 'You've got a nice tan,' and Madeleine laughed. It was the laugh when she had laughed about Kathi screwing around. And I was looking straight ahead. I kept wishing Lol was there. Then I forgot how to drive. And up ahead I saw my dad sitting with Kathi having tea in the road. She stood and walked towards the car but she couldn't see it and I couldn't stop the car. I woke up curled in a ball and the duvet was on the floor. The alarm had gone off. I couldn't find my voice to say shut up . . .

Lol stood up and went to the bar. I watched him and thought of the first time I'd seen him. Levis wrapped around his legs. I thought of him saying, 'Of all the bars in all the world you hadda walk into mine.'

He was talking to his sister, Tracey, then turned and winked at me, and stood looking over at me for a few seconds while I looked back at him. I felt as though I was with him and I felt as though I was without him. There was just that space between us. He walked over and put the drinks on the table. Lundy came over and said hello. 'I don't want to talk to you, man, I'm busy,' said Lol.

Lundy looked at us and his face broke into a lazy smile and his gold tooth glinted. He patted Lol's shoulder benignly, nodded his head and shuffled off towards the pool room.

Lol turned towards me.

'He thinks we're in love,' he said drily.

I smiled. 'Is he short sighted?'

'No.'

'Is he pissed?'

'No.'

I thought about it.

'Mistaken identity,' I concluded pouring my drink. The Beck's was cold and wet against my hand.

'No,' said Lol looking at me. 'He never forgets a face.'

Then he leaned across and kissed me and for a moment I thought I was back in the dodgems, my heart lurching, my body hunched against the delicious impact of it all.

On the way back to the flat, we held hands and I told him how I'd been promoted to director. We were on safe territory. We were talking about the film.

'Well, I'm not surprised. You're so bossy. That's what directors do, isn't it?'

I slapped him across the head and he took it.

'No, but seriously. Do you think it's because she likes you?' 'What's that got to do with it?'

I explained quickly about the shoot.

'Yeah, but . . . She's letting you direct it because she thinks you can do it. Not because you're a nice person,' he said as we strolled along the pavement. 'Which of course you're *not*,' he added grinning.

I was deep in thought. 'Do you think I'm selling myself short then?'

'Yeah. You know you can do it anyway. She's not doing you no favours, is she? In fact she's doing herself a favour.'

'What do you mean?'

'Well, that Charles bloke . . . he's the one I met in that poxy bar, isn't it? Well, she's putting him onto the solicitor because she doesn't think you're up to it.'

'That's not true,' I said indignantly.

'Wait. Wait. Don't fly off the handle. I'm on *your* side. But I mean I'm just saying. She probably thinks he can talk to the solicitor you know, man to man. Public school to public school. I dunno, I'm probably wrong, but it sounds a bit funny to me.'

I was looking at the pavement, my brow furrowed.

'I mean, you'd probably have a right go at the solicitor if he didn't do what you wanted. He'd probably run screaming out of the office,' said Lol trying to make me laugh. 'He should come and see me. I'll tell him all about it. All about how you push me around all the time. He'd feel sorry for me, he would.'

I dug him in the ribs and laughed.

'Finished studying the pavement now? What did you read at university on my taxpayer's money, then? Bleeding pavements?'

'I love you, Lol,' I said smiling at him.

He took my hand and dragged me into the middle of the empty street. He was grinning.

'Come out here and say that!' he challenged and we both laughed.

'No,' I said and we looked both ways to make sure there were no cars coming. I freed myself and ran back to the pavement, laughing.

'Why not?' he was still standing in the middle of the road like an idiot.

''Cos it's a secret.' I walked over and grabbed his hand, pulled him back to the pavement.

CHAPTER FIFTEEN

'There's a message for you,' said Derek as I climbed up the stairs. It was pouring with rain and the office was dark, but I was happy. I hadn't been home in days. I'd told them I was staying at Maggie's and I didn't give a damn for their tight lipped silences. Maggie said she didn't like the idea either, when I had rung her from Lol's flat.

'Give me a break, Maggie,' I'd said. 'I'm so happy.'

She'd grunted and said she knew all about it. Chloe and Hugh had reported that I'd been seen in the Trumpet by their spies and not bothered to say hello.

'We also live in Stoke Newington, you know.'

'Bushland!'

'We have phones and doorbells just like everyone else,' she'd said drily.

I promised to visit. After all, my family weren't talking to me anyway.

I watched the kettle boil and put a cigarette in my mouth.

'It's such a disgusting habit,' Lol had taken to saying, and I smiled to myself as I smoked.

'Who was it?' I asked Derek.

'Kathi. I think it was the Kathi of the film.' He looked especially bleary eyed this morning and I guessed he was in no mood for conversation. We had two days left before the viewing with the commissioning editor and it had to be brilliant. What the hell did Kathi want? It was lunchtime before I got around to calling her.

She picked it up on the second ring.

'Hello?' She sounded frightened out of her wits.

I felt alarmed.

'What took you so long?' she said nastily.

'Sorry, I've been busy. What's up?'

'I've got to see you straight away.'

'What? Look Kathi, we've got this viewing coming up and I'm really busy. Can't you tell me over the phone? What's up?'

'Fuck you. I've got to see you, all right? Just bloody get down here!'

She was hysterical. She was crying. Alarm bells began thundering inside my head.

'Ok, ok. I'll get a cab. It's all right, Kathi. Stop crying. It's ok.'

Everyone in the world was getting cabs because it was raining and three cab drivers looked at me disdainfully when I said Stoke Newington. The fourth took pity on me and set his meter. The traffic was heavy and frayed nerves followed us all the way down Euston Road.

My heart was pumping madly. My mind was racing. I had made shreds of a tissue in my hand and smoked five cigarettes by the time the cabbie turned into Brodia Road. I noted the man wasn't there. The one that always said Yaaright. Of course not. It was raining. I'd been here before when he hadn't been here. For God's sake. What did it matter, anyway?

She looked awful. Her make-up had run down her face and her eyes were puffed up. She had on a floor length blue candlewick dressing gown, at three in the afternoon. I shut the door behind me and followed her into the front room, almost holding my breath with the suspense of it.

She sat down on the settee and tucked her feet underneath her. I took the chair opposite. The gas fire was on and I could smell burnt toast from the kitchen.

'Kathi. Please tell me what's wrong. I can't bear it.'

She sniffed and looked at me.

'I don't want to do this film anymore. I don't want to do it anymore,' she repeated holding her head up, biting her lip.

'What? What do you mean? Why not?'

'I just don't want to, all right? What's the matter with you? Don't you fuckin' understand English or what? You fuckin' . . .'

I stiffened.

'Look, Kathi. You don't understand. We've nearly cut it. We're in the middle of negotiating for the second one. What's wrong?'

'No. You're the one who doesn't understand,' she said and started crying.

Alarmed I got up but she spat out between sobs,

'Don't touch me. Don't touch me.' She started to cry uncontrollably. 'I'm just dirt, I'm nothing. Go away. Fuck off.'

My heart was beating so hard I thought it was going to burst out.

I walked over and held her by the shoulders, shook her.

'What's happened?' I shouted.

'I've got fucking AIDS!' she shouted back.

'Charles, we have to talk. Right now.'

'Sure. Hey, Angie, where have you been all afternoon? I've been trying to get in . . .'

'I left you a note. I've been to see Kathi. Look, God, I'm so freaked, I've got to sit down. God. Disaster. She's got AIDS. She went to the clinic this morning. I don't know when they did the test. Anyway it doesn't matter. She's developed AIDS and she doesn't want anything to do with the film now. She's a complete wreck.'

'What? AIDS? Jesus Christ. Poor Kathi. What do you mean, she doesn't want anything to do with the film?'

'I didn't want to leave her like that but she said her sister was coming over. God, I was so frightened. She just kept crying like she wasn't going to stop.'

Charles took out a packet of Silk Cut and gave me one, took one himself. He took my hand, which was shaking.

'It's ok, Angie. Calm down. It must've been awful for you. Look, let's think about this now. She's hysterical obviously. She's got someone with her. That's good. We'll have to give her a couple of days before she'll probably even feel like talking. Do you think we should send something, flowers or something? Oh no, shit, that's wrong.' Charles was rubbing his forehead.

I looked at him.

'Charles, did you hear what I said? She doesn't want anything to do with the film any more. I mean . . . I don't know what it means.'

'It means we have to wait,' said Charles looking at me. 'Look, Madeleine's at Channel 4. I'll walk down there. I need time to think this out. Ok, look don't panic. Stay put. We'll be back as soon as we can.'

As soon as Charles walked out of the room I knew I had to ring Lol. Derek had left early.

'Come on! Come on! You can't be out! Oh God, please make him answer the phone.' I was rapping my knuckles on the desk. Every piece of my body seemed to have tensed and my throat was dry. Every second that the phone rang seemed a precious second lost.

'Hello,' he said languidly

'*Lol*! Oh God. Lol, listen . . .'

'Hey, what's up, Angie?'

There were tears rolling down my face. I was so scared I could hardly open my mouth.

'It's Kathi. You've got to . . . you've got to go and see her.'

'What the hell are you talking about? I'm not bloody . . .'

'Lol, please, don't make this difficult. Listen to me. She's . . . oh God. She's got AIDS. She's . . . I just saw her this afternoon.'

'Shit.'

'Lol, are you still there?' I felt full of panic.

'Look, I'm going. Now. I'll phone you later.' His voice was calm and steady.

Two days had gone by. Lol had not phoned. There was no answer at his flat. There was no answer at Kathi's flat. Derek was continuing the final cut of the film. The commissioning editor was still coming. That was the only thing we knew.

Madeleine had said we carry on as normal and that we were sure to get Kathi soon. She had said everything would be sorted out and there was nothing to do but continue to cut the film. I sat in the edit suite, trying to concentrate on the film, jumping every time the phone rang. Whenever the room was free I called Lol but there was no answer.

We'd all been briefed to say nothing to the commissioning editor. He came, made doodles on his pad through most of the film and then said it was the best thing he'd seen on modern sexuality. That it had bite, authenticity, originality. That it was beautifully shot and put together. That there would be no problem about the 'sequel' as he called it. He even requested a VHS copy for himself. While he and Madeleine exchanged Islington gossip, I sat in the darkness of the edit suite listening to my heart jump. I'd done it! My story, my contacts! Charles was joining in the conversation and smiling a lot at the man from Channel 4.

Even though it wasn't summer and all the doors were closed, the opulence of the Soho Brasserie was perfect for the celebration, half empty and warm against the tide of people stepping down Old Compton Street.

Sipping his glass of wine, Charles threw back his head and laughed.

'Bite!'

'Originality!' Derek downed his glass.

'Long Live Commissioning Editors who have no clues about a decent film but sometimes, just sometimes, manage to spot one!' Madeleine laughed and we all lifted our glasses to the toast.

'Well it's got to be said. I've worked on a lot of films and I've never heard such praise,' Derek said and we all drank to that as well.

'God, I feel a bit delirious.' Charles poured some more wine.

'It's allowed. Listen. I want to make a toast to all of you. You've all done really good work, especially Angie,' said Madeleine.

'Absolutely,' said Charles raising his glass to me.

'Look, I'm sorry to break up the party but I must go back and do that VHS copy for his Lordship,' said Derek, knocking back his wine.

'Nice,' said Madeleine. 'See you later maestro.'

Then there were three.

Charles excused himself, heading for the loos.

Madeleine leaned towards me.

'You're going places kid,' she winked. 'You know that kind of approval we got this afternoon is rare,' she said looking into my eyes. 'The Contemporary Dilemmas series is very prestigious, and our programmes are kicking it off.'

I nodded smiling. 'Madeleine, I don't want to put a downer on this but . . .'

'Kathi?' Madeleine raised a concerned eyebrow.

'Yeah.' I was worried about more things than she knew, feeling disoriented by the alternate feelings of excitement and anxiety.

'Listen, Angie,' she leaned towards me, her face suddenly serious. 'I've given it a lot of thought. Kathi's distressed. Of course, it's only natural. But don't you see? Now it's even more important that we go ahead.'

Charles was back and he too leant towards me. I became a fixed point in their triangle of advice and knowingness.

'Listen, the fact that she's developed AIDS makes the film stronger, not weaker. Don't you see?'

I looked at both of them helplessly.

'It's just that she was so adamant. She said she didn't want the film to happen . . .'

'Sure, sure. Of course. It's only natural. She's scared stiff. You've gotta talk to her, Angie. She trusts you. Explain to her. She's doing a great thing. She's helping other people in her position. She's demystifying the whole thing by showing you *can* get justice. It's so important. You can see that can't you?' said Madeleine.

'And, hey. I mean she's got power. Probably for the first and only time in her life. She's got the power to nail that guy. God, if it comes to it we could do another shoot. Ask her about how she feels now, now that she has full blown AIDS. It would fit in great,' said Charles.

'You're joking. You didn't see her, Charles. She was frightened out of her wits. It was amazing. I've never seen anyone so scared . . .'

'Sure, it must've been a real heavy number for you, Angie. But look at what could come from this. Listen, remember what I told you?'

I nodded.

'Right. I told you that we're making a film that has ultimately got to inspire and entertain, to engross people. I think you're losing that perspective again. I mean hey, you know, I feel sorry for Kathi, sure. But we're on her side. We're not against her. You've got to make her realise that,' said Madeleine.

My head was reeling. They were right. Everything they said made sense yet I felt a huge burden of responsibility on my shoulders and I didn't like it. If only Lol had phoned. Where the hell was he? What was going on?

'It's down to you, Angie. I mean she really trusts you,' said Charles. 'One of us will come with you if you like . . .'

'No,' I said shaking my head. 'Anyway, she hasn't even called yet.'

'She will. Listen, I've got faith in you to do the right thing,' said Madeleine and smiled.

CHAPTER SIXTEEN

The phone rang as soon as I stepped into the office. I
lunged for it, feeling the walls bending in front of my
eyes. I wasn't used to drinking at lunchtime.

'It's me,' he said.

'Yes.' There was a hardness in my voice I couldn't
control.

'I'm sorry I haven't rung till now . . .'

'It's ok,' I said as if I couldn't give a damn.

'Can we meet? Can you get away?'

'Yeah. Where?'

'Camden?'

I smiled.

'By the trees?'

'By the trees.'

Halfway down Camden High Street, opposite the antique
shop, were two young saplings inside a wire mesh cylin-
der. They were the lone survivors in a row of vandalism.

Framed by an old pine mirror in the window of the
antique shop, he was squinting at the street, hands stuck
inside Levis. He hadn't shaved.

There was that space again. The space full of
possibilities and impossibilities.

I crossed the road. He didn't take his hands from his Levis. I kept mine inside my pockets.

'There's a pub just up here . . .' He gestured away from me, not meeting my eyes.

I nodded. We walked.

Silence.

He pushed open the door of a dark musty pub that smelt of beer on the floor and stale afternoon smoke. A few workmen were standing by the bar in paint splattered overalls and a couple of old men sat at a table looking into their pints. The jukebox was playing a sad Irish tune.

I was looking at the rings on the table, trying to breathe evenly.

'I got you a lager. They don't have bottled beer . . .'

I shrugged and lit a cigarette.

He sipped his Guinness and looked at me.

'I'm . . . moving back to Brodia Road.'

The tune broke into a jig and one of the old men jumped drunkenly out of his seat to do a little half dance. There were cheers from the bar 'Go on, Paddy!' Then he collapsed wheezing next to his friend. The fiddle carried on.

Lol put his head in his hand.

'Are you going to say something?'

'No,' I said harshly.

'She doesn't want to do it anymore, you know. She's been going on and on about it . . .'

'Do what?' I almost shouted at him, my face twisted with rage.

'The film,' he said quietly.

'I thought *you* didn't want to have anything to do with the film, you bastard,' I said. I was raving.

'I'm just telling you what she . . .' He raised his hand helplessly and carried on looking into his glass.

'Why don't you just shut up about her for a minute? Hasn't she got a mouth? She can talk, can't she?'

He sighed.

'And don't bloody sigh like that! What have you been *doing*, Lol? Where have you *been*?'

'Up her sister's. In Tottenham.'

'Oh, that must've been nice. The four of you . . .'

'Angie, stop it. Stop talking crap.'

I laughed.

'Oh, I'm talking crap. So sorry. Sorry I'm not . . .'

'Angie!' He reached out to take my hand but I flinched away. 'She's in a bad way, Angie. I've never seen her like this before.'

'What do you mean?'

'Well, we went up her sister's. I dunno. She said she couldn't face being in Brodia Road. Said she thought they were all looking out their windows at her. And she was sitting there all curled up. Like a frightened animal or something. She wouldn't even let her sister touch her. And she just kept crying. She said, "What the fuck are you doing here?" and I said, "I just came round to see if I could help. Do something." And she said, "Give me back my life. Can you do that?"'

'What did you say?'

'I just sat there. Just sat there watching her. She was a different person. It was like suddenly all her front, all her bottle had just gone out of her. And she was sitting there shivering, her teeth chattering, however many blankets we put around her.'

I ground my cigarette out and lit another.

'At her sister's I just kept thinking and thinking. Sitting there in front of the tele with her bloke who just thinks Kathi's got a bad case of the 'flu. We were watching the afternoon tele, 'cos he's unemployed, and she took Kathi upstairs, to try and get her to sleep. I could hear her crying. I could hear her scared.'

I had both my elbows on the table, head in my hands, looking at the smeared rings.

'And I knew. I knew that I had to go back. Someone's got to look after her. Do the shopping. She's got to have some help.'

'What about the clinic? Don't they have counsellors?'

'Yeah. I rang them. They said that I should persuade her to come. But there's got to be someone around. I can't see no way out of it. I mean there's got to be someone there to look at in the evening, hasn't there? Angie, for fuck's sake it could have been me. It could still be me. Next week, next month. I don't know.'

I felt cold all over.

'Do you understand? I'm all she's got in her pathetic life. I'm practically all the family she's got. And I thought I was bloody useless as a husband, because I never really loved her. Not really. But I thought maybe I could be a friend, I dunno. Try and do something right for once in my life.'

'Do you love her now then?'

'What's love got to do with it? There's got to be someone there and it's got to be me. I bloody owe it to her, don't I? I spent ten years with that woman and I never saw her like that before. She was always so hard, like iron. She hasn't got any of it left anymore. Doesn't care about prosecuting Eddie. What does it matter? What's the point of revenge when you're dying anyway?'

He was looking straight at me.

'Can I talk to her? I need to talk to her,' I said suddenly detached.

He looked at my face searching for something but I smoked my cigarette, tight-lipped and professional.

'You don't see, do you?'

I turned my face to look at someone walking into the pub.

'You've got your whole life spread out before you like a

fairground. You can't imagine not being in control ever, can you?'

'What are you talking about?'

'Angie, it feels good to be tough. I know that. I've been there. But you get so lost in being tough and proud of yourself that you forget what it's like to be nothing, to need someone.'

'I think we'd better go. You've said everything there is to say on the matter,' I said calmly.

'Fuck you!' He slammed his fist down on the table. 'I'm trying to tell you what's been happening the last few days and you're not even listening to me. No you're not just walking out of my life like that. I'm not making it that easy for you.'

'What?' I stared at him incredulously. 'Who's walking out of whose life? Easy? You think you're making it easy? God, I just don't believe it. You're leaving and there's not one thing I can do about it. You're doing the right thing, the honourable thing, and I can't stand it,' I shouted and suddenly my voice began to croak and tears seemed to be brimming in my throat. 'You're leaving me. It's never going to be the same again. I need you too . . .' I said in a small voice.

'Angie, that's not true. You've got everything. You've got family and your culture and your success. I'm *all* she's got. Perhaps she's all *I've* got. Perhaps she's the only one who was *there*, who remembers me when I was tough, who got disappointed in me, fought for me, gave up on me. But, Angie . . .' He reached out and grabbed my hand, held it tight. 'I always used to hate people who were weak, pathetic. 'Cause I thought if I got too close, it'd make *me* weak. Soft in the middle, and I'd cave in. Yesterday she said, "I'm scared to go to sleep because tomorrow could be my last day. I could die tomorrow. The night's too long and then it's not long enough." You know I just looked at her, and I didn't cave in. I thought about you and how it was all useless and going nowhere. I thought I could be dead next month. But I didn't care. I felt this feeling inside me that was so big. I thought I don't need no crombie on my back and no blood on my hands to defend it. D'you know what I mean?' He was smiling at me.

I closed my eyes. A great pain rose up to my throat.

'That's your strength,' I said and started to cry.

He was holding my hand, smiling steadily at me. Brave, unshaven and brittle blue eyes; leather jacket coiled around him, white t-shirt stretching across his chest.

'Don't cry. I'm happy. I'm happy 'cos you're still here.'

'But I don't know what's happening. I don't understand . . .'

'Are we still friends?'

'Of course. Always.'

'Then everything's possible.'

'But Kathi . . .'

'Look. It's complicated. I want to do everything I can. Try. I'll be there on the settee if she needs to talk to someone in the middle of the night. If she wants to fall apart, she can do it in front of me. I won't mind. Maybe we can't see each other for a while. Maybe I'll tell her about us. Maybe you could visit her if you wanted. She likes you. Everything's "maybe" at the moment. I think the world of you. But I just need some time. To sort things out.' Lol was looking at me intently. I found a smile and put it on my face. Facts were sitting all around us.

We said goodbye and it was awkward. In the harsh light of the street he stood, his face to one side, looking at me, hands in his Levis. I lit a cigarette uselessly playing for time. One more minute. He picked up my cigarette packet and took a cigarette out, put it to his lips.

'I thought you didn't smoke,' I said tonelessly.

He shrugged.

'Anything for you, blue eyes,' he said in his impeccable Bogart voice.

And I didn't cry.

'I'll call you. Soon,' he added.

'Yeah,' I said.

CHAPTER SEVENTEEN

I don't know why I ended up at Amigo's. I stepped on the train at Camden Town and suddenly I was there. I ordered a margarita. I kept checking the double doors. Perhaps I thought Lol was going to walk in. Maybe Phillipa was going to emerge from the restaurant, not a hair out of place. I sat determinedly drinking margaritas. All I had to do was wait for the actors to bring the set to life. Newly arranged Christmas decorations winked at me from their mess of plastic holly and satin bows.

I stumbled out of Amigo's and walked. The alcohol in my head turned the pavement to sponge. There was a crisp smell of bonfires in the early evening air. Tambourines suddenly broke into 'God Rest Ye Merry Gentlemen'. A group of Salvation Army people in uniforms were collecting money. Although Christmas had started way back in September I realised I had only just noticed. They would be thinking about turkey and trees all over. Not just in Brodia Road. I kicked a stone. Anyway pakis and Jews didn't celebrate Christmas. I walked all the way to Phillipa's parents' house from Amigo's. Four miles.

'I'll make us a coffee,' auntie Miri croaked while I sat on the settee in the front room, opposite Geoffrey.

I looked at the ornate gilt frame on top of the tv. It had
a picture of Phillipa smiling. We had often drunk wine
and laughed at that frame, at its ostentation.

I looked away and started to cry.

'Sorry,' I said.

'We all miss her,' said Geoffrey distantly. He didn't
think much of me now, I could tell.

'I should have come. To the funeral. I couldn't . . .'

Auntie Miri set my mug next to me on the table, and
put her fat hand on my shoulder.

'She knew you were thinking of her, lovey.'

'I wished I could have done something . . . To make it
not have happened.'

'There was nothing you could do,' said Geoffrey. 'It
happened. No one could have done a thing.' He stood
up and walked across the room to take a cigarette from
the packet on the dining table. And I thought Geoffrey
didn't smoke.

I knew he had dialled the number and handed her the
phone.

'Hello,' I said wearily. The office was sticky and dark
against the sheet of morning rain. Stale with the stench
of cigar smoke and stewing coffee.

'I can't,' I heard her say to him. Was he holding her?
Would he do an impression to make her laugh?

'Kathi? Is that you?' I said, my voice shaking.

'I can't,' she said, her voice small and scared. 'Don't
make me.'

'Angie.' His voice was steady and without emotion.
'You'll make them stop this film, won't you? You'll do
the right thing, won't you?'

I couldn't speak. My mouth was full of anger and fear
and bile and silence.

'Still there?' he said and I remembered the last time he'd said that. In a sea of seconds I remembered everything. Every microdot of our short acquaintance and intimacy sped through my head. And I could not speak.

He put the phone down.

Charles was threading his fingers through his hair. I sat opposite him, words springing from my mouth on and on.

'*Charles*, she just doesn't want it to happen. I *spoke* to her. She's a mess. Her . . . her husband, he said it as well. *Charles*, look at me. She doesn't want this. She doesn't want . . .' My words seemed to slide past him. He was sitting there like a buddha.

Stilettoes scraped in the doorway. I looked up. Madeleine, eyes glowing with kohl and frost, arms folded, and watching.

'Ok,' she said, 'That's enough.'

Her voice rang around the room. Charles looked out of the window.

'Look,' she said striding towards me, 'I think this has gone far enough, young lady. I've had enough of carrying you. I've tried to give you a great deal of friendly advice. Many times. You have chosen to ignore it. Now you're behaving in a way I find completely unacceptable. It's unprofessional and neurotic. And . . .' she arched an eyebrow, her eyes staring coldly at me, '. . . I'm not putting up with it anymore.'

I looked at her stunned.

'Let me tell you what the score is. We're carrying on with this film. You wanna bail out. Fine. Stupid but . . .' she shrugged '. . . quite honestly I don't much care. The amount of headache you've caused all of us is not worth it. You had a chance, you blew it. Not many researchers with your limited experience get the chance to direct. Still I guess you haven't got what it takes.'

For a moment she lost control and her eyes lit up angrily.

'What the hell do you think we're doing here? We've spent a lot of money on this. That included your wages too, young lady. We've been paid to deliver a product.'

She sat down.

'We're going with this film and also with the follow-up. We'll stay faithful to the story and weave in the turn of events about how the interviewee pulled out at the last minute because she developed AIDS. We'll interview Eddie, get his reaction. It'll add to the drama. I'm sorry if you find this hard to take but Kathi signed the release forms and I'm sure you know what the implications of that are.'

She smiled, 'In fact, you got her signature if you remember.'

'Madeleine . . .' I thought I was about to go mad. Everything seemed to be going out of control. A release form wouldn't stand up in court, I was sure of it. But it was irrelevant. Kathi wasn't about to take up another case when what she was avoiding was prosecution and publicity in the first place.

'It's in her interests. She'll realise that. There are hundreds of people out there with AIDS, goddamn it! She could have shown them something inspiring and brave, but she chose the easy way out. I understand *her* fear, but what I can't believe is you. Caving in at the first sign of a weak link. Instead of putting your mind on the job, persuading her, working as a team with us, you're behaving like prima donna. Ok. But as I said, that's the bottom line. You have some paperwork to do, I guess, and we'll pay you till the end of the week as contracted, but Charles will take over as of then.'

Then she left.

I was looking at the floor but it refused to open up.

'Angie, you fool,' said Charles. I looked up. I was all cried out. There was nothing left but emptiness. Everything felt numb.

'I need a drink,' I said. 'Want to buy me one? Or do you think I'm a failure as well?'

'Angie, come on. I don't think you're a failure. You're just having a crisis of conscience. It's human. But you know, you're wrong.' He sounded so sincere. I was clutching at straws. I knew it then but I didn't recognise it.

The sixth margarita spilled onto my leg.

'Oopsie,' I giggled. Almost immediately, the smile drained from my face. I remembered the cold touch of tea on my bare leg as the wind blew around us on the roof. I pushed the thought away because it had no place anymore.

'Hey,' said Charles.

'Get me another one,' I demanded.

'You're the boss,' he said retying his ponytail and getting up.

The unpleasant irony of the remark mixed with the alcohol made me laugh so much that I rocked into someone beside me. The small Spanish bar was full of people laughing at tables with candles and rows of San Miguel.

'You're on a bit of a bender, aren't you?' said Derek slurping his beer. 'You can certainly put it away.'

I looked at him disdainfully. He had stayed inside the edit suite while Madeleine had delivered her lecture, then slunk out and agreed to come for a drink.

'So what?' I said.

'Look, all I'm saying is that Madeleine Davis is well known in this industry. It's not a good idea to cross her. I mean, you're at the beginning of your career . . .'

'I'm all washed up in this town, you mean,' I said putting on her New York accent.

Derek immediately glanced around furtively over his shoulder and I spat, 'I don't care if she's here. I couldn't give a fuck.'

Derek looked at me and shrugged. I stared at him, expecting more concern.

'Derek,' I said softly, 'didn't you say that the industry was full of people now who didn't know fuck all? That in film, people cared about what they did and how they treated people?'

Charles came back with the drinks.

Derek mumbled, 'Don't twist my words.'

'So. Say what you really think in a pub at lunchtime and then when it's time for wages, you keep your mouth shut like a good boy,' I said under my breath.

'What are you talking about?' said Charles.

'Nothing,' said Derek. 'Look, this Kathi, she's just an old slag anyway. I don't know why you're being so uptight about it.'

'No, you don't, do you?' I said taking a gulp, trying to push the bad taste from my mouth.

'Anyway, Madeleine's bark is worse than her bite,' said Charles waving his arm.

'God, I wouldn't want her to bite me. I'd probably never recover.' I laughed and they both smiled at my boldness.

'Look, I've got to be making tracks. See you both tomorrow,' said Derek.

'Creep,' I muttered under my breath once he had left.

'He's so crass,' said Charles. 'I suppose that's how he sees women. Slags or virgins or something. God.'

'Or battleaxes,' I said brazenly and laughed, clutching at wild unholy alliances. I wanted him on my side. He was all there was left. Even if he was involved with her on some level, tonight I wanted him on my side.

'I mean, God, I feel sorry for Kathi. People like Derek . . . God, that's why they stay in the same rut. I admire

you for standing up for what you thought was right.
But you see,' he took my hand and rubbed it, 'I don't
agree with you. Face it, Angie, if you got involved with
people on every film, you'd never work. Even social
workers don't get involved with every case. It's to do
with professionalism.'

Maggie, dead beat and rubbing her feet, flashed across
my mind. Lindsay's voice boomed in my head: 'Film
is about communication, changing people's minds.' I
wished I knew what I thought as clearly as Charles
evidently did. Perhaps it was to do with experience.
Perhaps the film was more important than the individual.
An individual who was ignorant and stupid. Who wore
too much make-up and high heels in the middle of the
afternoon.

'I want to go back and watch the film,' I said.

We made our way through the inky depths of Soho,
pulling our collars against the sleet. The office seemed
warm and comforting. I couldn't imagine being anywhere
else. I had spent so much energy and time in here.

'. . . Love hurts. Love scars . . .' The song filtered around
the small edit room while the wind and rain raged against
the window. I stared at the screen.

Charles pulled his seat closer till his shoulders were
touching mine. I giggled and opened up Derek's drawer,
found the bottle of whisky, drank straight from the bottle
and passed it to Charles.

'Mmm . . .' he said, wiping his mouth and leaning his
head on my shoulder, 'what a day.'

I could smell his aftershave and the sweet whisky on
his breath. His head felt warm and the rain beat on the
windows. He kissed the side of my neck. It was so easy to
kiss him back, lazily, without words, for comfort.

'I want revenge, I want justice, I want to make him pay.' Kathi's voice determined and full of guts boomed out.

Charles began to kiss my hair. I held his hand, trying not to think of Lol.

'Oh baby, I want you. You want it too. I want to be inside you. God, you turn me on,' whispered Charles. I sat rigidly holding his hand staring at the screen. Trying to imagine Lol watching this. Seeing Kathi like this. Remembering her like this.

'Love hurts, love wounds . . .' Charles growled to the music as he began to unbutton my shirt.

'To die is easy, to live you have to struggle,' went Kathi's voice and the camera panned across the bar to Eddie.

Charles groaned and put his tongue inside my mouth. I watched his body sprawled across his chair leaning into mine. Felt the ripples of hard muscle on his back as I ran my hand down his spine. He began to pull me on to the floor. We lay with our Levis locked into each other, his body pleasantly heavy and warm against mine. I closed my eyes.

Charles unzipped his jeans and began to fumble with my belt. He was hot against my skin.

'Oh God, you turn me on,' he whispered in my neck, rubbing my breast, kissing my nose.

'. . . brave woman who decided to take what happened in the bedroom into the courtroom . . .'

'You're great. Your skin's so soft . . .' said Charles.

'. . . His lips were soft. I wanted him, I did. He didn't force me into it . . .'

'Come on baby, baby,' whispered Charles as if he had forgotten my name.

I opened my eyes above his shoulder. Shots of posters saying Don't Die of Ignorance flashed across the screen. They were in the street near the Dog and Trumpet, where Lol had stood in the road in the dark and I had pulled him back to the pavement for safety.

'Charles,' I said tightly, 'Charles, hang on . . .'

But Charles was on top of me, poised, his hands by my sides, supporting himself on his arms. And then we were kissing. Wet, hungry kisses. He groaned and pushed himself into me and I relaxed, no longer hearing Kathi's words, no longer seeing Lol's face. I felt as though I was watching a play and understanding everything because I had seen a hundred plays like it.

Charles slipped out of me and lay on his back, his eyes closed, breathing loudly. He passed his tongue across the top row of his teeth as if he was killing time.

'We should have used something,' I said.

Charles sighed.

'Yeah,' he said resigned. 'But you know how it is.'

I stared at him unblinkingly.

'You just give in to the senses and take off,' he smiled.

I lit a cigarette.

'Is this as good as it gets between you and Madeleine?' I asked.

There was a silence.

Charles began to pull his jeans on.

'That's really none of your business,' he said. He buttoned his shirt. I zipped up my jeans. 'Madeleine's a very important person. You should be careful what you say.'

'Yes, I should,' I smiled.

'I'm sorry I've got to go. Are you coming or do you want to watch the film again? I can give you a lift to Finsbury Park if you want,' said Charles with the same charm and smile he had given me when he had been my colleague and ally.

'I live on the other side of town, Charles,' I said. 'See you tomorrow.'

Alone in the empty room, the wind shrieking into the starless sky I folded my arms. I was suddenly very sober. I wondered what on earth the film was about.

About revenge and drama? Or about safe sex and responsibilities? I laughed at the empty room. How come you were expected to talk about safe sex with a stranger when you hadn't yet learned to talk about sex? When sex was made up of baby words. When it was about walking on the wild side. Because speaking involved pieces of your precious self turning into impossible and painful gifts, making you weak with emotion not lust.

I pressed Play and Pause and Kathi's face looked at me full frame. The harsh colours of electronic resolution made her face pink and white and hard. Perhaps the doughy emulsion of film would have filled in her presence, as she swayed between the light of the electric bulb and the wash of sunlight at her doorstep.

I smiled at myself. I had begun to think like a film maker at the very point when my career was about to evaporate. I remembered Derek telling me about some archive film in musty film cans that he had opened once in a cutting room. It had been the old nitrate stock and had turned to crumbling ashes inside. He said he had sat down and cried. Grudgingly he had admitted that video lasted longer. You could transfer it, it was portable, hardwearing.

'It's a stubborn bugger,' he'd said.

'Hah!' I'd said, taking the position of the New World.

'Video,' he'd said pompously, getting into his stride, 'is a fuck magazine. Forever glossy and functional. Now film,' he had grinned at me, 'is a musty hardback with the scent of sepia and sweat and the thrill of thin paper.'

CHAPTER EIGHTEEN

The next day I walked up the stairs in a daze, the alcohol still milling around my system. It was highly unlikely that I would see Charles or Madeleine or Derek ever again. It was Friday and they were on-lining, making the one-inch master tape of the film for transmission. The only VHS copy lay on the table where I had left it last night. I had been contracted for one more week to finish off the paperwork. I sat and stared out of the window at the Chinese restaurant.

'Hi, sorry. I didn't realise anyone was here.'

I turned and saw an unfamiliar face at the door. A woman with brown hair and glasses hanging around her neck.

'Sorry,' she said. 'We're using the office next week. I've just come to drop the rushes off, but if it's inconvenient . . .'

'No, no,' I said getting up clearing the table of files and papers, 'I'll make some room.'

'Thanks,' she dumped a huge plastic bag full of tapes on the table. 'Are you finished now?'

'Mmm, they're on-lining today. The film's being trans-mitted on Monday night.'

'Gosh, pretty close. Mind you, at least you can't change

anything. At least you can have a social life at the weekend.'

We both laughed.

'No,' I said, 'we can't change anything.'

After she left, I sat staring at the plastic bag. Next week the film would have gone out. It would be Pick of the Week in *The Guardian*. I had sent a publicity package to all the dailies and the Sundays. Next week another production company would be here and our files and VHS rushes would be piled up on shelves waiting to be collected. Lol would be back at Brodia Road. Kathi would be thinking the night's too long . . .

I wanted to run away. Forget the whole thing and pretend it had never happened. I didn't feel like doing any paperwork. They could stuff their money.

'So. You can afford to throw money away? Since when did you get to be a millionaire?' Auntie Miri had scoffed at Phillipa. Phillipa had stayed quiet. I had sat next to her loyally keeping my mouth shut. I didn't know why she was being so stubborn. It was during the first week at Amigo's. Hank had held a meeting of the staff.

'We're gonna have a competition. I want all of you to go out and buy or make a hat. Make it as whacky as you like. I want everyone to wear their outrageous hats and I'll give twenty pounds to the best one,' he said.

An awed Oooo had rippled around the assembled staff and lots of chattering of 'sailors' hats, Carmen Miranda, stetsons, bowlers . . .' Phillipa had said, 'I'm not wearing a silly hat. If it's part of the uniform then you should provide it. You pay me to be a waitress, not a performing monkey.'

You could have heard a pin drop and suddenly to Hank's dismay everyone started doubting the credibility of the hats. Hank was furious and the idea was dropped and never spoken of again. Auntie Miri was convinced Phillipa would get the sack but it turned out Hank couldn't afford to lose his best waitress.

The phone rang. Charles. He wanted to check Kathi's full name for the caption. I gave him the information and we closed the call as if nothing had happened between us. In effect, nothing had. I looked at the phone and decided to leave. I could do without a week's pay. They could do the paperwork themselves. Blinking in the watery sunlight I strode towards the tube station, every step lighter, as Wardour Street receded behind me.

The tube was thankfully empty in the middle of the afternoon and I stared at the hurtling darkness from the grimy window. What could I do? So many people in the past few weeks had said the same words, yet each had meant something different. Do the right thing. Be professional . . .

I wanted to go home, to the quietness of No. 10 because no one would be home, to the lingering smells of onions, and crawl into bed. I felt as if I had been wandering around the past few days in a continuous mist of a hangover.

Suddenly the blackness of the underground yielded to daylight. I was only one stop away from Finchley. A middle-aged man with a flat cap sat absorbed in the *Sun*. Opposite him sat a couple with a pram. The husband had short back and sides, obviously army, home for Christmas. Across the aisle from me sat an old woman hunched by the window muttering to herself. Yesterday's newspapers danced along the ridged floor. There were sweet wrappers, a small Lucozade bottle and a pink comb that travelled up and down the carriage. The bottle rolled reassuringly as the houses and trees skimmed past. I remembered the girls at school and my delicious pleasure

at having power over Kathi. Her images, her man . . . Yet
nothing made sense now. I wanted to tell her there was
nothing I could do, it was out of my hands. I felt sick.
Suddenly there was a crash of splintering glass.

The old woman had picked up the Lucozade bottle and
smashed it against the floor. She was waving it in the air
and shouting. The man raised an eye over his *Sun*; the
young woman held her hand over her baby's head. The
old woman's eyes were red, her mouth twisted up with
rage. She pointed the broken bottle at me. My heart
jumped wildly. Then the hate started.

'You weren't born. You were spewed up. Fuckin'
cunts. Coming here. You're everywhere. Stinking up
the flats. Your *fuckin'* cars and your shops. You fuckin
cunts. Who do you think you are? You're a bunch of
cunts . . .'

My heart thumped wildly. I pushed myself back in my
seat, knowing the next stop wasn't for a few minutes. I
kept looking at the jagged broken bottle. I could feel
the other passengers looking. Everyone stayed in their
seats and the woman staggered up, her gnarled legs
splayed. She held on to the seat and started stamping
her foot, bottle in one hand. A stale smell of urine wafted
around her. She began to shout at the top of her voice.
Then she swung around and advanced toward me, bottle
pointed.

I sprang up and pushed her back away from me as hard
as I could. I looked straight into her red veined eyes. I
wanted to kick her till she stopped breathing, till the bottle
dropped from her hand.

She collapsed. I stepped back startled. She began to sob
and kick air. I moved towards the door. Finchley Station.
I gulped in the fresh air. Over my shoulder I saw the other
passengers move a few seats away from the helpless mess
crying on the dirty floor. For a second I felt an impulse, a
reflex to help her get up. Then the train thundered away.

I stood taking deep breaths on the empty platform. It was a day for guilt. I felt bad about pushing her down.

I came out of the station. Outside the Help the Aged shop, I saw a familiar figure examining a book by the door. I could have cried with relief.

'Hi, Maama ji,' I said.

Maama ji looked up.

'*Arrey*, Ungelliee. How nice. How nice. I haven't seen you for days. You always come home so late or else staying at Maggie's, come in, come in.' He ushered me into the musty shop.

'This is my niece. She works in the television business,' said maama ji to a middle-aged woman with a blonde chignon spraying a big bottle of Charlie in the air. They seemed like old friends which, of course, they probably were by now, as maama ji had bought up most of the shop over the last few years.

'Hello, dear. Isn't she pretty, Mr Kumar? This is what they do in Harrods, dear. It makes the shop smell nice and makes people buy more,' she said.

I nearly laughed out loud. Didn't the soft sell stop anywhere? Maama ji pulled me to one side. 'Silly woman,' he whispered. 'Look at this book. Interesting eh?' He turned the pages of the old book reverently: *The Wild Beasts of India*, published 1882 (third edition) with drawings of elephants.

I looked pityingly at him. If everything had been pulled from underneath him, would he too have become some ranting, sad venomous old man in the tube shouting at the wind.

We trudged the pavement in silence, maama ji hugging his plastic bag which held the book and two angora scarves. He had begun to buy things for the endless family in India.

'The grey one is Aquascutum,' he explained. 'Your maama ji in Delhi will be very happy with it.'

'You were born to shop, Maama ji,' I smiled. There was no reason to spoil the mood by telling him about the tube incident.

As soon as the central heating hit me in the face my heart sank. The house was buzzing with the washing machine and afternoon tv. Everyone was home.

'*Arrey*, we will go tomorrow as usual. Why are you raising your blood pressure?' Ma's voice came from the front room.

'I am simply making a reasonable point,' said dad, '*Arrey*, Shankar, Ungelliee come, come. I am glad I am off sick today.'

They all started saying hello excitedly as if they hadn't seen one another for years. The heating at the Nat West offices had failed and so ma had the afternoon off. They eagerly began to check through maama ji's purchases, as if it were a national holiday.

'Come, let us have another round of tea,' dad said expansively, reclining back into the settee, an eye on the chess game.

Ma began collecting up the tea tray and cups. They had obviously spent their stolen afternoon drinking tea.

'What are you discussing?' asked maama ji slipping into the seat next to dad.

'I was just saying we should do the shopping today instead of tomorrow, but your sister is such a creature of habit . . .'

Ma got up noisily with the tray. She was done with conversation. I sat down on the floor and stared at the tv.

Dad moved a chess piece on the board, crossed his legs, finished the last of his tea. 'It is getting too much on Saturdays now,' he started, obviously in the mood for a yarn. 'You know we have always gone on Saturdays because at five-thirty they reduce the vegetables.'

'Toofor won,' said maama ji rocking his head from side-to-side, the Indian way of nodding agreement.

'Well, now the place is so full up of that Indian housewife mafia. Now, even before they make the announcement, they have already stuffed their trolleys with ten cauliflowers! They anticipate the reduction, you see.'

Maama ji was nodding gravely.

'Tesco's will stop doing it. You wait and see. The Indians are looting the place.'

Both of them guffawed with laughter.

Maama ji was wiping his eyes, 'You know what Rakesh calls it? Pakistores!!'

They shook hands and guffawed again.

'Yes. Oh yes, Ungelliee I want to show you something I think will interest you,' said dad, reaching for his wallet.

I turned from the tv expectantly.

He produced a neatly folded piece of paper.

'Look at this. From last week Tesco's have started to have these receipts. They list all the things you have bought as well as the price! Computers, yaar!!'

Maama ji examined the receipt eagerly.

'*Arrey!* The time as well? Very useful.'

'Of course, of course. Modern fellows,' said dad proudly.

I looked at him witheringly. He would find *The Wild Beasts of India* 1882 (third edition) interesting as well.

'I got attacked today,' I said suddenly, frustrated with the mundane banality of the family set up.

Both of them looked up, shocked.

I told them the story quickly, playing up my great escape, and leaving out the fact that I had pushed her over. I expected at least a small round of applause. Instead, dad's face clouded over. 'These bloody people. None of them so much as moved? Pah, what a country. Even a soldier sits by while a young girl is being attacked,' he said.

I felt irritated.

'It was all right, Dad. I handled it. No problem.'

Ma was in the doorway, holding the tray, that old look of fear across her face.

'A bottle, you say?' she said defeatedly.

'Oh, *yes*,' continued dad unbelievingly. '*You* handled it. That's not the point. What is handling it?'

He lit a cigarette, and began to smoke tensely, blowing smoke at the bookshelf, his face averted. Maama ji was shaking his head at the carpet woefully as if someone had died.

I was about to shout it was no big deal, when I saw the look in dad's face, anger mixed with a kind of distorted pain. He couldn't save me from the world anymore and the others, strangers on a train, didn't give a damn about their own children let alone some damn paki . . . I wanted to tell him it wasn't the whole picture.

Later I sat in my room and watched the light fading behind the curtain, the windows steaming with condensation. All around me the spectre of multiple choice. The digital clock flipped over to midnight and the house was quiet and I made the decision. 'Someone's got to help,' Lol had said.

I turned the key and walked up the stairs unafraid. Against the winking red lights playing at the window, the room was quiet. The files lay placidly on the table; tapes silhouetted against the darkness, plunging into life as they lit up in the glow of the relentless screaming flashing outside. The green plastic box sat squat and smug in the middle of the table. I switched on the fluorescent strip light. Next to the box was a hastily written note in Charles's handwriting: 'DO NOT REMOVE — On-lined MASTER 'Love Hurts'. To be delivered to Channel 4 first thing Monday morning.'

I opened the catch and saw the bobbin coiled neatly with the video tape. Pulling a length of it I held it to the light but I saw nothing. Kathi's images were trapped inside electrons, not emulsion. The inch-wide brown tape felt powdery and silky in my hand. I pulled more and like a rushing stream it rolled and slipped around me. I twisted it, trying to tear it but it was resilient.

I thought of their faces: Madeleine, Charles, Derek, commissioning editor, angry, crazy, staring at me. I thought about all my hard work. I thought about my story, my contact . . . Lol, eyes lowered towards the pool table. The arch of his back. Then it was gone. It's a stubborn bugger, I thought and waited for panic to take a grip of me. The unwound videotape lay sprawled around me.

Then I heard 'God Rest Ye Merry Gentlemen', an electronic version. I disentangled myself from the reams of tape and ran to the window. The refuse collecting truck was reversing into Wardour Street from Shaftesbury Avenue. It always played a jaunty tune when it was in reverse gear and they had substituted it with the topical tune.

Three or four men in donkey jackets, emerged from the darkness, to pick up bulging black bags, two at a time, from the sides of the road.

'Got another one for us, love,' said a man as I closed the door behind me. The black bag in my hand felt as light as if it were filled with feathers. I touched my jacket pocket. The VHS master copy was there, safe. There was nothing left of the film upstairs.

'Can I?' I asked grinning.

'But of course. Be my guest darlin',' said the man and stepped back, making a gallant gesture with his hand.

I stood very still, poised. The man winked at me encouragingly. The hungry jaws of the machine opened to reveal shredded waste in its mouth.

Smiling, I threw in the bag with all my strength.

I stepped back as claws gouged and crunched at the bag. Strips of tape mixed with bones, milk cartons, bottles. We watched, arms folded, in satisfaction. Ashes to ashes.

'Well that's another bit of rubbish out of the way,' said the dustman clapping his hands, and bending over to grab more bags. The machine bleeped 'God Rest Ye Merry Gentlemen'.

The top deck of the night bus was full of night clubbers. Girls and boys with stale make-up and crumpled skirts laughed and shouted across the bus, eking out the night. The driver was negotiating traffic as though he were on his way to a fire. Passengers thrown against the windows shouted a delighted 'Whooo!!'.

Remembering that death defying bus ride of long ago, I turned and looked at the back of the bus, but Lol was not there. On the back seat were men in bouffants and dresses. One of them turned on his ghetto blaster. Heads turned around, arms stretched up, people began to jiggle in their seats.

'Action speaks louder than words.' The song blasted out and everyone joined in. I laughed and sang out of tune with the others.

Why had I done it? Lol wasn't going to come back. My name would be mud in the industry. Kathi wasn't my best friend. I thought of the VHS lying in its jiffy bag in the postbox in Wardour Street. I had scrawled on its cover — This belongs to you.

A clump of black men sitting in front of the men in frocks joined forces and blew the whistles around their necks. Someone leaned out of a window and informed the zooming world outside that action speaks louder than words. A woman in front dressed like Marilyn Monroe

got up and executed a bump and a grind, shaking her
voluptuous cleavage to tumultuous applause, whistles,
laughter.

The driver rang his bell repeatedly in irritation and
immediately everyone shouted: 'Action speaks louder
than *bells*.'

And amid the hubbub I felt uplifted, exhilarated. I was
young, gifted and . . . *brown*! Hell, I could always go back
to waitressing.

I climbed the stairs carefully avoiding the creaky ones,
the tune still nagging happily inside my head. There was
a slice of red light at the foot of Rax's door. I felt like
talking. I rapped softly.

'It's me,' I whispered.

Silence.

Then: 'Ok'.

I pushed open the door. The table lamp shrouded with
the red kerchief made the room macabre. Rax was under
the duvet, Kyle on the floor in a sleeping bag. They were
both wearing sunglasses.

'What's this, The Blues Brothers?'

'Shhh. Who?' they said in unison and I winced at the
already yawning generation gap.

'Never mind. Take the shades off,' I said, my heart
suddenly pumping.

'Jelly, will you keep it down. Shut the door.'

I sat on the floor at Kyle's feet. His head was rapidly
disappearing into the sleeping bag. He was obviously
leaving the talking to Cool Hand Rax.

'First of all, it's no big deal, ok?'

'What?' I said alarmed.

'Don't freak, man. Relax. It's in hand.'

'Yo,' said Kyle.

'Take them off.'

Rax lifted the shades from his nose. I gasped. Around his right eye was a brown and violet bruise.

'Oh my God.'

'Shh.'

'Kyle,' I ordered.

Kyle's baby dreadlocks peeped out from the sleeping bag. He looked away shamefaced, revealing his own mottled eye. It was like some creepy horror movie.

'First of all, it's in hand,' said Rax authoritatively.

'Oh my God. Has Ma seen . . .?'

'Don't be stupid. Look, we had a bit of an argument with those pasty white boys down at the centre. It's sorted.'

'Rax! Kyle! Have you gone completely mad? What is this? Gangland USA or what?'

'Chaa, man. We're finished with the Warehouse party business. Now listen. Don't say anything yet. I'm gonna tell the folks on Sunday when they're watching the video films. I've chucked it in at Telecom.'

'Oh my *God*!!'

'And Kyle, my main man, has chucked it in at Pakistores.'

'Stocked my last shelf last night,' said Kyle proudly.

I couldn't believe I was hearing this.

'We're going on the Enterprise scheme. We're setting up in business. Videoing Indian weddings. We got enough money out of the parties to buy all the equipment. I'm getting the cards printed next week. Can't fail, Jelly. You've seen all the Mercs and BMW's at the Indian weddings we've been to. Hasian rich!'

'Wedding Video we're called,' chuckled Kyle, 'Limited!'

'You're crazy,' I said. 'Enterprise culture, that's all in the city.'

'So, what you think we can get on the hotline to the Tokyo stock markets? Get serious, Jelly. We're gonna use our own market. Then we'll expand to West Indian weddings, Cypriot weddings. Can't fail, man.'

'We offer a whole package, see? Video and DJs for the party if they want it. We got soul, reggae, *bhangra*, world music. No problem,' said Kyle.

'Cool and legal,' said Rax.

They were undaunted, forging ahead on dreams and sunglasses. Nothing I could say was going to be anything but a drag. Their religion was serious money.

Sunlight. I pulled up the duvet, immobile with depression. Feigning sleep I listened to the trio getting ready for Tesco's. Predictably, Rax and Kyle had left the house early with their black eyes.

The door slammed shut, but dad and maama ji were talking at the top of their voices in the driveway as usual.

'*Arrey*, Maggie! Nice to see you. Wake up that lazy friend of yours,' said Dad. 'I am happy when this one comes, because I save on my telephone bill.'

'What are you talking about? Your mind is getting senile. They are both working girls now, they haven't time to sit on the phone. That was when they were at school,' said ma.

'Oh yes. Ah, it is all the same to me,' said dad.

'Come, let us prepare ourself for the Sari Mafia,' said maama ji and they shrieked with laughter.

I pulled on Levis and jumper, bounded down the stairs, opened the door before Maggie had a chance to knock.

'What's the Sari Mafia?' said Maggie grinning.

'Who knows or cares? Come in. God it's brilliant to *see* you. I'm totally depressed,' I said pulling her inside.

'Fuck that,' she said as I put the kettle on. 'Listen: *gossip*.'

'What?' I said, eyes shining.

'Huge and Chloe! *dee . . . vorce*!!'

'No!'

She nodded, slapping her hand on the table.

'Everything! Tell me everything!'

'Big scene last night in the Trumpet. Glasses smashed. Voices raised. Thrown out of the pub. You know what it was all about? Chloe's discovered women, she's become a *dyke*!!'

'Oh my *God*!!' I was jumping up and down on my chair. 'Scandal.'

'Serves him right. He's too bloody right on for his own good,' said Maggie mischievously and we erupted into laughter.

'Poor Huge,' she said.

'Yeah.' I was thinking about the Dog and Trumpet.

Reading my mind she said, 'Oh yeah. That bloke was there. Your squeeze.'

My heart knotted.

'He asked me if you were all right. Said he'll be in touch. What's all that about?'

I took deep breaths. I wanted to do a dance.

'You finished with him, then?'

'Nah. Yeah. Dunno,' I said grinning.

She kissed her teeth.

'No, Maggie. It's cool. "You gotta have *faith, faith, faith*".' I sang.

She grinned. 'When a love affair's reduced to a George Michael song, *boy* you're in trouble.'

I wagged my finger at her and we smiled.

'*Oh God*!' she said suddenly. 'I almost forgot. Had to leave Stokie because I know those two are going to try and make me split my loyalties this morning. You know what they're like. *But*, I wanted to show you my car . . .' she trailed off mysteriously.

'You've bought a car?'

'No. You know Cynthia's boyfriend? You know Mr Perfectly Beautiful, nice person, and loaded? Mark?'

'That one she used to treat like shit?' I asked remembering her older sister's sharp tongue.

'Still does. He loves it. Anyway he's taking her to Barbados for Christmas . . .' She paused to kiss her teeth. '. . . Anyway, he left me his car. Come on, let's shoot the breeze or whatever it is,' she said pulling me from my seat.

Big deal, a car.

'Maggie, I need to talk. There's a lot of things been happening,' I said suddenly serious, unable to engage with her mood.

'Go on,' she said in mid excitement.

'Nah. Not now. Later.'

She looked at me uncertainly, guessing it was a heavy number.

'You can drive,' she said generously.

My protestations died on my lips when she threw the front door open. A glittering spaceship was parked at the end of the drive. My mouth fell open.

'It's a Porsche,' she said.

'But is it real . . .?' I said.

We clambered inside, sank into the soft grey leather, tried the electric windows, blasted the street with the quadrophonic speakers. I turned the key and the car purred into action. Lol wasn't here. But it was fine.

'The clutch is *so*, so *sharp*,' I burbled as she reclined at my side, one elbow out of the window, sunglasses on, even though the sun was weak above us.

'It's *perfect*,' she sighed.

After the thrill of careering along the side streets, the rush of speed in our senses, we finally hit sluggish, Saturday afternoon traffic. And red lights. Maggie tapped the side of the window impatiently. We looked sideways at the red Volvo next to us, furry dice swinging, big gold rings on the driver's pudgy fingers.

Maggie turned to me and said slowly under her breath, 'Hello John. Got a new motor?'

I nodded knowingly. We were thinking the same thought: Burn him up!!

I cupped the gear stick, checked the mirror, watched him do the same. Looked straight ahead. Maggie's tongue was poised on her lip. The red turned to amber . . .

I stalled. The Volvo trundled away belching non lead free fumes at us. I pulled up at the side. The tight, heavy feeling across my shoulders was back.

I slumped over the wheel and accidently pressed a button. The windscreen wipers began their dance.

'Oh God,' I said into the steering wheel, 'I've lost the one bloke who made me feel different. I'm never going to work again. Rax's left his job and the folks are going to *freak*. And there's nowhere to hide.' I closed my eyes.

Maggie put her hand on my shoulder.

'Hey,' she said softly. 'We'll talk. Have a coffee. Everything can be worked out. Nothing's impossible. Whatever's happened, I'll bet you did the right thing. Bet you did exactly what you thought was right. That's good enough for me.'

I looked at her face.

'I sort of *did* something. I thought about it and it was the only thing I could think of, it seemed to put itself forward. And it made me feel clean. Clean.'

'You made a decision. Yeah. That's what grown ups do.'

I bit my lip. 'But what if it was the wrong thing to do? The *wrong* decision?'

She looked at me for a moment.

'Listen, girl, You're twenty-five, you've got soul, and you're driving a Porsche.' She paused. 'What d'you want? *Jam* on it?'

We laughed. Then we drove.

Founded in 1986, Serpent's Tail publishes the innovative and the challenging.

If you would like to receive a catalogue of our current publications please write to:

FREEPOST
Serpent's Tail
4 Blackstock Mews
LONDON N4 2BR

(No stamp necessary if your letter is posted in the United Kingdom.)